THE FOUR
WINDS SAGA

WIND
of
JUSTICE

RICH WULF

WIND OF JUSTICE
©2003 Wizards of the Coast, Inc.

Distributed in the United States by Holtzbrinck Publishing. Distributed in Canada by Fenn Ltd.

Distributed to the hobby, toy, and comic trade in the United States and Canada by regional distributors.

Distributed worldwide by Wizards of the Coast, Inc. and regional distributors.

Printed in the U.S.A.

Cover art by Stephen Daniele
First Printing: June 2003
Library of Congress Catalog Card Number: 2002114358

9 8 7 6 5 4 3 2 1

US ISBN: 0-7869-3073-X
UK ISBN: 0-7869-3074-8
620-17595-001-EN

U.S., CANADA,
ASIA, PACIFIC & LATIN AMERICA
Wizards of the Coast, Inc.
P.O. Box 707
Renton, WA 98057-0707
+1-800-324-6496

EUROPEAN HEADQUARTERS
Wizards of the Coast, Belgium
T Hosfveld 6d
1702 Groot-Bijgaarden
Belgium
+322 467 3360

Visit our web site at **www.wizards.com**

"I see a future as glorious as our past." — Hantei Naseru

PROLOGUE

The Year 99,
Month of
the Horse
Seikitsu
Mountain
Range

I did not think that it would end like this," Yasuki Hachi said, looking out at the blasted city. A twisting column of dark smoke rose from the walls, carrying the smell of sulfur and burned flesh.

"Death never comes when expected," Hantei Naseru replied as he joined the Emerald Champion at the edge of the wall overlooking the outer city.

The attack had come swiftly. The Imperial City was unprepared for combat, for only fools made war during the bitter winter months. An army unaffected by cold and the elements, unfortunately, cared nothing for such things. Daigotsu and his legions had come from the sea, riding the waves in warships crewed by demons and undead monstrosities. By the time the Great Clans mobilized to fight off the assault, the damage had already been done. The city burned. Countless lives were lost. The throne room had been desecrated by the foul touch of the Dark Lord. Though the Horde had been forced back to the sea, few considered it a victory.

Hantei Naseru, son of the late Emperor, was solemn as he studied the smoking city. Though he was the youngest of his siblings, his narrow face was lined with worry. The deep scar that lined his left cheek and the silken patch that covered his right eye added to the effect, making the young courtier appear much older than his twenty-one years. His emerald robes hung in tatters, stained with soot, grime, and blood. He was not a man accustomed to battle, but he was a son of Toturi and had fought his way out of the city with the rest.

"Lord Anvil," came a feeble voice behind him.

Naseru peered over his left shoulder at the sound of his nickname. A stooped elderly man stood beside a little girl. Soot and grime stained their clothes, but their faces were full of hope. They bowed deeply when they felt Naseru's eye upon them.

"Yes?" the Anvil asked, turning to face the two peasants.

"My apologies for disturbing you, Lord Anvil," the old man said, bowing his head humbly. "I was told that you were the one who organized the withdrawal from Otosan Uchi."

"Yes," Naseru said with a curt nod.

"You have my gratitude," the old man said, a tear streaming down his withered cheek. "If not for you, and for Hachi-sama's magistrates, my granddaughter and I would never have survived."

"Then remember this day," Naseru said, looking down at the old man with a serious expression. "When the time comes that the Empire must choose its new ruler, think upon what has happened here. Let your gratitude take the form of obeisance, and tell your fellows to bow before me as Emperor."

The old man looked up at Naseru for a brief moment, his expression confused. Then, with another deep bow, he nodded. "You have my loyalty, Hantei-sama," he said sincerely. "My granddaughter and I will serve you so long as we draw breath." The old man turned and climbed back down the crumbling steps. His granddaughter followed, pausing only long enough to stare curiously at Naseru.

"So you have not changed, Naseru," Hachi said in a grim voice. "Even after what you have seen here you are not prepared to surrender your claim on the throne. You only saved these people so that they would be indebted to you."

Naseru looked back at the city, arms folded behind his back. "You disappoint me, Hachi," he said, his voice a coarse whisper. "Had my sister or brother or that bastard Kaneka any ability to unite the Empire, they would have done so already. It is their failure that has brought about this tragedy. I saved those people because they are my country-men, and because it was honorable to do so. But if I can use the loyalty I have earned to repair this shattered Empire, I will not hesitate."

"Have you no compassion?" Hachi asked. "The flames have not even died in the city, and already you turn this to your advantage."

"Compassion?" Naseru, his eye burning with intensity, looked at Hachi. "What do you think happened to that old man's children, the parents of his grandchild? That man is too old to care for so young a child alone. Someone cared for them before, Hachi. Those people likely died in the invasion, because the Empire had no leadership. You say that I act as I do because I have no compassion. You know nothing of compassion. As you struggle to save each person you see, I fight to save an Empire. I will create a Rokugan where there will be no shattered families, no terrified orphans."

"Whatever you say," Hachi said, sounding unconvinced. Before the invasion, the Emerald Champion had been one of Naseru's strongest opponents. Though they had faced much together, the Anvil doubted if Hachi's opinion of him had improved much.

"Your sister, Tsudao, has fortified the First Legion in Kyuden Seppun," Hachi said. "There is talk that she is to pro-claim herself Empress with or without your consent and that Kyuden Seppun will be the new capital."

"Is that so?" Naseru asked wryly. "Then I assume you will go there to serve her."

"No," Hachi said. "As Emerald Champion I must remain impartial. I cannot risk tainting my authority by allying with an Emperor unrecognized by the Empire."

"You are wiser than they give you credit, Hachi," Naseru said with a small chuckle. "If what you say is true, then I must move swiftly." Naseru turned away from the wall, moving back toward the crumbling stair.

"Where will you go?" Hachi asked.

"Ryoko Owari," Naseru said.

"The City of Lies?" Hachi asked, surprised.

"The city has many names," Naseru mused. "With the destruction of Otosan Uchi, it has become the largest city in the Empire. It is the only suitable place to be the capital of Rokugan. Seek me there if you require me, Yasuki Hachi."

"Do you plan to declare yourself Emperor?" Hachi asked.

"We shall see," Naseru said, descending the rough stairs.

1 | GIFTS AND FAVORS

One Month
  Later

A samurai, clutching his katana in a two-handed stance, stood on either side of the Emerald Throne. To the right stood a bold warrior in armor of blood red and dark black, his face concealed behind a snarling mempo. To the left stood a smaller man in robes of dull brown, a mane of tattered golden hair hanging about his shoulders. The two warriors eyed one another warily.

"You know not what you do, Akodo Toturi," the red-armored samurai said with a dramatic flourish of his blade. "I struck down the Emperor for the good of the Empire. I would save us all from Fu Leng!"

"I do not believe you, Bayushi Shoju!" the smaller man roared, shaking a fist at his foe. "You have insulted my honor! Your geisha assassin tried to kill me!"

Seated in the deep shadows that filled the far end of the chamber, Hantei Naseru steepled his fingers calmly, trying not to appear irritated. He wore robes of emerald green worked with golden chrysanthemum symbols and a delicate wreath of gilded laurels. His katana and wakizashi lay on the floor to his side out of immediate reach as he watched the duelists square off.

"Do not be so selfish, Akodo Toturi," Bayushi Shoju begged. "The Scorpion Clan has sacrificed everything to accomplish what we have done today. For all our crimes and dishonor, the Empire will reap the rewards! The Celestial Order will be safe from Jigoku at last!"

"I do not believe you," Toturi cried, his voice full of rage. "For what you did, to me, to the city, and to the Emperor, you must pay!"

The two danced back and forth, their swords flashing in a brilliant display of swordsmanship. In the shadows, Naseru noted how their blades never seemed to come close to connecting. Toturi's blows, in fact, were particularly clumsy and Shoju was often forced to go out of his way to parry swings that otherwise would have connected with nothing but air. Finally, Toturi stumbled and fell before the Scorpion. Bayushi Shoju lifted his blade high and stared into its depths. A look of horror slowly dawned in his eyes.

"What have I become?" Shoju said. He drew off his scowling demon mask, revealing a handsome but tormented face. "This sword . . . this foul sliver of dark magic . . . it has corrupted my ambition. Nothing good can come from this."

The Scorpion turned and buried the sword in the back of the Emerald Throne with a single blow. The Scorpion's strength failed; he fell to his knees. The mask dropped from his hand, shattering on the stairs. He stared at the broken mask with hopeless eyes. He looked up to face Toturi, who had recovered his sword and was now ready to fight once more.

"Now you will die, Bayushi Shoju," Toturi said.

Naseru stifled a yawn.

"Kill me if you must," Shoju said, holding an imploring hand toward his slayer, "but please, listen to my words."

"Will you now beg for your life?" Toturi asked with a sneer.

"No," Shoju said. "I shall tell you of the prophecy. I shall tell you how to defeat the Dark Kami, Fu Leng. Then, if you wish, you may take my life for my crimes."

"I am listening," Toturi said, staying his blade.

Akodo Toturi and Bayushi Shoju froze suddenly. A smaller man wearing bright white face paint and colorful robes stepped into view between them, turning his back to the throne and samurai.

"And in that moment of wisdom," the narrator said, "Toturi began the path that would, after many other trials, lead him to the throne. With the aid of the Scorpion Clan, he overcame his weakness and became the greatest Emperor who would ever rule Rokugan. And so ends the tale of the Scorpion Clan Coup."

Applause filled the small theater. Toturi, Shoju, and the narrator bowed and made their way off the stage.

Naseru endeavored mightily to conceal his scowl as the room filled with light again. He clapped briefly before folding his arms in his sleeves.

"Well, my young lord?" asked Imperial Chancellor Bayushi Kaukatsu. The sour old man leered in Naseru's direction. "What is your opinion?" The chancellor smiled faintly. His hands toyed with a closed fan, tapping it against his chest. Around them, other high-ranking courtiers, mostly Scorpion, rose and began to mingle quietly. Kaukatsu and Naseru nodded to a few of them as they passed.

"It presented a . . . unique perspective," Naseru said carefully. He moved toward a quiet corner of the room, forcing Kaukatsu to follow. "Quite daring, I think, to portray Bayushi Shoju as the hero."

"Among the Scorpion, Bayushi Shoju *is* a hero," Kaukatsu said.

"How strange," Naseru said mildly. "My father considered him a regicide."

"Ah, but did not Toturi also gain the throne by killing the Emperor before him?" Kaukatsu asked. "The major difference, I think, was that Toturi was able to hold what he had taken."

"No," Naseru said. "I think the major difference was that

the Emperor my father slew was the vessel of Fu Leng, an embodiment of pure evil. The Emperor Shoju slew was an innocent old man."

"And of course that is the entire point of a play," Kaukatsu said, cutting the air with his own closed fan. "Why bother to tell a story again if only to tell it exactly the same way? I think that adding new flavor is a good thing."

"No doubt," Naseru said. "But some might complain at the lack of attention to detail."

"Such as?" Kaukatsu asked.

"I doubt Bayushi Shoju would have been so impractical as to wear a glass mask into battle," Naseru said. "Scorpion battle mempo are typically made from steel. Also, it was always my understanding that Shoju was a hideously disfigured man."

"True," Kaukatsu said, "but that is a harmless detail that most Scorpion would rather forget. It is an ancient superstition that any form of disfigurement is the sign of a wicked nature."

"In Bayushi Shoju's case, I would say that the superstition is correct," Naseru said.

"Oh?" Kaukatsu said. His stare fixed upon the black patch covering Naseru's right eye, but only for a moment.

"Is something bothering you, Kaukatsu-san?" Naseru said, turning his head slightly to the left so that the chancellor had full view of the right half of his face. "Did you wish to say something?" At his side, Naseru sensed the silent presence of his yojimbo, Seppun Isei. Imperial Chancellor or no, Isei was not the sort to endure any insult to his master.

Kaukatsu glanced at the yojimbo and smiled at Naseru. "Me? Bothered?" Kaukatsu laughed. "I am a sincere man, Naseru. If something bothers me, I will come right out and say it. I only wished to state my opinion that consistency has little to do with entertainment. Leave the attention to boring detail for the Ikoma historians and Miya heralds. A playwright's duty is to entertain!"

"I was not entertained by the rather dubious scene where my father disguised himself as a geisha to escape the city,"

Naseru said coldly. "I wonder if you would have dared perform this play at all if Toturi were still alive."

"I have nothing but the greatest respect for the Splendid Emperor," the chancellor said, as if the idea that the play had been insulting had somehow not occurred to him. "Did you truly find the play disrespectful? Say the word and I shall have the playwright punished."

"No," Naseru said. "I do not believe it would be prudent to punctuate my first day in Ryoko Owari with a harsh punishment."

"You are an Imperial heir," Kaukatsu said. "He is merely a playwright."

"I am an heir in contention for the throne with three other candidates," Naseru corrected. "And that playwright happens to be the favorite son of Shosuro Taberu, famed sensei of the Dojo of Lies. It is no wonder such mediocre work receives such praise. I would not envy the critic who condemns him."

"Impressive," Kaukatsu said. "You have researched this city and its inhabitants."

"Out of necessity, Lord Chancellor," Naseru replied. "I plan to remain in Ryoko Owari for some time, and I find it useful to be familiar with those in power."

"Then you will wish to visit Governor Shinjo Osema," Kaukatsu said. "The Unicorn Clan holds true power in Ryoko Owari."

"I have already paid my respects to Osema-san," Naseru said mildly. He looked about the room. "Yet I see many more Scorpion here in your palace than Unicorn. I expect a Unicorn governor may have difficulty enforcing his commands with a Scorpion Imperial Chancellor in residence."

"I must make my home somewhere, Naseru-sama," Kaukatsu said smoothly.

"And so must I," Naseru said, fixing Kaukatsu with a piercing stare.

"Then I welcome you to the City of Stories," Kaukatsu said.

"Also called the City of Lies," Naseru remarked dryly. "I do not like Ryoko Owari, Kaukatsu-san. It is a dirty, dangerous, crime-ridden city. Yet with the destruction of Otosan Uchi, Ryoko Owari has become the largest city in the Empire. No other city truly deserves to be the Empire's new capital. I will speak frankly, Kaukatsu. I know the Scorpion have a vested interest in Ryoko Owari, and some day I am certain you will seize this city back from its Unicorn government. I do not intend to interfere with your clan's operations. Ally with me in my quest for the throne, and I will turn my resources to enhancing your power base here. Ryoko Owari will one day be the jewel of the Empire, and the Scorpion Clan will be my right hand."

"An impressive if highly conditional offer," Kaukatsu said. "What if I refuse to aid you?"

"I will find a more agreeable samurai to serve as Imperial Chancellor," Naseru said.

"The role of chancellor is a lifetime appointment," Kaukatsu said.

"I know," Naseru replied. His eye narrowed. "Cease testing me, Scorpion. I tire of it."

Kaukatsu tapped his fan in his gloved hand.

"Am I being sufficiently clear?" Naseru asked.

"As clear as the shining waters of Golden Sun Bay," the chancellor said quietly.

Kaukatsu's fan opened with a snap, revealing the chrysanthemum of the Hantei, Naseru's favored symbol. The chancellor turned the fan subtly so that the entire room could see the symbol.

"It is refreshing to see a politician with courage and insight, Naseru-sama," Kaukatsu said. "I wish you well." The chancellor waved his fan idly a few times. Naseru noted that the reverse side of the fan featured the mon of the Shogun, Akodo Kaneka, Naseru's illegitimate brother and most hated enemy. The implication was clear. Kaukatsu had been prepared to declare his loyalty one way or the other this evening, and Naseru had passed his test. He had won the chancellor's loyalty, at least for a time.

"Now if you will excuse me, Lord Naseru, I must attend to my other guests now," Kaukatsu said with a short bow.

"Of course," Naseru said, returning the gesture. Inwardly, Naseru breathed a sigh of relief. Outwardly, he knew better than to show any such emotion with so many potential enemies nearby.

Kaukatsu closed the fan. "If you require anything further, you need only to call upon me."

"I will," Naseru said. Privately, the Anvil was preparing the strategy by which he would avoid the chancellor for the rest of the evening. He truly despised talking to the man, though if he intended to establish himself in Ryoko Owari such encounters were unavoidable. Kaukatsu bowed a final time and strode off through the chamber.

"He is too arrogant, my Lord," Isei whispered at Naseru's side. The yojimbo's tone seethed with barely contained rage. At the edge of the shadows, Naseru could make out the scar that bisected his yojimbo's face.

"Of course the chancellor is arrogant," Naseru said. "He is one of the most powerful and experienced politicians in the Empire. Keeping his loyalty will test even my abilities."

"You do not need him, my lord," Isei said. "He is dangerous and disrespectful."

"He is indeed." Naseru sighed. "But so long as he appears to be our ally, he may frighten other enemies away. Even Kaneka would be wary to attack us if the chancellor appears to be on our side. Many of the Bastard's supporters owe Kaukatsu favors not easily repaid."

"I see," Isei said quietly. Naseru could tell from Isei's tone that the yojimbo was merely agreeing out of obedience. Seppun Isei's strengths lay on more tangible battlefields and they both knew it.

"Ah, well," said Naseru with a sigh. "No sense hiding in this corner any longer. If we are to acclimate ourselves to this new city we must become acquainted with those in power. Come, Isei."

Hantei Naseru stepped forward, Isei two steps behind. The dour yojimbo's eyes scoured the crowd for any sign of a threat. Naseru seemed to be looking directly ahead, paying no attention to anyone. In truth, his senses were everywhere, taking in every detail. He mostly noted others' reactions as he passed and categorized them in his mind.

Some drew away, focusing more intently on their own conversations. They were rabbits. They sensed a new predator and froze or drew away, hoping that they would not be worth the effort to chase. Indeed most were not worth his attention.

Others noticed him and stumbled over themselves to move forward and meet him. They were dogs—predictable, unimaginative, and utterly loyal if they could be swayed. Naseru greeted them with courtesy.

Finally, others met his gaze for a bit too long, bowed a bit too low. Those were wolves, careful predators of the court. Naseru expected no problems from them tonight; they had already seen him deal with Kaukatsu. If they were wise they would plan well before confronting him again. If they were unwise, anything was possible. Naseru seldom wasted time wondering what fools would do; fools were innately unpredictable.

Naseru paused before a pack of dogs, supplied appropriate compliments for those whose names he recognized, and ignored the rest. Better to ignore a potential ally than compliment them falsely and make an enemy. There would be time enough to research the others later and pay them respect, if they deserved it. He recognized one samurai, a young Lion named Akodo Jusho. Jusho endeavored to engage Naseru in lengthy conversation, bragging about his conquests at Kyuden Tonbo. Normally, Naseru avoided conversations about recent battles; the risk of seeming to favor the faction telling the tale was too high. However, considering the fact that the Dragonfly samurai who had survived the battle of Kyuden Tonbo could be counted on two hands, Naseru felt he had little to risk.

In fact, speaking to Jusho gave Naseru a chance to display his own tactical expertise as he analyzed every detail of the Lion's description of the battle. After some time, a small crowd had gathered to listen. Naseru expected no less. He noticed a few courtiers he recognized, including Doji Kinnosuke and his wife, Atsuko. Kinnosuke was a well-respected merchant patron for builders and architects in Ryoko Owari, though his wife was rumored to be the true driving force in their business.

"You surprise me, Lord Naseru," Jusho said, after Naseru had finished analyzing a particularly critical part of the battle. "I did not think you were a student of warfare."

"Is it not a samurai's duty to excel in all things?" Naseru replied with a self-deprecating laugh. "To be truthful, I suppose I have an unfair advantage. It is difficult to be the son of the greatest tactical mind in history and not learn *something*."

The comment roused polite laughter. Naseru's father had been well loved by his people; complimenting him was always a good way to put a crowd at ease. A young Phoenix courtier hid her grin behind a fan. Naseru stared in her eyes for precisely four seconds, making sure the gesture was obvious enough that the more perceptive courtiers in the group would notice. He did not even know the woman's name, nor did he truly care, but before an hour had passed a thousand rumors would boil regarding the Anvil's intentions toward her. If she were smart, she would turn to his mercy and he would gain a new ally. If she were a fool, she would turn to someone else, and the Anvil would have smoked out a potential enemy.

"Pray continue, Jusho-san," Naseru said, looking back to the Lion. "I suspect that you were only just approaching the best part of the tale."

"Yes." Jusho nodded emphatically. "The final stand of the Dragonfly. Our foes did not offer their surrender. They did not lay down their weapons. They met us boldly and fought to the end. Though at the last they were only dozens against our hundreds, they gave their lives like samurai, and we offered them glorious death. I have never been more proud to be a Lion, noble Anvil."

"Indeed," Naseru said mildly, showing none of his distaste at Jusho's bloodthirsty zeal. Turning and coughing, Naseru rolled his eyes so that only the two Crane would see.

Doji Atsuko leveled a sultry gaze toward Naseru, shielded from her husband's attention by her silken fan and elaborate hairstyle. Naseru twitched a grin. She was a bit plump for his tastes, but her eyes and demeanor bespoke a cunning intellect. At her side, her husband merely smiled stupidly.

"Such a strange nickname, Naseru-sama," she said, interrupting Jusho in the midst of his description of a duel between his younger brother and a Dragonfly bushi. "How did you come to be known as the Anvil?"

"Surely no one here is interested in hearing my dull stories," Naseru said. "Jusho-san has not yet finished his description of the battle."

"I am certain Jusho-san will find opportunity to tell us of his exploits again in due time," she said, turning a dull gaze toward Jusho. Her blue eyes flicked back to Naseru and widened in interest. "But it is not every day that we have a chance to speak to an Imperial heir."

"And you have no idea what good fortune you have, Doji-san," Naseru said. "At times, my brother and sister can be most tiresome, and I suspect most think no less of me. I am quite the villain, or so it is told."

The group laughed at that. Naseru quietly noted whose laughter seemed most sincere.

"Brother? I thought you had two brothers, Naseru-sama," said a Scorpion courtier wearing a blue velvet fox mask. "Toturi Sezaru and Akodo Kaneka."

"I believe you miscounted," Naseru said firmly. "My father acknowledged only two sons." Naseru recognized the Scorpion as Shosuro Soshu, a minor functionary who had worked for one of the district governors of Otosan Uchi.

Akodo Jusho seemed somewhat uncomfortable at that statement. Of course he would be displeased by any implied insult toward the Shogun, a fellow Akodo. Naseru favored Jusho with a reassuring smile. "The Shogun may have many enviable qualities, but the facts are the facts. Perhaps Kaneka deems himself worthy to question the word of the Emperor, but I do not. Would you question the Emperor, Jusho-san?"

"No," Jusho said without hesitation. The Lion's brow furrowed.

"Indeed," Naseru said again, bowing his head toward the Lion. "You are a tribute to the honor of your clan, my friend. Now where were we?"

"My brother's duel!" Jusho said, happily, forgetting his internal crisis instantly.

"The story of your nickname," Atsuko interrupted.

"Ah yes," Naseru said, clasping his hands. He moved smoothly into the tale, as if its telling had been his idea all along. "This story may require a certain amount of background for the younger members of our audience." Naseru was silently amused as a few of the younger courtiers nodded at him. He was probably younger than every person here. Most assumed from his educated demeanor that he was much older than his twenty-one years. He encouraged the illusion.

"At the end of the War of Spirits, my father forged a treaty with the Steel Chrysanthemum," he continued, "Many concessions were made on that occasion, for my father's compassion in victory was as boundless as his tactical prowess. Among those concessions, Toturi agreed that one of his children would bear the Hantei name and would train in the household where the Hantei dwelled under house arrest. I volunteered for that duty, for I knew that my sister was too fierce and my brother too fragile to survive in the Steel Chrysanthemum's tutelage."

The tale was accurate, from a certain perspective. In truth, the concessions were made to soothe pockets of rebellious samurai who still supported the Hantei. Though Naseru had agreed to take the name, it was no secret that Toturi favored the choice because Naseru was the furthest from the throne. As Kaukatsu had said, details had no place in entertainment.

"Living with the Hantei must have been dreadful," commented another Scorpion. This one wore a porcelain mask painted like a kabuki actor. Naseru did not recognize him.

"The Hantei was a madman to be sure, but he also possessed the wisdom of nearly six centuries. I determined to make the best of a difficult situation and learn all from him that I could."

"How very brave," the Scorpion said sincerely.

Naseru gave the man a level look, noting his pale blue eyes, and moved on.

"I did not think of it as brave," he said, waving away the praise with his fan. "I thought of it only as an opportunity to help my father."

"Were you not afraid that the Hantei would use you against Toturi?" Atsuko asked.

"I counted on it," Naseru said, enjoying the confused looks the comment drew from the crowd. "You see, though I learned from the Hantei I also studied with Toturi. I never had any doubt that my father's instruction would hold greater influence. Each time I strode into the Chrysanthemum's lair, it was with total confidence that my father's lessons would protect me from dishonor. It was almost as if I were riding into battle with Toturi at my side. Could any man fail with the Splendid Emperor as his ally?"

"No!" Jusho exclaimed, as if on cue. Naseru so loved Lions.

"Indeed," Naseru replied, but he held up a cautioning finger. "However, do not believe that the Hantei did not attempt to exert his influence. He was a sinister man, and often attempted to turn me against my father. 'Naseru,' he once said"—Naseru's voice took on a somewhat hollow tone as he imitated the Steel Chrysanthemum—"'I will never escape this dungeon, but you will be my vengeance. You will be the anvil upon which I will forge a new Empire.' After the Hantei's death, I kept the nickname to spite him. I will forge the clans into a unified Empire once more, but it will not be in the name of the Iron Chrysanthemum."

"Then why keep his name?" Jusho asked. "The Hantei is dead. Why not call yourself Toturi Naseru?"

"Because my father made a promise," Naseru replied. "An Emperor's word binds all of Rokugan. No man stands above the Empire."

That line drew a quiet round of applause. Appropriate, Naseru thought. I have rehearsed it often enough.

"A moment of your time, if I may, Naseru-sama?" said a quiet voice to the Anvil's left.

Naseru turned to face the newcomer, noting that the man had been careful not to approach on his blind side. He was a small man garbed in fur robes dyed a dark purple. His face was lined with countless years, and he leaned heavily on a cane crafted of pure ivory. The mon of the Unicorn Clan was emblazoned upon his peaked fur cap. Naseru's eye widened in surprise.

Naseru knew few Unicorn by sight. Those who came to the Imperial City seldom remained for long; their clan was too restless by nature to stay anywhere for any length of time. This man was an exception. Naseru not only knew him, he was one of the few people the Anvil truly admired.

"Ide Tadaji-sama," Naseru said, bowing deeply.

"Sama?" Tadaji chuckled. "You give a simple old man too much honor."

"Quite the contrary," Naseru said. "You were my father's most trusted advisor. I learned by watching the way you commanded my father's court."

"I never command," Tadaji said, hobbling to one side. The others present immediately responded to the subtle gesture. They moved away to their own conversations, leaving the old Unicorn to speak to the Anvil alone.

"And yet you are always obeyed," Naseru said, smirking at the vanishing crowd. "The first of many lessons I learned. What brings you to Ryoko Owari, Tadaji-sama? I heard that after my father's death the Unicorn Khan appointed you as his personal advisor."

"You know that the Khan is an ally of your brother, Akodo Kaneka," Tadaji said. "I know how much you despise the Shogun. Surely you must wonder if I am an enemy?"

"Kaneka is not my brother," Naseru said sharply.

Tadaji sighed. "I have known you and your siblings since you were children. I have come to know Akodo Kaneka since he became allied with the Khan. The two of you are more alike then either will ever admit. The Four Winds are all worthy, in their own way."

"Four Winds," Naseru said with a wry smile. "If my mother ever returns from wherever she vanished to, I shall have some choice words with her for coining that colorful phrase. Calling us 'four' groups Kaneka equally with my true siblings and me. The title grants him more legitimacy than I care to admit, and I would prefer you not use it in my presence."

"Do you hate Kaneka so much?" Tadaji asked.

"As I said, he is not my brother," Naseru replied. "Did he send you to threaten me?"

"Kaneka does not know I am here," Tadaji said. "I have come of my own free will, to let you know that I am willing to propose peace between the two of you, should you seek it. I do not wish to see Toturi's children destroy one another. I fear the cost to Rokugan would be too high. Already your lack of unity has allowed Daigotsu to destroy the Imperial City."

Naseru scowled. "A tragedy that may have been avoided if my mother had remained on the throne as father intended," Naseru said. "Instead, she vanished without a trace. My brother believes she was drawn into the Heavens by her duties as an Oracle, but the fact remains that the rightful ruler of Rokugan vanished without naming an heir. But if you need any more proof that the reign of an unworthy Emperor causes tragedy, look no further than your own experience. You survived the Clan War, Tadaji. You remember what happened then. You know that an incompetent leader is often worse than no leader at all. You have a clear view of history, not like these . . . these short-minded fools." Naseru gestured at the empty stage.

Tadaji grunted noncommittally. "If Toturi had chosen to recognize Kaneka as his heir, would you have obeyed?" he asked.

"A pointless question," Naseru said. "The fact that it never happened proves that it was not meant to be."

"Hm," Tadaji grunted. "I find the reign of a bastard no more unlikely than the rule of a man trained by one of the Empire's most dangerous enemies." The old courtier studied

Naseru's scarred face with a careful eye. "All of your siblings are both flawed and admirable in their way, Naseru. As are you. None can say why your parents chose not to name an heir. The past cannot be changed, but we determine the future."

"How quaint," Naseru said. "Are you suggesting that I should abandon my quest for the throne and allow one of my unfit siblings to become Emperor, simply because it is easier?"

"I am suggesting nothing," Tadaji said. "Even I have no experience that will aid you in facing the crises you must overcome. I have come simply to offer my services as a peacemaker, to welcome you to Ryoko Owari, and to give you a gift." Tadaji reached into his thick fur cloak and drew out a bundle wrapped in rice paper and black silken ribbon. He offered it to Naseru.

"Unnecessary," Naseru said. "Your wisdom has been gift enough."

"The customary dance," Tadaji said. "Refuse the gift twice, and then accept. We both know the tradition, Naseru. It is an unnecessary gesture. Take it." Tadaji offered the package again.

"But I must refuse twice," Naseru said. "Coming up with reasons why is one of my few joys in life. It is the simplest game of the court, and the only one that remains entertaining after all this time. Keep your gift, Tadaji-san."

"You have refused twice," Tadaji said, feigning boredom.

"Indeed," Naseru said, taking the package with a quick grin. "My thanks, Tadaji-sama. Shall I open it?"

"Please do, but not here," Tadaji said. He gestured to one side; a servant in purple robes drew open the door to a private chamber. "It requires some explanation, and it would be best if you were not seen with it."

The two men stepped into the small room. As the door drew shut, Naseru peeled open the package. A pale green light shone in the Anvil's face. With a look of awe, Naseru drew out a curved dagger. From the end of the handle to the tip of the blade, the weapon was crafted of amethyst crystal. It glowed gently from within.

"What is this?" Naseru asked.

"It is called night crystal," Tadaji said. "Be careful; it is quite sharp. Draw it across a coin, if you have one, and see what happens."

Naseru reached into a small pouch behind his belt and drew out a copper coin. With a swift movement, he drew the knife across the face of the coin. A bright flash of sparks erupted and the coin fell in two pieces in his hand. "Fortunes," Naseru said, looking from the blade to Tadaji and back. "Even Kaiu steel is not this sharp. What samurai made this?"

"No samurai made it," Tadaji said. "It was found in the Way of Night."

Naseru's eye narrowed. "I have never heard of such a place," he said.

"A lie is the last resort of the defeated," Tadaji replied. "I thought I taught you better than that. I know that you sent your spy, Asako Misao, to investigate the Way of Night. I know what Moto Vordu did to him. Misao came back half mad, raving about crystals and ghosts and forgotten spirits."

Naseru frowned, studying the dagger for a long moment. He wrapped the knife in its paper and tucked it into his obi. "I sent Misao because I thought the Way of Night might hold the grave of my greatest ancestor," he said. "When he failed to discover it, I thought little more on the matter. Misao was never the most stable person, and I have much to occupy my mind."

"Well let this occupy your mind, then," Tadaji said. "Vordu is indeed dangerous, and you were wrong to ignore him."

Naseru's eye narrowed. "What game are you playing, Tadaji?" he asked. "What is the meaning of this gift?"

"The Way of Night is filled with artifacts such as those," Tadaji said. "Moto Vordu believes that the entire city serves some higher purpose and was created by a race of creatures that predates the Naga. Our Khan is an ambitious man and has given Vordu free reign to research the city as he pleases, so long as any new magic he discovers is turned to the benefit of the Unicorn Clan."

"How fortunate for the Unicorn," Naseru said. "With such weapons, no other clan will stand against you."

"With such weapons we will destroy ourselves," Tadaji replied fiercely. "I remember too well the days of the Clan War, when the Phoenix foolishly embraced the power of the Black Scrolls. Their clan was nearly destroyed. I do not trust Vordu. Whatever power lies in the heart of the City of Night, all of my instincts warn against using it."

"So tell your Khan," Naseru said.

"I have told him," Tadaji said, "but Moto Chagatai can be a difficult man. He is too occupied in helping Kaneka plan their conquest of Rokugan to listen to me. Usually he heeds my advice, but I suppose the weapons Vordu has given him outweigh an old man's paranoia. The Khan has forbidden me to interfere with Vordu in any way."

"Does that include asking me for aid?" Naseru asked, raising an eyebrow.

A shrewd smile crossed the old man's face. "I never asked you for aid, Naseru-sama," he said. "I was merely explaining the origins of my gift. However, should you choose to investigate of your own will that is your decision. As always, I wish you good fortune in all of your adventures."

"And what if I choose to ignore the Way of Night?" Naseru asked.

"That is your choice," Tadaji replied. "But I have confidence that you will make the right choice. Toturi was a just man, and you are your father's son."

Naseru chuckled under his breath.

"At any rate, I should take my leave of you now, Naseru-sama," Tadaji said, smoothing one hand over his fur cloak and peering at the door. "I must give my regards to that playwright. Clumsy and incompetent as he was, it's rare that we get any respectable new productions in Ryoko Owari. Good luck, Hantei Naseru. I do not mean to be trite, but I think that you will need it."

The old man hobbled away, cane clunking on the floor beside him.

Naseru watched him leave, his expression unreadable.

"What will you do next, my lord?" Isei asked quietly.

"Next?" Naseru replied, looking at his yojimbo. "Next, I plan to get some sleep. This party was dull anyway." One hand resting securely on the crystal dagger, Naseru stepped out of the small room and back into the crowd.

2 | THE SWORD OF YOTSU

Who are you?"

"I am Irie."

"Whom will you serve?"

"I will serve the Yotsu."

"How will you serve?"

"As their sword, carving away injustice and dishonor."

"The Yotsu have many swords already."

"There is much injustice in the world."

"One day you will fall, and the name of Yotsu will fall with you."

"When a samurai falls, she also rises."

"Then rise, Irie-san, and become Yotsu Irie, Sword of the Yotsu."

Irie opened her eyes. The darkness of the ruined city was palpable; only the small campfire in the center of the street warded it away. The shadows of several men and women in piecemeal armor surrounded her, all waiting patiently to see what she would do next.

Her hands were still curled about the naked blade resting

on its stand before her. At some point in the ceremony her fingers had closed upon the edge; now her own blood stained the steel. She peered up curiously.

"I said stand up, Irie-chan," Yotsu Seou, revered sensei of the Yotsu Dojo, said with a chuckle. "The ceremony is over."

Irie stood and peered around in wonder. The other samurai gazed at her with pride. Someone handed her a katana and wakizashi bearing the Yotsu mon; she eagerly tucked them beneath her belt. She was one of them now. The feeling was incredible; it made the pain in her hands seem like nothing.

"Bandage those," Seou said, tossing her a scrap of gauze. "That's Yotsu blood. No sense in wasting it."

"Yes, sensei," Irie said, wrapping her hands with an embarrassed chuckle.

"Well?" Seou said, peering about the assembled samurai. "Irie-san is one of us now. Shall we welcome her?" Seou hopped onto a fallen pile of rubble and rammed her fist into the air. "Utz!" she cried.

"Banzai!" the Yotsu shouted.

"*Utz!*" Seou shouted again, louder this time.

"*Banzai!*" the Yotsu replied.

"*UTZ!*" Seou shouted, even louder.

"*BANZAI!*" the Yotsu answered, their riotous cry echoing through the blasted streets of the Imperial City. They broke off into a chorus of cheers. Irie shouted with them, her own voice swiftly growing hoarse from the effort.

For the first time in over a year, she was happy. Many of the Yotsu came to congratulate her. Some clapped her on the shoulder. One small samurai-ko even embraced her. Irie was caught up in the emotion of the moment. These were not merely friends or allies; this was her family now. Someone produced a bottle of sake, and soon cups were passed around. The formal ceremony devolved into drunken revelry as the night continued. A circle of dancing samurai formed around the ruins of a burnt-out shrine. A samurai who introduced himself as Jun had climbed onto a rather precarious-looking tower and was howling Mantis sailing ballads on request. Most of the songs were incredibly lewd. Some referred to acts Irie had never even imagined. Irie listened with fascination, singing along as she picked up some of the words, never drinking the sake from her cup.

After some time, she set down the cup and wandered off alone.

This was home. This was family.

It was not her true home. It was not her true family.

Irie looked down at the daisho she now wore beneath her belt. They bore the symbol of the Yotsu house, the kanji for "ten thousand." She sighed, leaned against a crumbling wall, and wrapped her arms around her slim chest to ward off the cold. Only the dim light of the Yotsu campfire illuminated the broken streets of Otosan Uchi. After the city fell, most of the survivors had moved on. The Yotsu had remained; their dojo was one of a handful of structures still standing.

"Not attending your own celebration?" said a voice in the darkness.

Irie glanced around, startled. Yotsu Seou stepped out of the shadows. Her face was creased with age, though her hair remained raven black. She moved with a quiet, catlike grace; Irie knew from her brief training in the dojo how deceptively fast Seou could be. In the weeks since she had arrived at the dojo, Irie had modeled herself after Lady Seou. In a way, the old sensei had become like a mother to her. Not that Irie could ever forget her true mother, but it was comforting to put the pain aside when she could.

"I do not feel like celebrating," Irie said.

Seou nodded. "I see," she said. She sat across from Irie. "Do you wish to talk about it?"

"No," Irie said.

Seou nodded, waiting patiently.

"It is different than I thought it would be," Irie said at last.

"Oh?" Seou replied.

"I find it strange," she said, "but I feel somewhat . . . guilty."

"Because you are still alive," Seou said, "and the ones you love are dead."

"It is foolish," Irie said, eyes downcast.

"No," Seou said. "I know how you feel. I have lost my father, five brothers, two sisters, and countless friends. Each time a new samurai takes the Yotsu name I rejoice, but I also grieve for those who did not survive to share my joy."

Irie was quiet for a long time. In the distance, the songs of the drunken Yotsu echoed merrily. "How do you go on?" Irie asked finally, looking up at her sensei. "How do you find the strength to keep fighting, after all that you have lost?"

"I have the strength to go on *because* of all that I have lost," Seou answered. "The memories of my family carry me forward."

"My memories scream for vengeance," Irie said in a bitter voice.

Seou looked at Irie impassively. "Did I tell you the story of how the Yotsu were formed?" she asked.

"I have heard it," Irie said. "Your father rescued the Emperor's son from the Bloodspeakers. He was given a family name by the Emperor and appointed governor of the Yatoshin district of Otosan Uchi."

Seou glanced about the ruins with a wry smile. "The district has seen better days, I think."

Irie laughed, smiling despite her sour mood.

"There's more to the story," Seou said. "I was only a child when it happened, no more than five, but I remember that day more clearly than any other in my life. It was long before Toturi became Emperor, when Hantei XXXVIII reigned. My family lived in the Mountains of Regret. When winter began, an earthquake destroyed our home and killed my mother. It fell to my father to find us a new home. One night, my big brother Shoku pointed out a chain of campfires. My father told us to hide and went off to investigate. An hour later, he returned, took my brother Kyoden, and disappeared into the night again.

"This time, despite Shoku's watchful eye, I followed Father. I wasn't about to abandon Father so soon after losing my mother. It was dark, and the rocks were strangely slippery. When I looked at my hand in the faint moonlight, I saw that my palm was covered with blood, though I was not cut.

The entire *pass* was painted in blood, littered with the corpses of countless Imperial Guardsmen. They had been slaughtered by dark magic. The stench was indescribable."

"Slain by the Bloodspeakers," Irie said.

Seou nodded. "I had never been more terrified, but when I saw my father sneaking deeper into the camp, I knew I had to follow him. I had to protect him."

"But you were only a child," Irie said.

"I was a *samurai*," Seou said with a small chuckle. "I followed my father as he carried my infant brother through the camp, picking unseen through the tents of the evil cultists."

"They didn't see you?" Irie asked.

"My father was a fine hunter, and I was his best student," Seou said with some amount of pride. "We were not seen. Father stopped by a large cage of bamboo. A young woman huddled in the cage, holding a child the same age as my brother. Both wore bloodstained robes marked with the symbol of the chrysanthemum."

"The Empress?" Irie asked.

"Yes," Seou said. "Hochiahime. Her caravan had been attacked, all the guards slain. When she saw Father, tears welled in her eyes. 'I told you to run, ronin,' she whispered. 'There is nothing here but death.' "

" 'I cannot abandon you,' Father said, kneeling before her."

" 'You have no choice, Yotsu,' she said to him. 'If the Bloodspeakers find me missing, they will scour the mountains until they find you. You cannot escape their black magic.' "

" 'Then let me rescue the child,' Father said. 'I will replace him with my own son. By the time they realize the difference, I will be in Otosan Uchi.' "

" 'Your son will die,' the Empress said."

" 'Then he will die serving the Empire,' my father replied. I remember how little Kyoden laughed as his fingers curled around the bamboo bars. Without another word, Father bent the bamboo, pushed Kyoden through, and took the Empress's son."

Seou sat silently for a time, staring at the fire in the distance. "It was what the Empress said next that stuck in my mind. 'Live,' she said. 'Take my son to his father. Tell them to mourn me and the child I would have borne.' "

Irie sat where she was, quietly absorbing the story as she watched her sensei.

"It was the truest display of bravery I have ever seen," Seou said finally.

"Your father was a brave man," Irie agreed.

"That's not what I mean," Seou said. "My father's actions were heroic, but they stemmed from duty, not courage. The Empress was truly brave. She could have allowed my father to rescue her. The Bloodspeakers would have followed, would have killed us all. Instead, she chose to face her death, to give us all a chance to survive. As I followed my father back through the camp, I took one last look at Hochiahime. Her eyes were full of pride, hope, and joy. There was no fear, none at all. When times are difficult, I draw strength from that memory. You can draw strength from the past as well as pain, Irie. Try. Tell me of something that gives you strength."

"All right," Irie said. She thought for a long moment. "I remember when the Shadowlands Horde attacked the city. I had only been here for three days. I still did not know the streets, so I did not know which way to run for safety. The city was overwhelmed in minutes, legions of demons and undead destroying everything in their sight. I was certain I would die until, by random chance, I found the Yotsu dojo. The Yotsu samurai fought fearlessly. I knew I could do no less, so I joined the defense of the dojo."

"A fine story," Seou said, "but I know that one. Isn't there anything from your life before?"

"It is easier not to remember," Irie said.

Seou frowned. "Your problems are our problems now, Irie-chan," she said. "If your accent is any indication, you are either Dragon or Phoenix."

"Something like that," Irie said.

"That is a long way to travel," Seou said. "What brought you to Otosan Uchi?"

"I came seeking the man who killed my family," Irie said.

"Do you still intend to seek him out?" Seou said.

"I swore to carve away injustice and dishonor," Irie said. "My family will not rest until I have vengeance."

"And neither will you, I suspect," Seou said. "I wish you good fortune in your quest."

"You do not intend to stop me?" Irie asked.

"As you said, it is the Yotsu's duty to carve away injustice and dishonor," she said. "Go fulfill your vow to your family. When the deed is done, the dojo will still be here."

"Thank you, Seou-sama," Irie said, bowing her head gratefully.

"No need," Seou said. "Do you have enough money for the journey?"

"A samurai does not concern herself with base needs such as wealth," Irie said.

"Clan samurai need not concern themselves," Seou replied, "but ronin like us need every advantage they can get. Here, take this." Seou reached into her belt, drew out a small pouch, and threw it to Irie.

Irie's eyes widened when she saw the gold coins that filled the pouch. "Seou-sama, this is—" she began.

Seou silenced her with a wave of her hand. "We are sisters. What is mine is yours. I ask only that you return home safely. In the meantime, I must return to our errant siblings." She looked off in the direction of the boisterous Yotsu samurai. "I think if they drink much more, their singing might collapse the rest of the city. Think of what supplies you will need. In the morning, you may leave."

Seou departed soundlessly across the broken streets. Irie remained where she was, enjoying the silence and the darkness. All that Seou had asked was that she return safely. Irie felt a pang of guilt as she realized she would be unable to fulfill even that simple request. If she was successful, it was unlikely she would survive.

"Soon," she whispered, knowing that her father and brothers could hear her voice. "Soon we will all be able to rest. Soon, Hantei Naseru will die."

3 | VILLAINS

The Year
1159, Month
of the Tiger
Present Day

Naseru and Isei strode toward the front gates of the governor's mansion. Two Unicorn bushi tended their posts with varying levels of inattention. One nodded wearily, leaning on his spear. The other sat on the steps, drawing patterns in the dust with his toe. The guards stared at the two samurai for several moments, then hurriedly snapped to attention. Bowing and mumbling apologetic greetings, they opened the gates wide. Naseru and Isei passed through the wall into the courtyard beyond. Somewhere, a bell clanged loudly.

"Ah, another warm greeting from the vigilant governor," Naseru grumbled under his breath.

The palace doors flew open and a group of samurai in white and indigo armor marched out. At the head of the group strode a tall man with nervous eyes, still lacing on his breast plate. His long hair hung loose about his face. Naseru had the impression that the man had just dragged himself out of bed.

"Governor Osema-san," Naseru said, bowing courteously. "Did I wake you?"

"Lord Naseru, you have returned!" Osema said, gasping for breath. He carried his sheathed katana in one hand as he glanced about for any threat. "We did not expect you for several hours. You should have sent word. I would have dispatched my magistrates to escort you."

"I tired of the chancellor's entertainments earlier than expected," Naseru replied. "I sent no word because I felt I was in no danger."

"Then the Fortunes favor the bold," Osema said. "The streets of Ryoko Owari are not safe at night . . . or at any other time for that matter. A personage of your importance should not have traveled alone."

"I appreciate your concern, governor, but it is unnecessary," Naseru said. "Between my yojimbo and my relative anonymity in this city I assure you I was quite safe."

"Anonymity?" Osema asked. "You are a son of Toturi! One of the Four Winds! The entire city knows your name."

"But they do not know my face," Naseru replied. "My enemies cannot attack a name."

"Don't be so sure," Osema replied. "Ryoko Owari is built on lies. No one is safe here, not even me!"

"I see," Naseru said, nodding sagely. "Then I thank you once again for your earnest protection and sound advice. You are an island of truth in a sea of deception, Osema-san."

Osema paused, not certain exactly how to reply to the unexpected flattery. "Yes," he said finally, nodding confidently to punctuate the statement. He turned to address his troops. "The Anvil is safe. Return to your posts."

Naseru watched as the Unicorn samurai scattered. They were presumably eager to return to sleep or to whatever other duties did not involve chasing after shadows.

Osema noticed the Anvil watching the departing samurai, and a worried look crossed his face. "Naseru-sama, do you require an escort to your quarters?" Osema asked, pausing at the door. "I could call back some of my magistrates."

"I am certain that Isei will be protection enough. Unless you believe that Kolat assassins await me under the stairs."

Naseru feigned a wide-eyed, suspicious look and glanced about the hallway.

Osema seemed to consider this for a moment. "I sometimes forget your notorious sense of humor," he said. His face twisted in a crooked grin, as if he were uncertain how to accept a joke. "I will see you in the morning, Naseru-sama."

"Good night, governor," Naseru said as Osema passed into the doors. The Anvil stooped to remove his shoes, extending one hand to delay Isei as the governor continued on.

"Sama?" Isei said quietly. The yojimbo glanced around. "Is there danger?"

"Only of being bored to death," Naseru whispered. "I think I've had enough melodrama for one night. Let us wait until Osema is a good way ahead before we enter."

"Ah," Isei said, nodding toward the governor's retreating back. "The governor is a very . . . meticulous man."

"A polite way to put it," Naseru said. "I would call him paranoid."

"I think he suspects you are up to something," Isei said.

"No doubt," Naseru replied. "My reputation precedes me, it seems. I cannot stand people who are paranoid without cause. As if the rest of the world has nothing better than to do than conspire against Shinjo Osema. How insufferably arrogant."

Isei gave his master a pointed look, though he was careful not to say anything specific.

Naseru laughed. "I saw that," he said. "The difference between myself and Osema is that my paranoia is built on very solid ground. The rest of the Empire really is out to get me." Naseru smoothed his wide haori vest over his shoulders as he entered the halls of the governor's palace.

"Of course, sama," Isei said, drawing another laugh from his master. Isei fell into line a step behind his master.

"Mock as you wish, Isei," Naseru said. "Shinjo Osema does not have to deal with mysterious gifts from the mysterious Ide Tadaji, tests of loyalty from the sinister Bayushi Kaukatsu, and war stories from the insufferable Akodo Jusho."

"I thought the party went relatively well," Isei observed.

"Of course you thought it went well," Naseru said. "You didn't have to kill anyone."

Isei shrugged.

"While we're on the subject, I think we should make arrangements to meet with Doji Kinnosuke," Naseru said. "Perhaps we could arrange for him to build us suitable accommodations in the city. A home worthy of the son of Toturi."

"His wife seemed to approve of you," Isei commented.

"You think so?" Naseru remarked blandly, as if such a thing had not occurred to him. "At any rate, this is an entirely new city. We have many matters that require our attention, and the lovely Atsuko-chan is merely one item on a very long list. Let us return to our chambers and consult with Bakin."

"Naseru-sama," said a husky voice from the room to their left. "I wondered when you might return."

"Fortunes," Naseru whispered. "That couldn't be. . . ."

Naseru turned just as a young woman emerged from behind a sliding screen. She wore a rich dress of golden silk and her hair was elaborately tied back with gem-laded pins. She moved with the grace of one trained in the courts, the clinging material of her dress displaying every curve of her small body without appearing lewd or forward. Her full lips smiled slightly, unadorned by makeup. Her natural beauty was exquisite without such aid.

"Hoketuhime-chan!" Naseru exclaimed, his tone genuinely delighted. He bowed to the young woman more deeply than etiquette required. She replied with a pleased blush. Not all women could blush at whim. It was a skill Naseru admired.

"Lord Naseru, do you have time to enjoy some sake?" Hoketuhime asked. "My friends would be honored to meet you."

The young woman gestured for the Anvil to enter the room. Within, two more pretty young women sat at a small table. One wore robes of deep forest green. The other wore a form-fitting gown of dark red and a black veil that concealed the upper half of her face.

"Ah, but I am a stranger here," Naseru said humbly. "I would not wish to intrude upon your friends."

"Silly," Hoketuhime chided. "Who would not be pleased to meet the Son of Toturi?"

"Many people, actually," Naseru remarked under his breath. "But the hour is late," he said more clearly. "I have much business to attend to, sadly."

"Oh," Hoketuhime pouted and rolled her eyes at the floor. Her eyes were clear blue, a result of generations of intermarriage between the Imperial Families and the Crane Clan. "Such a shame."

"No shame at all," Naseru replied. "I only refused twice out of custom. Surely the opportunity to dally with such beautiful maidens must be a precious gift from the Fortunes. I only fear I will be unable to repay them with a gift of equal value." He raised one hand, barely caressing the edge of Hoketuhime's perfect cheek with the backs of his fingers. The woman in green giggled.

"You rogue," Hoketuhime said, smiling playfully. "You're teasing me."

"Of course," Naseru said. "I have all the time in the world." He followed Hoketuhime into the room, pausing only long enough to glance back at Isei. The yojimbo's grim frown was tilted slightly on one side. That was about as much amusement as Isei ever showed. The yojimbo silently took up his post in the hall beside the door.

"This is the fellow I was telling you about," Hoketuhime said as she returned to her place at the head of the table. The other women rose and bowed to Naseru, and he returned the gesture before they were all seated.

"So I am the subject of legend now, Hoketuhime-chan?" Naseru asked.

"In some circles," she replied coyly, "and you should not call me 'chan.' I am the daimyo of my family now, and you are the heir to the throne. We are children no longer."

"Bah," Naseru said. "Most of my memories of our youth are quite fond, Hoketuhime. May I not keep them?" He looked at her imploringly.

Hoketuhime blushed again. "You have not changed a bit," she said. "Hantei Naseru, might I introduce Bayushi Mitsuyo, a recent acquaintance who lives here in the city. She is here on business, guarding one of her clan's caravans on its way to the Dragon provinces."

"A pleasure," Naseru said. The woman in red inclined her head slightly.

Hoketuhime continued. "And this is Moshi Nao, an old friend from Toshi Inazuma."

"A Mantis," Naseru said to the young woman. "There are not many of your clan in Ryoko Owari."

"I have never met an Imperial heir," Nao said, a slightly giddy tone to her voice. Her eyes were very wide, as if she feared the city would vanish at any moment and she had to look at as much of it as possible as quickly as possible.

"I pray I meet up to your expectations," Naseru said. He leaned closer to her, squinting slightly. "You have green eyes," he observed. "How extraordinary."

"Many women of my family have green eyes," Nao said, carefully averting her eyes to the table with a pleased smile.

"Have a care, Nao," Hoketuhime said with a small smile. "The Lord Anvil is a fool for women with exotic eyes."

"I think I must plan a visit the Mantis Isles soon," Naseru concluded. He looked to Nao again. "I don't suppose you would want to come with me?"

"I couldn't," she said. "I am here with my grandfather. I am arranged to be married."

"Congratulations," Naseru said sincerely. "A brilliant victory for one man and a tragedy for all others. That explains your association with Hoketuhime-chan. Your future will be bright, I think. She is an expert at arranging marriages."

"You are too kind," Hoketuhime replied.

"You must know one another from Otosan Uchi," Nao said, her voice full of wonder. "Hoketuhime told me much about the city. I wish I could have seen it before it was destroyed."

"Indeed," Naseru said, his tone somber. "There was no other place quite like it. To see it in ruins was almost as much a shock as my father's death. Otosan Uchi was like a dear friend to me. I have many memories there."

"As do I," Hoketuhime said. "Most I would rather forget. However, with you, Kaukatsu, and myself here we could rebuild the Imperial Court. Give us a year, and Ryoko Owari will be the new Otosan Uchi."

"An ambitious plan," Naseru said.

"Oh," Hoketuhime said meekly. "So you did have such a thing in mind? You did not intend to ask me if the Otomo family would support your bid to declare Ryoko Owari the new capital?"

"Not without a drink," Naseru said wryly, drawing a laugh from Nao and Hoketuhime. The Scorpion grinned but did not laugh.

Nao pushed a small porcelain cup toward the Anvil, but he pushed it aside. Reaching into his robe, he drew out a small china cup. Setting it on the table, he poured himself a cup of sake. Nao regarded him with a puzzled expression, glancing at Hoketuhime for help.

"Do not be insulted. Naseru is a something of a collector of obscure customs and traditions," Hoketuhime said. "It's a game to him. What's this one, Crane?"

"Not Crane," Naseru said, "Truth be told, I do not remember where the tradition of carrying one's own cup originates, but I am rather fond of it." He sipped his sake, studying Bayushi Mitsuyo over the lip of the cup for a moment. The Scorpion watched him quietly, her eyes unreadable behind her thick veil.

"The Crane do have a surprising number of drinking traditions, however," he said. "For instance, the Doji believe that it is unlucky to pour one's own sake, and quite fortunate if one's sake is poured by a beautiful young woman." His eye flicked to Nao. She quickly looked away, trying to appear as if she had not been staring at him.

"And what was the origin of that?" Hoketuhime asked, looking from Nao to Naseru, then back.

Naseru set his cup down. "The tale dates to two brothers of the Doji family, Shojiro and Taikan," he said. "One evening, before a battle, they drank sake to build their courage. Shojiro poured his own sake and due to overindulgence he died in battle the next day. Taikan's sake, on the other hand, was poured by a beautiful young courtier of the Kakita house, who watched him carefully and made certain he drank in moderation. As a result, Taikan won the battle and became one of the most decorated generals the Crane have ever known." Naseru paused to consider his own story. "Strange, that. The Lion have a reputation as talented generals, but in all the tales they are soundly defeated, time and again, especially by the Crane."

"Of course the Crane win in all the stories," Hoketuhime said, sipping from her own cup. "The Lion have better generals, but the Crane have better storytellers."

Naseru laughed and raised his cup. "A toast," Naseru said, his eye twinkling as he looked at Hoketuhime. "To old friends and to new ones."

The others returned the toast happily. They passed the time in idle conversation, with Naseru flirting idly with Moshi Nao and drawing irritated comments from Hoketuhime in return. Bayushi Mitsuyo spoke very little, her voice muffled by her thick robes. After an hour, Mitsuyo quietly excused herself. Naseru was as unconcerned with her absence as he had been with her presence.

At last, Moshi Nao rose to leave. Again, Naseru flattered her by rising as well. Hoketuhime also stood. "I am sorry to cut the evening short," Nao said, bowing her head, "but I must return to my quarters and make certain that my grandfather is properly attended to. He is quite elderly and I fear he may have fallen ill during the journey here."

"Is that so?" Naseru said. "I will arrange for the city's finest physicians and shugenja to attend him."

"Oh, no," Nao said, shaking her head quickly. "I could not possibly repay you."

"Nonsense," Naseru said with a grin. "If your grandfather helped raise a daughter as beautiful as you, he must be preserved for the good of all the Empire."

"Many thanks, Naseru-sama!" she said, bowing quickly.

She quickly left the chamber, obviously excited to bring her grandfather the good news.

"She forgot to refuse your gift twice," Hoketuhime said, peering out through the shoji screen as Nao departed.

"I noticed," Naseru said, pouting slightly. "I love that game."

"You were flirting with her," Hoketuhime said archly. She sat beside him. Alone with Naseru, Hoketuhime was more relaxed. She no longer sat prim and straight in her seat, no longer measured every movement with calculated precision. Naseru's shoulders also relaxed. His calm expression drooped into a frown.

"Of course I was flirting," Naseru said. "She was exquisitely beautiful. Terrible shame she was so dull."

"You're terrible," Hoketuhime said, smiling at him as she drew one of the long pins from her hair. A lock of dark black spilled over her left shoulder.

"I prefer women who can think for themselves," Naseru said. "Otherwise, what's the point? Must be the same reason I can't see the sport in fishing. If you catch a fish, eat it. Don't congratulate yourself for outsmarting it."

Hoketuhime laughed. "Are you truly going to send the physicians for her grandfather?" She leaned against his arm. Her exquisitely cut dress fell to reveal a scandalous amount of flesh. Her dark eyes watched Naseru.

Naseru's brow wrinkled in thought. "I promised, therefore I must," he said, smiling down at her. "I should guard my tongue more carefully. Why did I promise that? How strong is this sake?" He plucked up the bottle and examined it.

"You hardly drank any," Hoketuhime said. "You hardly ever drink any. You just watch everyone else drink."

"You're too observant for your own good," Naseru said, grinning at her. "So you are arranging a marriage for the Moshi?"

"Yes," she replied. "There's a young Scorpion named Kwanchai who sounded promising, though he is apparently missing."

"Bayushi Kwanchai?" Naseru asked with a small smile.

"The fool who injured Shiba Aikune at the Test of the Emerald Champion?"

"The same," she said. "He comes from an impressive family."

"More's the pity," Naseru said with a deep sigh.

"The marriage will serve both families well," Hoketuhime added.

"And to blazes if neither of them cares for the other, I suppose," Naseru said dryly.

"You know that has always been the way of things," Hoketuhime replied. "Samurai marry for the same reason that they do everything—duty, honor, and clan."

"I know," Naseru said. "But still, it does not seem right. My father never forced my sister to marry. He let her make her own choice."

"When you become Emperor, I suppose there will be changes?" Hoketuhime asked.

"I think we both know how much chance I have of becoming Emperor," Naseru said. "I have many friends, but I have too many enemies. My sister is neither truly loved nor truly hated. She will gain the throne by default, I'm sure of it. If that happens, I suppose it is for the best. I only hope she is strong enough."

Hoketuhime laughed.

"What?" Naseru demanded. "Are you laughing at me?"

"I'm laughing at the Empire," she said. "So many people are convinced that you're some sort of evil, soulless villain. I think they would be surprised at the good you do."

"What good?" Naseru asked. "My sister kills Tsuno, brings food to starving peasants, inspires hope. I just plot and scheme." Naseru waved a hand dismissively.

Hoketuhime seized his wrist in one hand. "And adjudicate legal disputes and collect the taxes and hear the grievances of provincial governors and a thousand other things that the other Winds couldn't be bothered to do. Your problem, I think, is that you *enjoy* letting people think that you're a villain."

She leaned her head on his shoulder. Her hand rested on his. He clasped her fingers in his own.

"Villainy does have a certain charm," he said. "People do what I say. Fear is quite the efficient motivator." With his free hand, he poured her a cup of sake. "Plus, many women find a villainous man quite attractive."

"So you think," she said. Hoketuhime picked up the cup between two fingers. "That tale you told about the Crane brothers. Was it true?"

"I made it up," Naseru said. "I have no idea why the Crane don't pour their own sake, but that story seemed as good a reason as any."

Hoketuhime laughed. "You are a better man than you admit, Naseru. You give everything to the Empire, and unlike your brothers and sister, you have the scars to prove it." One finger traced his chest and his throat, and trailed to his face, touching the silken patch that covered his eye. He could feel her warm breath on his cheek.

Naseru turned away from her. "You should go," he said, his voice thick. "If your husband discovered you were here, the scandal would bring shame to both our families."

"I mean nothing to him," she said, her hand falling away. She lowered her head, staring down at her knees. "He obeys my commands, but he does not love me. He seldom speaks to me. I think he fears me. He is a boring fool chosen only because my father wished to please the Matsu."

"Your father was a fool," Naseru said fiercely, his hand tightening on hers. "We must live with the promises our fathers make, but we must live with our own choices as well. I think if I remain near you for much longer we will make a choice we will both regret in time."

She looked up at him again, eyes full of sadness. She would not cry. In the Imperial Court, Hoketuhime was called the Winter Princess. She had a reputation as a cold, calculating woman. Naseru knew the truth as well as she knew him. It wasn't that she had no emotions; she simply controlled them better than most. She certainly had more experience needing to do so. When he looked into her deep blue eyes, he could see all the pain and sadness she hid from the rest of the Empire; it echoed his own. He found it difficult to look away.

"You have not left," she noted.

"I am gathering my courage," Naseru said. He quickly plucked his sake cup from the table and downed its contents in a gulp. "Ah, there it is." Leaning closer, he kissed Hoketuhime softly on the cheek, then stood.

"You were right. I plan to forge Ryoko Owari into the new capital of the Empire," he said. "I will not force you to aid me. You owe me nothing, Hoketuhime-chan."

"Silly boy," she said, gazing up at him from beneath her thick eyelashes. "You already know I will help, even if you do not ask."

He smiled crookedly, turned, and left. There was nothing further to say.

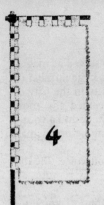

4   FRIENDS AND FAMILY

Like a shadow, Isei joined him in the hall. The yojimbo made no comment on the exchange that had taken place within.

"Which way did the Scorpion go?" Naseru asked.

"Toward the garden," Isei said, as if he had been expecting the question. He pointed down a hallway to the right. "That way."

Naseru nodded and turned right. Isei followed. After several moments, they emerged into the gardens of the governor's palace. Shinjo Osema did not strike Naseru as the sort of man who enjoyed luxury, but the former Scorpion governors of the city were quite the opposite. The gardens were lush and beautiful, with countless fountains, raked stone paths, and shrubberies carved into exotic forms. Some of the floral sculptures had not been tended in the months since the Unicorn had taken over the city. Shrubs that once resembled horses or rabbits now resembled shaggy oxen and porcupines.

Here and there beside the path stood shrines to various

Fortunes and notable souls who had once served as magistrates in Ryoko Owari. Naseru noted that a large number of magistrates seemed to die in the line of duty in the City of Lies. He followed the rock path that seemed the most recently disturbed. Not far along the path he found a young woman in red robes and a dark veil bowing before a small shrine in prayer.

"Naseru-sama," the Scorpion said in a soft voice. She did not look up, but sensed his approach. "This is quite an honor."

"Oh, stop it," Naseru said in a clipped tone. "I know it's you. Now stop spying on me and take off the veil, Sunetra."

The Scorpion laughed. Rising nimbly to her feet she pulled off the mask. Striking blue eyes sparkled from an angular, mischievous face. When the veil was removed, her entire mannerism changed. She moved with restless energy, constantly shifting from foot to foot like a dancer. She even seemed to stand two inches shorter, her brow hardly coming to Naseru's chin.

"When did you suspect?" she asked. Even her voice had become fuller, more melodious.

"You gave three clues," Naseru said, holding up three fingers. "I first suspected you were here when the random Scorpion began shilling me at Kaukatsu's mansion."

"Ah, yes," Sunetra said. "My cousin, Sorai. How did he do?"

"Very well," Naseru replied, "though complimenting my bravery was a bit much."

"I'll warn him to be more subtle next time," she said. "What was the second clue?"

"Any Scorpion who truly hailed from Ryoko Owari would have known that the custom of carrying one's own cup comes from this very city," Naseru said. "You hail from Bayushi lands and lived mostly in Otosan Uchi, so the custom was unfamiliar to you."

Sunetra swore. "Well, I feel like a fool," she said. "I knew I should have researched the city more."

"The third mistake was the veil," Naseru said. "You should have chosen a mask that covered your entire face."

"What?" Sunetra asked, bewildered. "Why?"

"Your lips," Naseru said. "Any man who could see them once and forget them doesn't deserve to be a man."

"Flattery?" she asked with a smirk. "Save that one for the Moshi. She might be impressed by it."

"I think I will," Naseru said. "Other than that, the disguise was very good. Excellent touch, changing your posture and pace."

"Basic Bayushi training," she nodded. "The Soshi techniques are even more advanced. Were you fooled at all, Isei-san?" She smiled at the yojimbo imploringly.

Isei folded his arms and sighed.

"Still, there is the obvious question," Naseru said. "Why were you in disguise? Why did you not report to me in person?"

"Otomo Hoketuhime knows your secrets," Sunetra said. "I was hoping she would share."

"Must you always pry into my past, Sunetra?" Naseru asked, more irritated than angered.

"I am curious by nature," she said. "I must compliment you, by the way. Whatever you said to wrap the Winter Princess around your finger was quite effective."

"Sunetra," Naseru said, his voice taking a dangerous edge. "Leave Hoketuhime alone."

"She is quite taken with you, Naseru-sama," Sunetra said. "She said the two of you met in the house of the Steel Chrysanthemum. Is it true?"

"We have work to do," Naseru said more firmly. "Cease this annoying behavior."

"Hai," Sunetra replied, taking the hint. "What do you need me to do?"

"Stay nearby," he said. "I am certain we shall require your talents soon. Visit Shinjo Osema and tell him you are with my entourage. He will provide you with a room, though I'm certain he will conclude you are a spy of some sort."

"I *am* a spy," she said with a smirk.

"Then tell him that," Naseru said. "I think it may put his mind at ease."

"Should I tell him I'm an assassin as well?"

"One day at a time, Sunetra."

Sunetra laughed. Bowing to Naseru a final time, then smiling at Isei, she returned to her prayer. Naseru and Isei left the garden, heading back toward the stairs that led to their rooms.

"You take a risk placing any more trust in her," Isei said once she was out of earshot. "She is too curious."

"Spies are supposed to be curious, Isei," Naseru said.

Isei shrugged. "She will bring you trouble, my lord," he said.

"Then keep her from doing so."

"Yes, my lord."

The two men continued up the stairs to the guest chambers Osema had prepared for them. The floors creaked as they moved—nightingale floors, designed to alert against the presence of assassins. Naseru wondered if the floors had been present since the Scorpion ruled the city or if Osema had them installed. At the sound of their approach, a spindly old man appeared, keeping his eyes carefully downcast and bowing deeply as he greeted them.

"Hantei-sama," the old man said. "Your presence illuminates the dreary evening. How was the play?"

"Entertaining, Bakin," Naseru said. "The kabuki was not bad, either."

"How wonderful, Hantei-sama," the man said. "This letter arrived for you." He offered a scroll of pure white paper, sealed with red and white mask. The seal was that of a wolf—his brother, Sezaru.

Naseru did not touch the scroll at first. "Who delivered this?" he asked.

"It was not delivered," Bakin said. "It simply appeared. When I touched it, I somehow knew that it was for you."

That sounded like Sezaru. Naseru accepted the scroll. When he had been younger, Naseru often found it difficult not to be jealous of his brother. Sezaru was a powerful shugenja, a holy man who could work magic by speaking to the elemental spirits. He could call lightning from the sky on a clear day and crack a mountain with sheer force of will. When he grew older, Naseru began to learn that he had certain distinct advantages over his brother. Naseru did not argue with himself aloud when he thought no one else could hear. Naseru did not fall into a catatonic stupor for days at a time. Naseru did not wake up screaming, ranting about visions that never were and people who never existed. He envied his brother's power, but he pitied him as well.

Naseru loved his brother, but there was no denying that Sezaru was insane. Months ago Sezaru had launched into a personal vendetta against the Shadowlands, determined to hunt down those who had summoned the beast that murdered their father. Naseru had approved; not only did the fight remove Sezaru from the race for the throne, but it gave the shugenja something useful to do. Naseru knew from his time with the Steel Chrysanthemum that power and boredom made a deadly combination. Should Sezaru ever take the throne, the Empire would suffer.

Dismissing Bakin and Isei, Naseru sat at a small desk and broke the seal on Sezaru's scroll. He felt a small tingle pass through his fingers when he did so, and wondered vaguely what would have happened had anyone but the intended recipient opened it—probably something dramatic and lethal. That was Sezaru's style. Naseru squinted his eye and leaned close to read his brother's jumbled, chaotic handwriting.

Naseru-san,

I hope that this letter finds you well. Though you have chosen to ignore my claim to our mother's throne, I wish you no ill.

I will not demand that you set aside your own claim, for I know that only your own reason and wisdom will bring you to such a decision. It is not the intent of this missive to argue over politics or trade empty threats, but to share information.

I have discovered the identity of the man who slew our father.

Yes, I say a man. Those who witnessed Toturi's death claim that a savage beast beheaded him, but that creature acted at the bidding of another, an entity known as Daigotsu, the same Dark Lord who led the recent attack on Otosan Uchi. During the battle in the heart of the Forbidden City we encountered Daigotsu and learned his terrible secret.

The truth of Daigotsu's identity is so sensitive that I dare not write the information in this letter. For you to know at this point will cause you greater harm than good. Instead, I merely urge you to exercise caution in any and all confrontations with Daigotsu or his minions. His designs on Rokugan are terrible indeed.

In some way Daigotsu has taken the stuff of nightmares, bound it to oni, and created a new type of demon that draws strength from our weakness. There are eight of these onisu, each a powerful beast that represents the darkest aspects of one of the Great Clans. Acts of dishonor and sin cause them to grow in strength. The four-armed creature that slew our father was one of them. Its name was Fushin, the Onisu of Betrayal, and it draws power from treachery.

Fortunately, I have discovered the weakness of these creatures. Many months ago, I encountered Yokubo, the Onisu of Desire. My yojimbo was able to injure it because he desired nothing. Presumably the other onisu have similar weaknesses. Reports of encounters with the onisu during the attack on Otosan Uchi seem to support this theory.

Possibly more dangerous are the ogre-like beasts called Tsuno that have plagued the Lion of late. They often appear in the company of the onisu. Their strength is incredible and some of them practice powerful magic. I believe the Tsuno shugenja—called "Soultwisters" among their kind—aided Daigotsu in the creation of the onisu.

I hope this information comes of use to you, my brother. I believe these creatures may have dark designs for all the children of Toturi. We should not be enemies. When I rule as Emperor, I would have you as my advisor. I would trust no one else.

Toturi Sezaru, The Wolf

"Bah," Naseru said, tucking the letter into a nearby brazier as he committed it to memory. "When *I* am Emperor, I will build you a nice, remote monastery where you can talk to yourself in peace."

As the flames licked at the paper, Naseru's eye narrowed in thought. Something seemed strange about his brother's letter. It did not surprise him that Sezaru had chosen to warn him about the Dark Lord and the oni; though he and Sezaru had their differences they were still brothers. Yet he felt there was something missing.

Had the letter been written by anyone else, Naseru would have suspected its intent was merely to put him on guard, to alert him to a threat that would not come. Sezaru was above such tactics. The Wolf never threatened, and Sezaru had been very direct with his warning. There was no implication that he had sent similar missives to Tsudao or Kaneka. He had chosen to warn Naseru only.

"If there are only eight onisu, why waste them in an attack against me?" Naseru wondered. "I am hardly a threat to the Dark Lord."

Two possibilities emerged in Naseru's mind. The first and simplest possibility was that Daigotsu had some personal vendetta against him, that somehow he had angered this Dark Lord and become one of his enemies. That was very possible. Naseru had made many enemies in his brief career. If that was the case, he took some comfort in the thought. Vengeful people were driven by emotion and were prone to making foolish mistakes.

The second possibility was that Naseru posed some threat to Daigotsu's power. That was almost laughable. Of all the Winds, Naseru was perhaps the least likely to attract the attention of the Dark Lord. The Shadowlands threatened Rokugan in a direct fashion, via hordes of undead, oni, and Tainted samurai. A politician like Naseru was no threat. Short of using his influence to rouse a strike force of Inquisitors and Witch Hunters there was little he could do against Daigotsu—unless, of course, he possessed some heretofore unrecognized key to the Dark Lord's defeat and did not realize it. Speculation along such lines was worthless.

He needed more information. Without knowing more about the Dark Lord, there was no way to know how to react to his brother's letter short of finding Sezaru and asking him. Naseru knew full well how difficult it could be to find Toturi Sezaru. The room darkened as the flames burned down. Naseru watched the blackened parchment curl and contemplated his next move.

5   THE KOMUSO

Komuso were a special variety of monk particularly common in Ryoko Owari. These anonymous itinerant holy men were known for wearing wide basket hats that covered their faces, concealing their identity so that it would not interfere with their message. These strange individuals traveled from place to place, teaching the wisdom of Shinsei wherever they went. The komuso knew no home temple and owed allegiance to no lord. Many made their living by playing the shakuhachi, a long flute, and begging for what donations they could to survive.

It was much easier for a komuso to make a good living in the City of Lies than many other cities. This was not so much due to the fact that the citizens of Ryoko Owari were particularly pious; far from it. Rather, the fact that komuso were faceless, anonymous, and able go anywhere they wished in the city without being questioned made them excellent spies. No one would ever dare call them spies, of course. Such an accusation would be an affront to the Brotherhood of Shinsei. However, those who did business with the komuso often found that their observations could have very practical applications.

Magistrates generally gave those dressed in the regalia of a komuso little trouble, but genuine komuso were expected to police their own. It was all too easy for a ronin or peasant to take up a flute and a basket hat and pretend to be a holy monk. Upon encountering one another in the streets of the city, komuso would quote obscure passages of the Tao to test one another's authenticity. Those whose memories failed them quickly discovered that the Brotherhood's reputation for martial prowess was not unearned. The local magistrates often found the corpses of false komuso floating in the city's bay, aptly named the Bay of Drowned Honor.

The dangers of impersonating a komuso were the farthest thing from the mind of the man who sat crosslegged at the edge of the city docks. He wore a heavy basket hat and simple robes. He played a shakuhachi flute through the small hole near his mouth; the haunting music drifted lazily across the bay. The komuso took no note of the fishermen preparing for the day's labor nearby. One paused to listen to the komuso's song for a time, then dropped two zeni on his plate.

"Copper?" the monk said, drawing his flute from his basket and looking up at the man. "Would you give Shinsei copper? What do you expect me to eat with that? Sand?"

The fisherman scowled. "It's all I have," he said.

"Liar," the komuso said in an amused voice. He poked the man in the chest with the end of the long flute. "You have three koku hidden in a box under the docks. You've been saving it, stealing the best fish for yourself and selling them to that Tortoise ambassador. I think your lord would be most agitated if he discovered such a thing, don't you?"

"What?" the fisherman said with a start. His gnarled hands balled into fists. "Listen, I don't know who told that, but—"

"Careful," the komuso said. "I wouldn't lie to me again. You have already betrayed your lord's trust and your own honor. Lie to a servant of Shinsei and your sin will be thrice compounded." The monk began playing his flute softly once more. He tapped the clay donation plate in time with one toe.

The fisherman stood by the komuso's side in impotent fury. Finally coming to a decision, he glanced around the docks, reached behind his back, and drew a short knife from its sheath. He flipped the weapon in his hand and advanced.

The komuso stopped playing and looked back at the man. Though his face was covered, something in the way the little man silently stared sent a chill of fear through the fisherman. The knife fell from his hand, sticking upright in the dock with a shuddering sound.

"Go bring me the money you have stolen," the komuso said. "Next time you haul in the catch, I want you to double the amount that you set aside. One share for your Tortoise and one share for me. Is that clear, Izo-san?"

"Yes . . . yes, sir," the fisherman said, now trembling.

"Good," the komuso said. "Now get out of my sight." He returned to his song.

The fisherman nodded and ran back down the dock as fast as he could. A few of his fellow laborers watched him with some curiosity. Just then a Scorpion wearing a blue velvet fox mask and robes of bloodred silk stepped onto the docks, glaring at the peasants in a condescending manner. Noting the wakizashi he wore on his hip, the fishermen bowed and found more pressing business elsewhere. The Scorpion ignored them, heading directly toward the komuso. Stopping several paces behind the anonymous stranger, the Scorpion knelt and bowed, pressing his forehead to the wooden planks.

The little man drew the tip of the flute from his basket. "Good morning, Soshu-san," he said without looking back. "How are your headaches?"

"Better, my lord," the Scorpion said, sitting upright. "I have news for you."

"I am listening," the komuso said.

"The Anvil has arrived in the city, just as you said he would," Soshu said. "He has taken quarters in the governor's mansion and has made an alliance with the Imperial Chancellor, Bayushi Kaukatsu."

The komuso played a short trill on his flute and gestured over his collection plate. Two small cubes wrapped in black paper appeared there. Soshu licked his lips.

"Tell me more," the komuso said.

"He also met with Tadaji," Soshu offered, eyes fixed on the black cubes.

"Emperor Toturi's advisor?" the komuso asked.

"Yes," Soshu said. "He gave the Anvil a gift. He did not unwrap it in public, but the spirits told me it was crystal."

The music stopped. "Crystal?" the monk said, peering over his shoulder. "Are you sure?"

"Yes." Soshu nodded. "Naseru concealed it, but I saw it clearly."

The komuso gestured over the plate again as he continued playing. Two cubes became four. "Did you overhear what they discussed?" he asked.

"No," Soshu replied. "I dared not approach too closely. Even when they were not in a private room, they stood in shadows."

"As do we all," the komuso chuckled between notes. "Take your payment, Soshu-san."

The courtier scuttled forward on his hands and knees and collected the cubes. He hid them in his kimono with no mind for his own dignity. "Will there be anything else?" he asked eagerly.

The komuso's song stopped again. "Yes," he said. "Steal the Unicorn's gift from the Anvil. Bring it to me here in three days, and I will supply you with all the opium you will need for the next three winters."

Soshu's eyes widened. "M-my lord," he stuttered, "is this a serious offer?"

"Quite serious," the monk said. "Perhaps it may seem a bit generous, but you are my friend, Soshu. I know how bad your headaches get. I only wish to help."

"Thank you, my lord," Soshu said, pressing his head to the planks again. "I will not fail you!"

"Three days," the komuso said. "Now go on your way. May the blessings of Shinsei be upon you."

"Yes, my lord," Soshu said. He pressed his head to the dock a final time, rose, and quickly scurried back the way he had come.

The komuso watched Soshu leave, chuckling softly. When he had first discovered Shosuro Soshu two years ago, the man had been one of the most talented young courtiers in Otosan Uchi. Someday, he might have been appointed as provincial governor, or perhaps hatamoto to an honored lord. Instead, he was barely a shadow of his former self, an animal who sought nothing more than the next mind-numbing high that the opium would bring. Now he was even willing to resort to theft to acquire what he needed, never even pausing to consider the risks involved. Shosuro Soshu was no longer a man. He was nothing more than a beast. He would not return in three days; that much was obvious.

Behind the basket, the komuso smiled.

6 FROM THE SHADOWS

Seppun Isei yawned so wide his jaw cracked. Rubbing his chin with a sour grimace, he peered out the window into the courtyard below. His eyes quickly adjusted to the early morning light and scanned every corner for any sign of a threat to his master. There was none, of course, nor did he expect any. It was too soon; Naseru had only just arrived in this city a few days ago. It was unlikely that any assassin who attempted to attack the Anvil so quickly would make it past the governor's guards and defenses.

In Isei's experience, the most dangerous assassins were the ones who bided their time and learned the routine of their quarry. Naseru had no routine in Ryoko Owari as of yet, and thus presented no pattern for such an individual to exploit. However, there was always the remote chance that a fool could get lucky, so Isei was no less vigilant. Closing the window, Isei crossed the nightingale floor, opened the shoji screen, and peered into the hall in either direction. He saw only old Bakin, seated by the main entry to Naseru's quarters and idly smoking a pipe.

"Bakin, if you see anything amiss . . ." Isei whispered.

"Close the screen," the old man said with a chuckle. "Yes, Isei-sama, I remember."

Assured that there was no immediate threat, Isei slid the shoji screen three quarters closed. The dim light of the dawn through the window slits was all he needed to see. Any more light than that would simply give away his location. With a satisfied nod, he returned to his post just outside Naseru's bedroom door. A low snoring echoed from within. For the last two days, Naseru had not slept. During the days, he conducted meetings with important samurai from the city. During the night, he made plans. Naseru rarely slept. He would work until he became too exhausted to continue and then find somewhere peaceful to collapse.

For the moment, at least, the Anvil was most likely not leaving his chambers. The old yojimbo folded his arms across his chest and stood with his feet at shoulder's width, staring straight ahead. For nearly two hours, he did not move. The morning light crawled across the floor of the chamber. As a finger of sunlight touched the toe of his foot, his stare came into focus, settling upon the figure watching from just beyond the shoji screen. The muscles in Isei's jaw tightened. "What do you want, Sunetra?" he whispered.

The Scorpion stepped into the room, making no noise on the nightingale floor. She crouched near the wall, watching Isei curiously from the shadows. "Were you sleeping?" she asked.

"Resting," he corrected her.

"You sleep standing up with your eyes open?" she asked. "Impressive."

"What do you want, Sunetra?" Isei repeated; the tone made it more of a dismissal than a question.

"I wish to know more of that woman Naseru spoke to last night," Sunetra said.

"She is Otomo Hoketuhime, daimyo of the Otomo," Isei said. "She arranges marriages on behalf of the Imperial Family."

"I know that," Sunetra said in an irritated tone. "I wish to know who that woman is *to him.*"

"Then ask him," Isei said.

"You know he will not tell me," she said.

"Then it is none of your business," Isei said.

"So you say," she replied, "but like you, it is my duty to protect the Anvil from dangers he cannot see. I know that the Steel Chrysanthemum was held under house arrest in a minor palace of the Otomo in Dragon lands. Is that where they met? Was she Hantei XVI's student as well?"

"I fail to see how gossiping about Lord Naseru's past serves to protect him," Isei said.

"I need to know what significance she has to him," Sunetra said. "I do not trust that woman."

"I agree Lord Naseru should be more careful whom he trusts," Isei said.

"You know I am loyal to him," she said, bristling at the implied insult.

"If you are loyal to him, trust him," Isei retorted. "Do not pry into his past."

"Easy to say," Sunetra said. "You have known him since he was a child. You know all there is to know about him."

"Stupid girl!" Isei snapped. "Don't you realize there are some things that are better left forgotten?"

Sunetra's blue eyes widened in surprise. Isei glanced at the floor, his face reddening in shame from his outburst. The sound of footsteps approached from outside. Bakin's bald head peered around the shoji screen.

"Hello?" the old servant said. "Is there a problem, Isei-sama? I heard a cry."

"There is no problem," Isei said.

The old servant frowned, noting the tension in the room. "The fault is mine," he said with aplomb. "Obviously my ears deceived me. I apologize, Isei-sama."

Isei nodded abruptly.

Bakin turned to the Scorpion. "Lady Sunetra," he said warmly. "I shall serve tea for you, if you like."

"Thank you, Bakin," Sunetra said.

The old servant bobbed his head a final time and withdrew, closing the shoji screen. Isei scowled. In an instant, his blade was in his hand. The Scorpion looked down at Isei's sword, her eyes full of curiosity rather than fear.

"What is it?" she asked. "What is happening?"

"Something threatens Lord Naseru," Isei whispered, nodding to her sword as he reached for the screen leading to Naseru's room. "Time to prove your loyalty, Sunetra."

Confused, she nodded to the yojimbo.

With a loud kiai shout Isei charged into Naseru's chamber, katana held high in both hands. Sunetra rolled inside, a short knife clutched in either hand. Naseru sat behind his low writing desk, a look of fear contorting his face. A second figure crouched beside him, dressed in jet-black clothing and a mask covering all but the eyes. He held a short sword in one hand, pointed at Naseru. Ide Tadaji's crystal dagger lay on the desk atop its wrapping paper.

"Stay back," the man in black said, pressing his sword against Naseru's chest.

"Naseru-sama?" Isei called out. "Are you injured?"

"Not at all," Naseru said softly. The Anvil's feigned terror melted into a frown of bored annoyance.

A short knife appeared in the Anvil's palm, which he swiftly drew across the wrist of his distracted captor. The masked man cried out in pain and dropped his sword. Staggering backward, he reached for the knife tucked into his belt. In that instant, Isei charged. He made a single broad slash with his katana, cutting the man in half just above the waist. Isei turned a full circle with his gore-drenched sword in both hands. Seeing no other attackers, he flicked the blood from his weapon and returned it to its scabbard.

"Governor Osema shall be most distressed when he sees what you have done to his carpet, Isei-san," Naseru said, gazing at the fan-shaped pool of blood. He was still seated behind his desk, wiping his bloodied knife on a silk cloth.

Sunetra crouched by the upper half of the man's body and removed one of her knives from his eye. Isei was impressed; he had not even seen her throw the weapon. "How did you know that Naseru was in danger, Isei?" she asked, looking up at the yojimbo.

"I was in no danger," Naseru said, calmly folding the crystal dagger in its paper.

"Sunetra entered, but Bakin did not notice," Isei replied, speaking to Naseru rather than the Scorpion. The yojimbo stared at the ceiling; he seemed to be searching for something.

"I should hope Bakin did not notice." Sunetra chuckled. "He's just a simple old peasant."

"An old peasant who lived in the Imperial Palace," Naseru corrected. "Bakin survived four slaughters of the Imperial Court, two palace coups, three palace fires, an earthquake, and two invasions by the Shadowlands, one of which happened to be the Second Day of Thunder. He is not simple, by any stretch of the imagination."

"There," Isei said, pointing at the ceiling. One panel was moved slightly aside. "The thief came in through the ceiling, just as Sunetra must have. Is there a crawlspace above?"

Sunetra nodded. "Just wide enough for someone to enter if they know what they're doing," she said, "but it's full of traps. The Scorpion who used to live in this palace had them installed so their agents could come and go undetected."

"You don't know Ryoko Owari customs but you know the secret passages in the governor's palace?" Naseru asked her with an amused grin.

"I have my priorities," Sunetra replied.

"If he knew of the passage, he must be a Scorpion," Isei said, gesturing at the dead man.

"He is Shosuro Soshu," Naseru said, rising from his seat. Isei looked at his master in surprise. "I recognized his voice. I rely on hearing more than sight."

Sunetra peeled away part of the man's mask with the tip of her knife and nodded. "It is Soshu," she said. I recognize him. It surprises me to see him try something like this. He was just a bureaucrat."

Isei winced as Sunetra peeled the dead man's mask away with her hand. "You should leave the body to the eta, Sunetra," he said. "Such things are impure."

"Eh, I had planned to visit Bayushi's Shrine today," Sunetra said. She dropped Soshu's mask with a wet plop. "If I'm going to purify myself anyway, then surely there's no harm in fouling myself a bit further. Especially if we can learn something."

Isei was revolted. He had enough battle in his time that the sight of corpses did not disturb him, but the glee Sunetra took in searching the dead man's body was unsettling, to say the least.

"Fascinating woman, don't you think?" Naseru whispered so that only Isei would hear. The Anvil stood beside the yojimbo, watching Sunetra search the mangled corpse with an intrigued eye. Isei scowled.

"Are you all right, Naseru-sama?" Isei asked.

Naseru looked at Isei curiously. "Hm? I am fine. Why do you ask?"

"Well, you seem very calm," Isei said. He chose his words carefully to avoid offense. "Earlier you looked . . . to be in danger."

"I looked afraid, you mean," Naseru corrected with a short chuckle.

Isei lowered his head. "Yes," he said.

"Honest Isei," Naseru said with a sly grin. "I take no offense. Rather, I take it as a compliment that I was so convincing. Fear does not come easily to me, but I had hoped that by playing to his ego, letting him think he had startled me, I could encourage him to reveal something."

"That was risky," Sunetra said, looking back over one shoulder.

Isei wasn't certain what bothered him more: that his lord had risked his life in such a manner or that the bloodthirsty Scorpion's thoughts echoed his own so closely.

"The risk was acceptable," Naseru replied. "I could tell by the way he held his blade that he had never killed a man in his life. I could tell by the look in his eyes that he did not intend to do so today. He was a thief, not an assassin. He was no match for me, even without your welcome aid."

"Was he trying to steal the dagger, then?" Isei asked, nodding at the package on the desk.

"Indeed," Naseru replied. The Anvil stooped and picked

up the weapon, weighing it in one hand. "What's more, he asked me where I might find others like it."

"It must have been Kaukatsu," Isei said. "I knew his show of loyalty the other night could not be trusted."

"Ha!" Sunetra laughed, glaring back at Isei. "Typical. Just because Kaukatsu is a Scorpion you automatically assume he is to blame?"

"Soshu served the Scorpion, and Kaukatsu is the highest-ranking Scorpion in the city," Isei retorted.

"I do not think it was Kaukatsu," Naseru said. "I would hope the Imperial Chancellor has better thieves at his disposal than this. Perhaps someone paid Soshu to do this."

Isei frowned. "The thought of a samurai selling his services for money makes me ill."

"Well, this should make you feel better," Sunetra said, reaching into the pouch on Soshu's hip. "I do not think our would-be thief was being paid in gold." She held out her hand, displaying two cubes of black paper. One was misshapen from being torn open and mashed shut again.

"What is that?" Isei asked.

Naseru leaned forward and sniffed softly. His eye narrowed. "Opium," he said, taking one cube between two fingers. "I doubt it is the medicinal variety."

"The packaging is strange," Sunetra said, peeling at one corner of the other cube. "It has some sort of writing on the inside. I think it might be gaijin."

Naseru frowned. "I think you should show that to Shinjo Osema, Sunetra-chan," he said. "Our esteemed governor may have some thoughts on this matter. At any rate he will wish to be informed of the stains on his carpet."

"Yes, Naseru-sama," Sunetra said, tossing the cube in the air and catching it in the same hand. Rising quickly, she left the room at a dash.

Isei drew his blade, still in its scabbard, from his belt and prodded at the loose tile in the ceiling. Glancing over one shoulder, he saw Naseru at the far end of the room, studying the bloody corpse. During the War of Spirits Naseru had survived many assassination attempts. The surviving followers of Hantei XVI had sought to wipe out Toturi's dynasty. Ironically, Naseru had also faced threats due to his own association with the Steel Chrysanthemum, killers sent by overzealous Toturi loyalists who believed Naseru had schemed with the Hantei to usurp his father's dynasty. As he was one of the Four Winds in contention for the throne, his enemies were countless. His brothers and sister might be too honorable to hire killers, but many of those who supported them were not. Isei's career as a yojimbo had been an eventful one since Toturi had ordered him to protect his youngest son. He wondered why this killer concerned his master more than so many of the others.

"Well?" Naseru said, glancing back at Isei.

"I think we should have Bakin hire some carpenters to nail up this opening," Isei said. "Sunetra said some of the crawlspaces were trapped. Perhaps we could move some of the traps. It would be a nasty surprise for anyone else who tries to come in this way."

"A fine idea, but that was not what I meant," the Anvil said. "I mean what do you think about this?" He held the opium cube in one hand and gestured at the body with the other.

"If it is foreign-grown opium then it is probably of Senpet origin, imported via a local trade cartel," Isei said. "Probably Unicorn or Scorpion. Both clans have had contact with the Senpet in the past, despite Imperial decree forbidding contact with gaijin."

"Do you think Osema's magistrates will find anything?" Naseru asked.

"Doubtful," the yojimbo said. "Any group so used to breaking Imperial edicts will be used to dealing with Legionnaires as well as Emerald Magistrates. Osema and his city magistrates are too loud and belligerent. The smugglers will hear him coming and scatter."

"You think so?" Naseru asked, placing the opium cube in his obi pouch.

Isei nodded. "Which makes no difference, since you plan on finding those responsible yourself."

"Of course," Naseru said. "Whoever sent our thief must be

rooted out quickly before they realize that Soshu failed. What do you think is our best course of action?"

Isei's brow furrowed. "Send Sunetra," he said. "She will know where to find information that you or I would miss."

Naseru looked somewhat surprised. "Sunetra?" he said. "You said she was too curious."

Isei nodded. "Yes, but she is nearer to hand than any I would trust sooner," Isei said.

Naseru nodded, tucking the wrapped crystal dagger into his kimono.

"If I had warned you not to rely on her, would you have listened?" Isei asked.

"You did not warn me, so the question is pointless, Isei-san," Naseru said. "I value your advice and protection, so it pleases me that we are of one mind on this. When Sunetra returns, I am certain the governor will have questions for us. Once that is dealt with, we shall find out who is at the heart of this."

"And when we do?" Isei asked.

"We shall show him what it means to trifle with a son of Toturi," Naseru said, a merciless glint in his eye.

7   ARRIVAL

Yotsu Irie stared about in wonder. She had never seen anything quite like Ryoko Owari. Otosan Uchi had been larger, of course, but she had seen only a fraction of that city before it was destroyed. Ryoko Owari was almost as large and fully alive. The streets teemed with peasants hurrying about their business. Merchants stood on street corners selling just about anything one could imagine. The crowds parted periodically to allow a magistrate on horseback to ride past. What struck her most, however, was how altogether filthy the city was. The people were filthy, the buildings were filthy, and the occasional brightly colored palanquin bearing wealthy samurai only punctuated how truly dirty the City of Lies was. Before its destruction, the people of Otosan Uchi took pride in the capital, keeping it spotless and pristine. Here, it was almost as if no one had really cared in some time.

Ahead and to her left Irie saw an old man kneeling in the mud, begging. A thick bandage was wrapped around his eyes. "Two zeni, sama, two zeni," he whimpered to a passing merchant.

The fat man turned and spat at the beggar. One of his paired budoka bodyguards kicked the old man in the chest, knocking him back in the mud.

Incensed, Irie strode toward the merchant. Walking up behind him, she placed one hand firmly on his shoulder.

"What?" he cried out in alarm. The budoka both reached for the stout tonfa on their belts. All three paused when they saw the daisho Irie carried.

"Samurai?" the merchant stuttered, bowing deeply. The budoka followed suit.

"You owe that man an apology," Irie said, pointing at the old man, who was feebly smearing the mud from his face with a dirty rag.

The merchant looked up at Irie again, his expression souring as he noticed the lack of clan mons on her armor. "No," he corrected himself. "Not samurai. Ronin."

The two budoka laughed.

"You mock me?" Irie demanded. She could feel her face growing hot. A small crowd had gathered to watch the exchange from a safe distance. She did not want to resort to violence, but it would be difficult to back down now without losing face.

"Me? Mock a ronin?" The merchant laughed. "I would never do such a thing. Why don't you come by my offices later, little girl? Maybe I can give you a job guarding one of my boats." He snickered, causing his multiple chins to jiggle.

Irie shrugged and bowed low. The merchant and his guards laughed again, thinking that she had bowed out of respect. Then Irie stood, a large ball of mud in one hand, and hurled it at the merchant. It struck him in the face, dripping down onto his fine robes. "Ronin I may be, but I am still samurai," she said. "I am a Yotsu, the Emperor's sword. You are nothing but dirt."

The merchant spluttered in rage. The two budoka growled and lunged forward. Both men were far larger than the slim Yotsu, but Irie's face showed no concern. She drew her sword, still in its scabbard, and darted close to one budoka so the other would have to circle around his friend to reach her. She parried the first budoka's tonfa with her scabbard and then clubbed him across the stomach, knocking the wind out of him. Lashing out with her left foot, she caught the other man squarely between the legs just as he reached her. He stumbled away, giving Irie time to deliver a wicked palm strike to the first man's jaw. His head snapped back and he fell in a heap. The other man was recovering from Irie's attack when he saw his friend fall. He hesitated. Irie gave a sharp cry and feinted toward him. The man tripped over his own feet trying to get away, then crawled rapidly away on his hands and knees, leaving all dignity behind.

"Worthless!" the merchant snapped, kicking the fallen budoka in the midsection. He fumbled for the box hanging at his belt. "Thirty koku to any man who—"

A sharp hiss of steel interrupted the merchant's words. Irie's katana was now unsheathed, only a finger's width from the fat merchant's throat. "Do not finish that sentence," Irie snarled, her eyes fixed on the fat man's.

As soon as steel was bared the gathered crowd quickly found business elsewhere. Fights were a popular spectator sport in Ryoko Owari, but when katanas were involved it was all too easy for a spectator to lose a limb.

"Please, samurai-sama," the merchant squeaked. "Spare me."

"You were going to pay thirty koku to end my life," Irie said with a grim smile. "Now you will pay that much to save your own."

"Money?" The merchant smiled nervously. "All you want is money?" He fumbled for the box hanging from his belt again. Gold coins spilled into his hand. "I can easily pay you. I can gladly pay you!"

"Not me," Irie said. She pointed at the kneeling beggar. "Him."

The merchant's jaw dropped. "Him? Such treasure would be wasted on him! He is nothing more than a filthy eta!"

"Fair enough," Irie said. She seized the handle of her sword in both hands and raised it quickly over her head, prepared to strike the merchant down.

"Wait!" the merchant cried, cowering before the blade. "I will do as you say!" He scurried to the old man and dumped his coins into the begging plate. The old man cocked his head to one side, uncertain if he could believe the sound of so many gold coins falling in his plate.

"Now get out of here," Irie snarled at the merchant. "I will check on this old man again. If I find that he has come to any harm I will hold you responsible."

"Yes, sama!" the merchant said, bowing repeatedly. "Thank you for your mercy!" He turned and ran.

Once he was gone, Irie turned to the old beggar. He, too, was gone. The young ronin looked left and right, but there was no sign of him. The streets had returned to normal, except for the three Shinjo magistrates now riding toward her. They did not look pleased.

"You there!" one of them shouted. "Halt."

Irie sheathed her katana and stood her ground. The three samurai looked down at her with angry expressions. The leader moved beside Irie and glared down at her. Like most Unicorn, he was short and squat. No doubt he remained on horseback so he would not have to look up at her.

"We hear you were creating a public disturbance," the man said tersely. "Is this true, ronin?"

"I acted only as bushido demanded," Irie replied, squarely meeting the Unicorn's gaze.

"Bushido does not make the law in Ryoko Owari," the Unicorn replied. "You will surrender your daisho and come with me, or we will be forced to subdue you."

The streets quickly cleared again. Only a few faces peered from half-opened windows.

Irie scowled. She did not plan to surrender her swords, not when she was this close to her quarry. Neither did she wish to begin a fight with three samurai who were only doing their duty. Such an act would dishonor her blade, not to mention that she had no hope of defeating three mounted Unicorn bushi. Irie bowed her head in defeat and knelt. She drew her blades, still sheathed, and set them on the muddy road.

"Do you have traveling papers?" the Unicorn asked.

"I do not require them," Irie said. "I am a magistrate. I have a charter." She drew a scroll from her belt and offered it to the Unicorn.

The Unicorn sighed as he examined the papers. "This is a local magistrate charter for the city of Otosan Uchi. Does this look like Otosan Uchi?" The Unicorn clicked his tongue. "This is a serious offense, ronin."

Irie bowed her head further. How could she have been so foolish? She should have known better than to make trouble in such a dangerous city.

"What is this?" called out a cocky voice. "Three on one? Is this another brilliant victory for the Unicorn?"

Irie risked looking up to the source of the voice. A tall, muscular samurai in loose-fitting robes walked down the street toward them. His face was hidden behind a hideous scowling oni mask. Two more masked samurai flanked him on either side. All wore the armor of Scorpion bushi, and all but the leader carried long spears—the sort normally used against cavalry.

"This is none of your affair, Churai," the Unicorn leader said. "This is magistrate business."

"I beg to differ," the samurai replied. He walked casually, but Irie could not help but notice his left hand rested on the hilt of his katana. She had heard stories that the most deadly Scorpion duelists were left-handed. "You are Yotsu Irie, are you not?"

Irie sat back on her heels, a puzzled look on her face. "I am," she said.

"There, you see?" Churai said, his voice smug. "She is a personal guest of my master, and thus his diplomatic immunity extends to her. I do not have any documents to this effect, of course, so I am certain that my master would understand if regulations forced you to detain his honored guest."

"She attacked a merchant," the Unicorn said. "She caused a public disturbance. Justice must be done."

"Justice is, of course, a grand goal, yes?" Churai said. "I am certain it would be no trouble for my master to cancel his busy schedule so that he could collect Irie-chan from the prisons. What was your name again, magistrate? My master might wish to know who he as to thank for maintaining such a firm dedication to the letter of the law even when it threatened his own career. Justice and all that."

The Unicorn coughed. Churai and his five Scorpion waited patiently.

"I will let you off with a warning this time, Yotsu Irie," the Unicorn said, as if it was his own idea. "Do not cause a disturbance again." He rolled up her charter and pointed it at her.

"Hai, sama," Irie replied, gathering her swords and standing. She took the scroll from the Unicorn and bowed again. This time, she found herself bowing to his back as he was already turning to ride away. Clearly these Unicorn did not intend to remain in the presence of the Scorpion for longer than was necessary.

Irie turned to face her rescuers. The Scorpion watched her cautiously from behind their masks. Churai's eyes glinted with amusement. "Thank you," Irie said, uncertain what else she could say.

"Think nothing of it," Churai said with an exaggerated bow. "I am Bayushi Churai, Sensei of the Red Crane Dojo, Master of the Folding Leg technique." He sounded as if he had rehearsed the introduction many times and was rather proud of it. "I am pleased to make your acquaintance, Yotsu Irie. You will come with me now."

"I have to confess, I am confused," Irie replied. "You said I was a guest of your master, but as far as I know that is not true. I came to the city of my own accord."

"This is true," Churai said, "but my master is a powerful man, and little transpires in Otosan Uchi or Ryoko Owari without his knowledge. You are his guest now, for he has deemed it so. Now that you owe him a favor for rescuing you from those Unicorn savages, you cannot deny his hospitality."

"Of course," Irie said. "But if you do not mind my asking, who is your master?"

"Is it not obvious?" Churai said with a laugh. "I serve none other than Bayushi Kaukatsu, the Imperial Chancellor. Now come with me, Irie-chan. The chancellor is an impatient man."

8 STRANGE VISIONS, DARK BARGAINS

Naseru stood at the top of a staircase, at the head of a long hallway. On either side, closed shoji screens seemed to stretch on forever. He peered back down the stairs behind him. All was inky blackness. Ahead, he could make out lights and figures moving about behind some of the screens. He did not recognize the hall or remember how he had come here. Perhaps it was one of many labyrinthine corridors in the governor's palace?

Naseru stepped forward, stopped at the first screen, and pushed it aside. Within, a young boy and girl chased one another around the room. The girl was tall and lanky with long pigtails. She wore a golden yellow kimono with grass stains on the elbows and knees. The boy was short and wiry. His long white hair hung loose to his waist. They giggled as they chased one another around a tiny model of a castle.

When they noticed that the screen was open, the boy and girl turned and looked at Naseru. The girl smiled shyly and folded her arms behind her back to hide the grass stains. The boy took on a fierce expression and stepped between Naseru and the girl. Naseru stepped into the room, leaned close, and studied the toy palace. It was a perfect model of the Forbidden City, right down to the tiny kakemono paintings on the walls. Tiny metal figurines of Imperial Guardsmen stood watch over the tiny castle. Even their quivers seemed to hold miniature arrows. Naseru imagined that he could almost see their tiny chests heaving with breath. Such a masterpiece was impossible, even for the greatest toy-makers of the Kaiu. This was clearly a dream, and a strange one. One could learn much from dreams; the real Sezaru had taught him as much. Naseru decided to play along with this for now and see where it went.

"Who are you?" the little boy demanded, interposing himself between Naseru and the toy castle. "What do you want?"

"Hush, Wolf," the little girl chided. "This is our little brother. Don't you recognize him?"

"Jiro?" the boy said, brightening. He had referred to Naseru by his child's name, the name all second sons held for a time. "Is that really you? They said you were never coming back! Sword, Jiro's back!"

The little boy danced merrily around the room. After a moment, Naseru noticed that Wolf's feet never really touched the ground. He hovered aloft on invisible air spirits.

"Who said I wasn't coming back?" he asked, turning his question to the little girl. If these really were counterparts of his siblings, then Tsudao would be the more reliable source of coherent information.

"Father said so," the little girl said. "He said you were going away and never coming back."

"He did?" Naseru asked.

"And why wouldn't Toturi say so?" said a harsh voice from behind him. "The boy who would have been Toturi Naseru never returned. He became Hantei Naseru instead."

Naseru peered back over one shoulder. A tall, broad-shouldered figure stood in the shadowed hallway. His armor was black and dark brown. His hair was tied back in a formal topknot. His face was sharply angular and weathered by the sun.

Naseru gasped. "Father?"

"Close," the man said, stepping into the room.

"Kaneka," Naseru whispered.

"Bastard!" Sword shouted, running forward to hug Kaneka's right leg. "Wolf, our brother's here!"

"Bastard!" Wolf shouted, running up to hug Kaneka's left leg.

Kaneka smiled and absently tugged one of Sword's pigtails. She winced and kicked him in the shin.

"You have no place in this family, Kaneka," Naseru said coldly.

"Really?" Kaneka asked. "Why is that?"

"You are an abomination," Naseru said with a sneer. "You are a stain upon our father's name. Your arrogance has torn the Empire apart."

"Because I seek Toturi's throne?" Kaneka asked. "Do you think it is yours to give? Even if I were never born, Tsudao's claim is more legitimate than yours."

"I don't really want to be Empress today," Sword said. "I want to go riding with Paneki and Dejiko."

"You heard her," Kaneka said with a smile. "She doesn't want my throne. And what of little Wolf?"

"I'd like to be Emperor!" Wolf said eagerly, clapping his tiny hands. "We won't have any wars like we did when Daddy was Emperor, because anyone who defies me will burn!"

"I'll help!" Tsudao said. "I like helping people."

"You two are so adorable," Kaneka said, smiling down at them fondly. "Go play."

Sword and Wolf giggled and ran off down the hallway, hand in hand.

"No," Naseru said, shaking his head. "Sezaru and Tsudao would not say things like that."

"Wouldn't they?" Kaneka asked. "That's how you portray them to your friends in the courts. You place your claim on our father's throne above theirs because Tsudao is too naïve, Sezaru too unstable. You do not trust them."

"Only because neither of them will stand against you," Naseru said. "Neither Tsudao nor Sezaru realizes how dangerous you are. You expect to rule the Empire, but you do not even know your own place."

"I am dangerous?" Kaneka asked. "Interesting. Allow me to list the ways I am a danger to the Empire. My teachers were Akodo, the heroes of the Empire. I built an army from nothing." He counted off the points on his fingers. "I ended the war between the Crab and Crane. Samurai proudly swear their swords to my name. Now let's consider your accomplishments." Kaneka began counting on his other hand. "Your teacher was a pitiful madman. Everything you have you inherited or extorted through political favors. Your pathetic attempt to make an alliance between the Lion and Phoenix brought war to all the northern provinces and exterminated a Minor Clan. The only samurai who follow you are the ones too lonely, desperate, or terrified to find anything better. I am not a danger to the Empire, Naseru. You are." With a final, disdainful chuckle, Kaneka turned to leave.

"Do not turn your back on me, ronin," Naseru said. He advanced on Kaneka and seized his shoulder with one hand.

Kaneka whirled about, striking Naseru in the chin with the back of one armored forearm. The Anvil stumbled backward, landing unceremoniously on the model of the Forbidden City. The tiny model collapsed under Naseru's weight.

"I am a Lion, not a ronin," Kaneka said through gritted teeth as he advanced on Naseru. "I am a Lion, as Toturi was a Lion. That is why you hate me, Naseru. Because I understand Father better than you ever could. Toturi abandoned me, Hantei Naseru, but *you* abandoned *him*."

Kaneka spat on the floor at Naseru's feet, turned, and left. Naseru scrambled to his feet and drew his katana as he charged for the door. "Bastard!" he shouted, leaping into the hallway.

The hallway was empty. Akodo Kaneka was nowhere to be seen. That was probably just as well. Given Kaneka's reputation as a fierce duelist, there was little chance Naseru could have defeated him. Taking rein of his temper, Naseru sheathed his sword and looked at his surroundings. He looked back into the room where he had found Wolf and Sword. The model of the palace was destroyed now, as the true Forbidden City had been destroyed. Naseru imagined he could see smoke drifting from the model, that he could smell the scent of burning flesh as he had that day in Otosan Uchi.

Naseru closed the shoji screen softly, pushing the memories away. He rubbed the side of his face, surprised by the sensation of pain he felt from Kaneka's blow. He had never felt pain in a dream before. Glancing at his hand, he saw blood on the tips of his fingers.

The sound of whispers from farther down the hallway drew his attention. He advanced with one hand on his blade. The voices came from the next screen to his left. Sliding it open only a little, he peered inside.

The room was cast in shadows. A small fireplace set in the floor in the center of the room illuminated the chamber. A tall man in the deep red armor of a Scorpion stood just beyond the screen, his back to Naseru. He spoke to another figure Naseru could not see.

"The plan proceeds apace, young lord," the Scorpion said, his voice smooth and slick as oil. "Tomorrow we will make our offer to the Steel Chrysanthemum."

"Excellent," the other person replied. Naseru did not recognize the voice, but it sounded like a child's. "Does Toturi suspect what we plan?"

"The Emperor's attention is fully occupied with the Hantei armies," the Scorpion said. "He seeks to keep enemy forces out of Otosan Uchi, not to prevent allies from escaping. By the time he realizes we have gone, we shall have added our strength to the Chrysanthemum. Shall I have your steed prepared?"

"Indeed," the other said.

The Scorpion bowed and turned to leave. Naseru quickly darted to one side. The Scorpion walked past him and headed for the stairs, taking no note of the Anvil's existence.

Stepping forward again, Naseru peered back into the chamber.

"Soon," the stranger said to himself. "Soon all of my patience will be repaid. My father's throne will be mine." The stranger stepped toward the fire. The light revealed his features. He was no more than seven years old. He wore robes of dark black and a white porcelain mask. Naseru recognized the mask. It was the same disguise he had worn when he first offered his loyalty to Hantei XVI. The mask was not true porcelain but carefully sculpted grease paint, an effect intended both to prevent the possibility of Naseru becoming accidentally unmasked and to impress the Steel Chrysanthemum.

"No," Naseru said stepping into the chamber. "This is not the way it happened."

"Isn't it?" the younger Naseru said, peering up at his older self curiously. The mask had begun to melt from the heat of the fire. A trickle of black makeup ran from Naseru's right eye like a tear.

"It was a ruse," Naseru said. "The intent was to lure the Hantei out, to cause him to make a mistake."

"Ah," the little Naseru said. "I only ask because the way you describe it, it seems like an awfully complicated plan. You stayed at the Hantei's side for over a year. Are you saying you lived a lie for a whole year?"

"It was necessary to gain the Chrysanthemum's trust," Naseru said fiercely.

"That's funny," the younger Anvil said, laughing as he peered into the fire. He scratched his cheek with one hand, badly smearing the makeup and staining the sleeve of his robe. "I know the way we think. The game isn't nearly as deep as we make it appear. There are no plans, only ideas and contingencies. Our idea was to ally with the Hantei. We were prepared to betray him, and when the tides of battle turned against him, we did. However, had things gone against Toturi, I think we gladly would have betrayed Father as well."

"No," Naseru said. "I did what I did for the Empire. My father's Empire."

"If it pleases you to remember things that way, please do so," his younger self said with an earnest chuckle.

"I have had enough," Naseru said. He turned and left the room. He looked both ways, seeking a path out of this dream. Finding no obvious escape, he gave a resigned sigh and continued to his left.

"We have always served the Empire," the younger Naseru said, falling into step beside his older self. "We lie, betray, manipulate. What a fine Emperor we shall be! I can hardly wait. And why should we? Let us dispatch assassins to kill the other Winds and be done with it."

"Silence," Naseru snapped.

"Why are you so bitter?" the younger Naseru said. "Because the assassins you sent to kill Kaneka failed? We can find stronger ones next time. I bet for enough money you could even find someone strong enough to kill Sezaru."

"I did not send assassins to kill Kaneka," Naseru said.

"You didn't?" little Naseru replied. His face expressionless behind his ruined mask, he drew upon the shoji screen to his right. In the chamber within knelt a man in pale blue. His face twisted in deep meditation beneath his snow-white hair. A tall woman in identical blue armor paced the room before him, her expression one of frustration. Her short-cropped hair was jet black, though the tips were off-white. In the corner of the room, a peasant servant watched them both apprehensively.

"It makes sense, Marui," the man said. "We should accept his offer."

"And die in a ditch like common assassins?" she replied with a sneer. "I will not have it, Eloka. There must be another way."

"After our failure at Toshi Ranbo it is the only way to atone," the man replied. "It is the only way to take our revenge upon the Lion who disinherited us."

"Bah," Marui said. "It was the Lion Champion who took the city of Toshi Ranbo, not Akodo Kaneka. Killing Kaneka accomplishes nothing."

"It will keep a Lion off of the throne," Eloka said. "Naseru has promised that when he takes the throne, the custom of the Hantei taking a Kakita bride will be renewed. Our clan will be restored to its former power."

"Is such a sacrifice worth our honor, Eloka?" Marui asked.

"Honor will not feed my children," Eloka said. "Even if we fail, the koku Naseru offers us will allow my sons a second chance. Think of your own family. Your sister. Your infant brother. Would you let them live in poverty? Would you become a *farmer* to support them?" Eloka spat the words in disgust. For a samurai, peasant labor was a fate worse than death, a surrender of one's place in the Celestial Order.

Marui stopped pacing and did not answer for a long time. "Naseru guaranteed that Kaneka would be alone?"

Eloka nodded. "We need only challenge him. Our mastery of the Kakita technique will do the rest. The Son of Toturi, legitimate or not, at least deserves to die in an honorable duel. Naseru demanded that much. Even yet, I would prefer not to face him alone, Marui. If you were at my side . . ." Eloka looked away, his face somewhat flushed. "I feel I could face anything."

Marui rubbed her chin with one finger. "You intend to face him with or without me, don't you?" she asked.

"Hai," Eloka said. He looked at her, his pale blue eyes pleading.

Marui folded her arms across her chest and returned Eloka's gaze uncomfortably. "Give me time to think about this," she said.

"We have two days," Eloka replied.

The younger Naseru slammed the shoji screen slut abruptly, startling his older self. "They died," he said. "Akodo Kaneka cut them both down without a second thought and kept riding. He doesn't even remember their names. People challenge him all the time."

"They knew the risk," Naseru said.

"I suppose you are right," his younger self agreed. "Their lives were over anyway. There are only two choices for a dis-inherited samurai—to die or become a ronin. You did them a favor when you killed them."

"I did not kill them," Naseru said, turning and continuing down the hall.

"Of course you didn't," his younger self agreed happily. "If it pleases you to remember things that way, please do so."

Naseru walked faster, forcing his younger self to walk more quickly to keep pace. "What is the point of this dream?" he asked.

"What do you think the point is?" his younger self replied.

"You babble like a Dragon," Naseru said, stopping abruptly and glaring down at his counterpart. "Either state what business you have, phantom, or begone!"

"Very well then. Sayonara," the younger Naseru said. He opened the shoji screen behind him and stepped back into the darkened room. For a moment the younger Anvil's half-melted mask appeared to hover in the darkness, and the shoji screen closed.

Naseru stood alone in the shadows, peering in both directions. The dream was not through with him yet. He could only keep walking and see what happened next. He was pondering whether he should follow his younger self when a shrill scream sounded from further down the hallway. Without thinking, Naseru charged down the corridor. Another scream sounded from the room to his right. Naseru could see bright light within and two figures moving. He kicked the shoji screen aside and entered the chamber.

To his surprise, he found that he recognized this room. These were the private bedchambers of Hantei XVI, from the palace where he dwelled in the lands of the Dragon. The room was sparsely decorated and stank of the bitter incense the Chrysanthemum favored over bathing. Sake bottles lay broken upon the floor. Otomo Hoketuhime lay sprawled upon the sleeping pallet, clutching her torn kimono to her chest. Tears streaked her face and blood streamed from her nose. The Steel Chrysanthemum stood above her, stripped to the waist with a dagger in hand. Though bent by age, his arms and chest were still lean with muscle. He whirled about as Naseru entered, a mad look in his eyes. Hoketuhime looked up plaintively and sobbed.

"You," the Hantei roared, pointing his dagger at Naseru. "How did you get past my guard?"

Naseru realized with a start that his katana was in his hand. It was soaked with gore from tsuba to tip. Naseru touched his face and discovered blood streaming from a cut on his cheek. Seppun Isei stood at his side. The yojimbo's face was grim and determined, his own blade held low at his hip. Isei's eyes were fixed on the Hantei. Naseru became carried away in the memory, forgetting for the moment that this was a dream.

"Step away from her," Naseru demanded.

"So," the Hantei said with a shrill laugh. "The smallest pup of the Black Wolf has teeth after all? Have you come to kill me, my son?"

"I said step away," Naseru repeated angrily. "I will not repeat myself a third time."

"But I thought you enjoyed that game," the Hantei said with an amused smile. "Why should I step away? She is mine. The Otomo offered her to me as a bride. I shall do with her as I will."

"My lord, give the word," Isei growled in a low voice. The yojimbo seethed with calm fury. Naseru had no doubt that if he gave the word Isei would slaughter the Steel Chrysanthemum and take the blame for the entire affair.

"Wait outside, Isei," Naseru said.

The yojimbo nodded sharply, never questioning his master. "Fortunes be with you, Naseru-sama," he said as he withdrew.

"Pick up your sword," Naseru said, nodding to the katana resting on its stand near the window. "Die like a samurai if you cannot live like one."

The Steel Chrysanthemum chuckled and made no move toward the blade. "I do not fear death," he said. "Like your yojimbo, I came back through Oblivion's Gate. I know what awaits me in my next life. My soul is prepared. Is yours? Surely even your father will not forgive a crime of this magnitude. By killing me, you violate the treaty your father made. And for what?" He sneered down at Hoketuhime. "For this."

"I told you to pick up your sword," Naseru repeated.

"Did you think I did not notice?" the Hantei said, turning to face Naseru again. "Do you think I did not see how you coveted this little one? Why do you think I forced the Otomo to promise her to me? I did it for you, my son."

"You are not my father!" Naseru shouted, taking a step toward the mad Emperor.

"You are distraught, Naseru-san, and I forgive you," the Hantei said in a chillingly sweet voice. "I do this for you. You hope to be an Emperor, but you allow yourself to be distracted by mere flesh. You are as weak as your first father ever was. I will help you become strong." The Steel Chrysanthemum turned and seized Hoketuhime by the wrist. "An Emperor must think only of himself, Naseru-san. Never of others. Nothing else matters."

The Steel Chrysanthemum held the dagger high.

"No!" Naseru shouted, charging toward the Hantei.

Halfway across the room, Naseru realized his mistake. Hantei XVI looked up with a savage grin. With a flick of his wrist, the dagger flew from his hand toward Naseru. Something heavy and burning hot struck him in the face; pain lanced through his entire body. Naseru writhed on the floor in agony, blood streaming over his hands as he clutched the handle of the blade lodged in his skull. Rolling onto his knees, Naseru clutched the handle tightly and tore the weapon free. He peered up, half blinded by blood, to see Hantei XVI watching him calmly. The deposed Emperor had retrieved the katana from its stand and now clutched it in a traditional Crane dueling stance. He had kicked Naseru's katana out of reach, behind him.

"Still alive?" the Hantei asked with a note of surprise. "I knew I should have used poison. Before you die, know that your foolish compassion has destroyed Toturi's Empire. You have broken your father's treaty with this base attack on the true Imperial Presence. My hidden supporters will flock to me. In one month's time, the Steel Throne will be mine."

The Hantei stepped closer to Naseru and lifted his sword high. Naseru looked up into the eyes of his killer.

A confused look spread across the Steel Chrysanthemum's face. He peered down as blood began to stream from his abdomen. Staggering forward one step, he peered behind him. Otomo Hoketuhime scowled savagely as she drew Naseru's katana from the Steel Chrysanthemum's back. The dying Emperor hissed like a snake and lifted his sword to behead the girl. Gathering his strength, Naseru leaped at the Emperor, throwing him back on the sleeping pallet. Lifting the bloody tanto, he buried it in the Steel Chrysanthemum's throat with all his strength. Naseru pushed on the blade until he felt the old man's body cease struggling beneath him.

When the deed was done, Naseru closed his eye and drifted into unconsciousness, weak from loss of blood and exhaustion. The last things he remembered were Hoke-tuhime's quiet sobs and the hiss of the shoji screen as Isei returned to carry him to safety.

"Murderer," said a voice. Through the haze of pain, Naseru wondered if it was his own.

Naseru opened his eye again. He stood in a rugged valley. Clouds filled the sky. Corpses of animals lay strewn around him. They were like lions, but they were the size of horses, with bright golden fur. Their chests were broader than normal lions, and their eyes larger, more intelligent. The slaughter stretched as far as he could see in every direction. Samurai in gore-soaked armor guarded the battlefield. Peasants patrolled with long spears, burying them in the hearts of the creatures to make certain they were dead. The buzzing of flies was deafening. The stench of rotting flesh turned Naseru's stomach. The nearest beast stared up at Naseru with lifeless, red-gold eyes. Lion samurai sometimes had eyes that color, if the blood of the Kitsu family was strong enough in them.

"That is the last of them," growled a rough voice behind him.

Naseru turned to see a tall samurai bury a massive golden

katana in the skull of one of the creatures. The man wore black armor like Toturi's, but his face was thin and angular like Naseru's. A black silken patch covered his right eye. Naseru recognized the man from the statues in the Hall of Ancestors.

"Lord Akodo," Naseru whispered, staring up into the eyes of the First Lion, his most illustrious ancestor. Akodo walked past Naseru, oblivious to the Anvil's presence. The nightmares of that terrible day in the Hantei's chambers were familiar to Naseru, but this grisly battlefield was something altogether new. "What is this? Where am I?"

"Is it not obvious?" asked a languid voice.

"Another mysterious voice." Naseru turned with a scowl. "This seems to be a recurring theme. Whoever you are, you certainly have a sense of melodrama."

"Thank you," came the reply. Naseru turned to find a small man perched on a rock nearby. He wore the wide basket hat of a komuso. A shakuhachi flute was slung over one shoulder.

"Who are you?" Naseru demanded.

"Who do you think I am?" the komuso replied.

"What do you want?" Naseru asked, annoyed.

"To teach and to learn," the monk said, spinning the long flute idly in one hand. "You learn the most interesting things about people from their nightmares. Did you really kill the Steel Chrysanthemum? I find that extraordinary. I always viewed you as the weakest of the Four Winds, but here I discover that you have more murder in your heart than Toturi Sezaru and Akodo Kaneka combined. I like you, Hantei Naseru. That is why I wish to offer an alliance."

"Ally with you?" Naseru said with a laugh. "Truly I must be spending too much time in the court if even my dreams are seeking to gain political advantage with me."

"I am quite real, Naseru," the komuso said. "I command powerful maho."

"Black magic?" Naseru replied, eye narrowing. "You expect me to ally with a servant of Fu Leng. Do you take me for a fool?"

"Quite the opposite," the stranger said. "I think you are wise enough to see the value in my offer despite the unfortunate origins of my power, especially when I am so honest."

"State your case," Naseru said. The last thing Naseru intended was to make any sort of deal with this person, but better to keep him talking than enrage him. If this odd monk truly was a maho tsukai, there was no telling what power he might command.

"My offer is simple," the komuso said. "The Shadowlands are a bleak, dreadful place. Daigotsu is a heartless master, driving even the most valuable of his servants"—he rested one hand on his chest to indicate himself—"to the brink of exhaustion. My associates have no imagination. They do not seek to better themselves, but are satisfied with the life of a slave. I am not. I seek to escape the Shadowlands, to cast off my Taint. In return for safe haven, I offer you information."

"I do not have the power nor the inclination to grant you safety," Naseru said.

"Perhaps not . . . but as Emperor you could easily grant me amnesty. The information I offer can go a long way to placing you upon the Steel Throne. I do not ask you to make any promises now, simply to listen. Judge the value of what I offer before you decide."

"I am listening," Naseru said.

The komuso nodded graciously. "The beasts that surround us in this field are called kitsu, members of a proud race that held dominion over the lands of Rokugan long before the fall of the Kami. After the War against Fu Leng, the Emperor dispatched Akodo to bring peace to the land. The first Lion hunted the remnants of Fu Leng's legions, slaying countless beasts that threatened the safety of the people. When Akodo saw the kitsu, he mistook them for such beasts. The result is what you see here." The komuso held out his hands to display the valley. "Genocide."

"What is your point?"

"Well, to begin with, I hope it makes you feel better," he said. "Compared to Akodo the Slayer, your crimes are not so damning. Look around you. Murder as far as the eye can see.

Yet the Empire remembers Akodo among its most beloved heroes."

"I have heard this story," Naseru said. "The surviving kitsu made peace with Akodo, but the damage was already done. The kitsu race dwindled until only five remained. Those five forgave Akodo and took human form. They founded the Kitsu family of shugenja."

"An odd family, that one," the komuso mused. "Your brother trained with them for a while, did he not? Strange. The Kitsu are usually very selective about admitting only members of their exclusive bloodline to their temples."

"*What is your point?*" Naseru demanded.

"Forgive me," the komuso said, pressing a hand to his sternum and half bowing, his oversized basket hat wobbling dangerously. "Perhaps I have strayed too far from my purpose, but I do so love a good story. This is merely background so that you can better understand what is to come. The story becomes more interesting a few decades later."

The little monk hopped down from his stone. When his feet touched the ground, the scene changed. They now stood in a mountain pass, surrounded by Lion samurai. Their eyes were intense, fixed on the far end of the pass. Most were far past their prime, though they still held their katanas straight and true. In the distance, the clash of steel on steel could be heard clearly. The monk strode calmly through the army toward the sounds of battle. The samurai did not notice him, though they made room as he passed.

"Do you know where we are?" the strange little man asked.

"I suspect you are about to tell me," Naseru said, following the tsukai. The samurai paid no attention to the Anvil either, though they absently moved from his path.

"We are in the Seikitsu Pass," the komuso explained. "In a few minutes, Akodo One Eye will die here. Do you know the story?"

"Of course," Naseru said. "He fought an army of ogres here."

"Ogres," the komuso said with a small chuckle. "Of course."

"To me!" shouted a voice from deeper in the pass. The waiting Lion samurai shouted as one and charged. At the heart of the pass, Naseru could see one warrior standing taller than the others. It was Akodo, though his mane was gray and his face was lined with age. He dueled with an enormous creature clad in sleek plated armor, wielding a large two-handed blade. Sharp horns curved from its head, and steam billowed from its fanged muzzle. Dozens of similar creatures charged the ranks of Lion samurai that surrounded Akodo.

"These are not ogres," Naseru said. "These are Tsuno."

The komuso nodded. "A forgivable mistake. The two races are somewhat similar in appearance."

The Lion troops screamed and died as the larger creatures tore them apart with jagged claws and enormous swords. The battle now boiled around Naseru and the monk, but even the Tsuno ignored them. The Anvil paid no attention to the battle, watching his strange guide intently. The komuso leaned against the wall of the pass and grinned at the slaughter.

"How can these be Tsuno?" Naseru asked. "Daigotsu created the Tsuno eleven centuries from now."

The monk shrugged. "That is what the Crab think, simply because they had never seen the Tsuno before. The Tsuno allow the Crab to think what they will. It works to their advantage. Look at their eyes, Naseru."

A Tsuno collapsed on the earth near the Anvil. Naseru looked down at the dying creature. A pair of red-gold eyes stared back, identical to those of the dead kitsu. Naseru had never looked closely at a Tsuno's eyes during the attack on Otosan Uchi. He had never been foolish enough to get so close.

"Physical form does not bind kitsu as it does humans," the komuso said. "If you are willing to believe that five kitsu became men, then the idea that a thousand kitsu could become Tsuno is no less reasonable."

"So they seek revenge upon Akodo for killing their brethren?" Naseru asked.

"That is not their main purpose," the komuso said. "The fact that Akodo stands against them here is nothing more than a coincidence, one of many events throughout history that convinces me without question that fate has a sense of humor. Perhaps it was simply Akodo's karma. For his thoughtless murder of the kitsu he was destined to be slaughtered in turn by the Tsuno. You must admit, there is a certain poetic justice inherent in that."

Naseru studied the face of the dying Tsuno. The battle continued around him, oblivious to his existence. The Anvil looked up at the monk skeptically. "If the Tsuno are kitsu, then where were they when Akodo killed the rest of their kind?" Naseru asked.

"A good question," the komuso said. "You do not get all the answers today. Not until we have a deal."

"Why would I grant you any deal?" Naseru asked. "Your information is useless. So the Tsuno were once kitsu? What significance is this to me?"

"Follow me," the komuso said, "and see what your ancestor did not."

The komuso strode forward into the pass. Though the Lion and Tsuno still did not notice him, they parted as he passed.

Naseru followed, watching the battle with fascination. Even if this were a dream, it was remarkably detailed and realistic. He was watching history unfold—the last battle of his most glorious ancestor.

They descended farther into the pass. The komuso paused near the center of the Tsuno horde. There, a group of the creatures hurried to clear the boulders from the mouth of a collapsed cave. When the komuso saw that Naseru was following him, he scrambled up the rocks and disappeared through the half-buried opening.

Naseru stood where he was. He had risked listening to this bizarre person this far, but he was uncertain if he was willing to follow a self-proclaimed maho tsukai into a darkened cave. The monk's basket hat appeared in the opening once more. "Stay where you are, if you like," he said, "but choose quickly. Akodo's dying roar will collapse this pass very soon, and you will be much safer in the cave."

"Let the pass fall; it will not harm me," Naseru said. "This is only a dream."

"If you say so," the monk replied, retreating into the darkness again.

Naseru scowled and followed. The opening in the wall was not large enough to admit the burrowing Tsuno yet, but Naseru was able to enter on his hands and knees. He crawled into the pitch darkness, following the sounds of the komuso's footsteps. After nearly a minute, the sounds stopped. A bright light filled the cave, radiating from a dark green flame that sheathed the tip of the monk's flute. The light was reflected a thousandfold from the enormous crystal gates that stood before them.

"These gates lead to the City of Night," the komuso said. "A thousand years from now, Moto Vordu will find this cave and open this seal."

Naseru stepped forward, staring up at the door in wonder. An enormous bas-relief image was carved into its face. It depicted a gathering of strange, inhuman creatures dancing about the streets of a city laid out in a strange spiral pattern. Naseru recognized some of the creatures, mystical beings out of Rokugani myth. Near the center he saw a leonine creature standing beneath a circle. The creature was obviously a kitsu.

Echoing through the tunnel from far above, Naseru could hear a cacophonous roar as Akodo called down the wrath of the Celestial Heavens. The entire chamber shook. Small trails of dust trickled from the ceiling. Naseru looked down at the komuso with a bored frown.

"Is that all?" he asked. "You arranged all of this to show me a door?"

"Do you fail to understand?" the komuso asked, a disappointed tone in his voice. "Do you not grasp the significance of what I have given you? Are you not amazed by the implications?"

Naseru shrugged. "I see nothing that convinces me I should accept your offer, tsukai," Naseru said. The sound of

crumbling stone echoed far above them, the death cry of
Seikitsu Pass. "How do I know this is not a lie?"

"You think I created all of this?" The monk laughed. "I
assure you it is real. I have no intent to deceive you, Hantei
Naseru. A lie is the last resort of the defeated."

Naseru raised an eyebrow at the monk's familiar words.
"Indeed," he replied. "I have no doubt that what you show
me contains a great deal of truth. Truth clouded so that I will
see what you wish me to see. You offer to make a deal with
me, to betray the Dark Lord himself. How do I know that
once I have helped you gain your freedom you will not
betray me as well?"

"How do you know that the price will not be worth the
risk?" the monk countered in a mocking voice. "Your skepti-
cism is expected, Anvil. If you do not believe me, then find
the truth for yourself. My offer still stands. We will talk
again."

With that, the fire died. The tunnel was cast into total
darkness.

An instant later, the light returned. Naseru found himself
in his windowless bedchambers in Ryoko Owari. Bakin
stood nearby, holding a small lantern in one hand. Naseru
scowled as he surveyed the room, as if he expected to find the
komuso waiting for him here.

"My lord?" Bakin said, a worried look on his face. "You
told me to awaken you at this time. You have an appointment with the Lion ambassador today."

Naseru groaned as he sat up on his sleeping pallet. Since
arriving in Ryoko Owari his schedule had been clogged.
Between meetings with local politicians, planning for the
construction of his new home here, Scorpion thieves invading his chambers and maho tsukai invading his dreams, what
sleep he had gleaned had provided little rest.

Bakin pursed his lips as he examined Naseru. "You are
tired, my lord. I can return in another hour if you desire
more sleep."

"No," Naseru said in a rough voice. "Sleep can wait till
another time."

"Of course, my lord," Bakin said, his disapproval clear in his voice.

"And the Lion ambassador can wait till another time, too," Naseru added. "Send for Bayushi Sunetra. I need to talk to her at once."

9 GAMES AND PREPARATIONS

"Your move," Bayushi Sunetra said, placing a black stone upon the go board.

Her opponent, a gangly young Unicorn magistrate whose duty it was to patrol the garden, chewed his lip as he stared at the pattern of white and black stones. Sunetra regarded him calmly, reclining back on one elbow. The Unicorn plucked a white stone between two fingers and moved to place it on the board. It was a good move; it might not save him from losing at this point, but it would certainly be a step in the right direction. Sunetra shook her head almost imperceptibly and gave a little sigh. The Unicorn hesitated, looked over the board again, and put the stone somewhere else. He settled back on his heels with a satisfied grin.

"A skilled move," Sunetra cooed. "You are quite good at this game."

The Unicorn beamed with pride.

Sunetra placed another black stone on the table, trapping several of the Unicorn's pieces simultaneously. The

"I think I would make a fine governor," Sunetra said with a small laugh. She studied the board, rolling a white stone among her fingers.

"I think I would be terrified to see you in a position of leadership," Naseru said humorlessly. "Sunetra, what can you tell me about the Tsuno?"

Sunetra looked up, stone inches above the board. "Tsuno?" she replied, surprised by the question.

Naseru nodded. "Your clan were the first to face them," Naseru said, "when my father was murdered on the road to this very city."

"I was not there," Sunetra said, putting her stone down. "The only Tsuno I have seen were when Daigotsu attacked Otosan Uchi. They were bigger than the largest Crab samurai and fast as lightning."

"Did you see their eyes?" Naseru asked, placing his own stone without hesitation.

"No," Sunetra said, placing a stone. "I fought them with a bow. I did not wish to get close."

"I saw them," Isei said.

Naseru looked up at his yojimbo. "Do you remember the color of their eyes?"

Isei nodded. "Deep orange, almost golden, with a bit of red."

The Anvil was silent. He knew better than to question Isei's memory; the yojimbo remembered every foe he had ever faced in perfect detail. Naseru's expression became thoughtful. He absently set a stone on the board, not even appearing to notice when Sunetra captured it.

"Is there a problem, Naseru-sama?" Sunetra asked.

"I am beginning to believe the origins of Ide Tadaji's gift are more complex than I first suspected," he said. He picked up a black stone.

"That dagger," Sunetra said. "Is it made of night crystal?"

"How do you know about night crystal?" Naseru asked, setting his stone down.

"I have seen it once before," she said, wrinkling her nose at the move he had made. "There was a man I knew who . . .

owned a piece of night crystal. He lives in Ryoko Owari now."

"That seems an extraordinary coincidence," Naseru said.

"Perhaps," Sunetra said, and placed a stone on the board. "I was planning to visit him later today. I think he may have some leads regarding that opium we found."

Naseru frowned. "Could he be the one who hired Soshu?" he asked.

"I seriously doubt it," Sunetra said. "What is this about? Why are you asking about Tsuno?"

"We have enemies in this city, Sunetra," Naseru replied. He plucked up a black stone and rolled it thoughtfully between his fingers. "Even my dreams are no longer safe."

"Your dreams?" Sunetra asked. Her blue eyes were now wide with curiosity. "How strange."

"Such is my life," Naseru said with a shrug. He placed the stone. "How soon can we meet with your friend?"

"Calling him a friend would be something of an exaggeration."

10 THE CHANCELLOR'S OFFER

What do you think?" Bayushi Churai asked as he led Yotsu Irie through the courtyards of the chancellor's mansion.

"It is impressive," said Irie, tyring not to show how overwhelmed she was by the opulent splendor of the rich palace Bayushi Kaukatsu called his home.

"Of course it is impressive," Churai said. "Kaukatsu has mastered a simple truth: This world is a material one. If one cannot impress others with one's wealth and power, then that wealth has been wasted. Not as if you can keep it after you die, yes? Might as well live in luxury!"

The Scorpion chuckled as he continued onward. The building was relatively small. Kaukatsu would never insult Shinjo Osema by building a home larger than his, but Irie had difficulty imagining the governor's mansion could be more lavishly decorated. A huge fountain of pure white marble stood in the courtyard, a plume of water spouting twenty feet into the air from the mouth of a ningyo statue coiled in the water. More statuary, the figures of great

Scorpion warriors and scholars, stood on either side of the courtyard. As Irie was led inside, displays of Scorpion ceremonial armor greeted her. Crimson lacquered plates with impressive masks and silken kakemono paintings depicting simple nature scenes hung at regular intervals on the wall.

Churai noticed Irie's eye on the nearest painting, a dragonfly hovering over reeds. "The Chancellor prides himself on his collection," Churai said. "Did you know kakemono are valued as much for the identities of their previous owners as the quality of the work itself? You see here?" He pointed at one of the chops in the corner of the painting. "This symbol represents its most famous owner, Otomo Konyo, cousin of Hantei XXXIII." Churai gestured at another chop. "The artist, you see, was only a minor noble of the Dragonfly Clan. Hardly worth remembering at all, yes?"

"Where is the chancellor?" Irie asked tersely, interrupting Churai's amusement.

"Of course, where are my manners?" Churai said. The Scorpion was still clearly amused with himself. "I can hardly expect a ronin like yourself to appreciate fine art, yes? Come this way. The chancellor awaits."

Churai walked quickly through the halls and Irie followed. She concluded that either the hallways of the mansion were unnecessary complex or Churai was leading her via a circuitous route. Was he trying to get her lost, or was he simply trying to impress her by displaying as much of the chancellor's wealth and possessions as possible? The answer, as usual where Scorpion were concerned, was probably some mix of both.

Irie said nothing, hoping to avoid engaging the arrogant Scorpion in any further conversation. Churai was mercifully silent during the rest of the tour, leading her finally to a small chamber near the center of the house. Two servants appeared seemingly out of nowhere, opened the shoji screen, and vanished. The room beyond was remarkably simple compared to the rest of the house. There was a low, simple table with a cushion on each side and a lantern in each corner. A thin man in rich silken robes the color of fresh blood sat at one side of the table, sipping from a cup of tea. A mask, simple in design but crafted from pure gold, covered his eyes and forehead. Irie could hear the haunting tones of a biwa floating from some hidden room.

Churai stepped into the room and fell to one knee, balancing with one fist on the floor in a warrior's bow. Irie did likewise beside him.

"Lord Chancellor, this is Irie of the Sword of Yotsu otoko-date," Churai reported.

"Ah," Kaukatsu said, setting down his cup and turning to face Irie with an eerie smile. He studied her face intently for several moments before inclining his head in a very slight bow. "I have been waiting for you, my dear. Churai, that will be all."

"Hai," the Scorpion said. He rose quickly and stepped back into the hall. The shoji screen slid closed behind him.

"Join me," Kaukatsu said, gesturing at the empty seat. The statement was polite but firm; it was clearly not open to discussion. Irie did as he bid, though her mind was still racing as to what this important man could possibly want with her.

A servant stepped forward with a pot of tea, looked at Irie curiously, and grunted. Kaukatsu glanced up at the servant and chuckled at Irie. "My servant is surprised to see that you do not carry your own cup."

"Should I?" Irie asked.

"It is a custom of the city," the Chancellor said. "Please accept one of mine, as a gift." Kaukatsu lifted a delicate teacup from a nearby tray and passed it to Irie. It was crafted of fine porcelain and painted a bold green color, highlighted by golden dragonflies in flight.

Irie was stunned by the gift. The craftsmanship was exquisite; even her parents had not owned a piece so valuable. "I cannot accept this," Irie said, not touching the cup. "I am not worthy of such a gift."

"Nonsense," Kaukatsu replied. "In Ryoko Owari it is a custom that all samurai carry their own cup," he said. "A custom, I confess, invented by my own clan to protect themselves against being poisoned. At any rate, I would prefer to keep my clan's customs alive even if the city is no longer technically ours. The cup is a trifle, nothing more. I will not miss it. Your friendship will be treasure enough to replace it ten times over."

"With all gratitude, I do not intend to stay in the city for long," Irie said. "I will not be needing it."

"Then I insist you keep it as a remembrance of your visit to the City of Stories," Kaukatsu said with a hopeful smile, "so you might tell your friends that the Bayushi are hospitable hosts."

"Then I must accept," Irie said, picking up the cup gently. She turned it over in one hand, marveling at its beauty. The servant cleared his throat patiently, reminding Irie to set the cup down so that he could fill it with tea. The servant did so and retreated into the shadows of the room.

"You seem uncomfortable, Irie-chan," Kaukatsu observed as she sipped the delicious brew.

"I am rather confused, Kaukatsu-sama," she replied. "Why am I here?"

"I once lived in Otosan Uchi," Kaukatsu replied. "In the short history of their brotherhood, the magistrates of the Sword of Yotsu have gained my family's respect. Your order and my family share a love of order and a thirst for justice that can never be quenched. Yotsu Seou sent me word of your imminent arrival. It was the least I could do to show you my hospitality."

"Thank you, Lord Chancellor," Irie said, though she suspected the chancellor's motivations were not so simple.

"I also wished to take this opportunity to offer some advice, if you would have it," Kaukatsu continued. "In Otosan Uchi you were a magistrate, but here you are merely another ronin. Few of the citizens of Ryoko Owari know the name of Yotsu or what it means. I would encourage you to exercise discretion during your visit here, lest more incidents occur like the one with the three Unicorn."

Irie blinked. "How did you know about that? I only just arrived."

"And while Churai was leading you indirectly around my

home, one of his lieutenants came here and reported everything that happened," Kaukatsu said. "That is another lesson you must learn. Always assume your enemy is prepared for your arrival."

"My enemy?" Irie replied, surprised. "Are you implying that you are my enemy? You said you wished to be friends."

"I am both enemy and friend," Kaukatsu said. "Yet another lesson. Everyone is your enemy here. This is not a safe city for a samurai without a clan. If I were you, I would recommend the City of the Rich Frog, Tonfajutsen, or perhaps Nanashi Mura. If you are seeking to make a name for yourself, all three of those cities are safer by far for those without a clan's favors to call upon."

"I am not here to make a name," Irie said, a bit more tersely than she intended. "I am not seeking favors. I am here seeking justice."

"And how do you expect to find it when you cannot even see what lies before you?" Kaukatsu asked. "Do you recall the blind man to whom you forced the merchant to give his koku?"

"Yes," Irie said.

"His name is Seiji, also referred to as 'Vile Seiji' by the governor's magistrates," Kaukatsu replied. "He has been useful to my agents as a source of information in the past. You may have noticed how quickly he vanished when the Unicorn appeared. Far more quickly than one might expect a blind man to make his escape in a crowded city street, wouldn't you say?" Kaukatsu sipped his tea, letting the question hang.

"He wasn't blind," Irie said, her tone mildly resentful.

Kaukatsu chuckled. "Tell me, Irie-chan. What makes you think you are a match for Hantei Naseru?"

Irie shifted uncomfortably on her cushion. "I don't know what you mean." She sipped her tea.

"Then allow me to elaborate," Kaukatsu replied. He looked slightly to one side, over one shoulder, in the direction the servant had gone. "Leave," he said simply.

There was the sound of a shoji screen opening and then sliding shut once more. Kaukatsu sat silently for several moments. Irie waited nervously. What was this man about to say that could not be risked in the presence of servants?

Finally, Kaukatsu broke the silence. He rested his elbows on the table and clasped his fingers as he began his tale. "Three years ago Hantei Naseru arranged an alliance between the Phoenix and Lion Clans—the greatest shugenja and greatest bushi of the Empire, side by side. The intent was to send their forces beyond the Kaiu Wall, to help the Crab destroy the Shadowlands once and for all. Such was not to be. War erupted between the Phoenix and Dragon Clans. The Lion, bound by their oath to the Phoenix, entered the war at the side of their shugenja allies. The Dragon had only one ally to call upon—the humble Dragonfly Clan, whose holdings marked the border between Dragon, Lion, and Phoenix. The Lion burned Kyuden Tonbo and killed every Dragonfly samurai."

"I know this story," Irie said in a bitter voice.

"Ah," Kaukatsu said. "Do you know this one? Several hundred years ago, there was to be a marriage between a Phoenix shugenja and a Lion general. However, the Phoenix chose to abandon her family's oath to the Lion. She married her Dragon lover instead, and out of their arrogance the Dragonfly Clan was born. The Lion were infuriated by the insult, though the Dragonfly were always careful never to goad the mighty armies of the Lion into open conflict. They knew that the Emperor's Right Hand would easily overwhelm them. The Lion were likewise wary to move upon the Dragonfly, for such an act might draw them into a simultaneous war against the Dragon and Phoenix, who were allies at the time. The Dragonfly Clan hovered tenuously on the borders between three Great Clans, surviving only because their feud with the Lion was less important than the Lion's reluctance to throw half the Empire into war. And so it went for over four centuries, but the Lion never forget a grudge. Some might say that the Lion cannot forget, not with the voices of their immortal ancestors whispering in their ears. When the opportunity came, and the Phoenix turned against the Dragon, the Dragonfly's fate was sealed. Only a few Tonbo still live. Those who were fortunate enough not to be in Kyuden Tonbo at the time—diplomats, magistrates, the odd young samurai-ko on a warrior pilgrimage . . ." Kaukatsu looked at Irie. "I have been watching the survivors of the Dragonfly Clan carefully, Yotsu Irie. I suspected that sooner or later one of them might prove useful to me."

"What is your point?" Irie snapped.

"I am simply curious," Kaukatsu said. "So curious, in fact, that I am willing to ignore your dishonorable impertinence in the face of your betters."

Irie's eyes narrowed but she said nothing.

"Why do you blame Hantei Naseru for the death of your clan?" Kaukatsu asked. "Why not blame the Lion officers who led the attack? Why not the Dragon commander who failed to send sufficient forces to protect the Dragonfly? Why not blame the Phoenix Elemental Council for declaring war in the first place? Why not blame my clan for not coming to the Dragon's aid? Why not blame your own dishonorable ancestor for breaking her oath to the Lion so many generations ago?"

"Because none of them intend to become Emperor, as Naseru does," Irie said in a low voice. "The Anvil plays games with people's lives and cares nothing for the result. My father warned Naseru what would happen to the Dragonfly if the Lion and Phoenix were to ally, but Naseru would not listen. He claimed that the potential gain was greater than the loss. Now my family lies dead, and what has the Empire gained? Nothing. The alliance between Lion and Phoenix is broken and the Shadowlands Horde still exists. I would kill Hantei Naseru myself before I let him take the throne. Do you intend to stop me?"

Kaukatsu laughed brightly, as if Irie had made some fine joke. "If I wanted to stop you we would not be having this conversation, Little Dragonfly. I wish to aid you. Why else would I have sent Churai to retrieve you? Had Churai's intents been hostile, he would have left you to the mercy of the Unicorn, or perhaps even aided them."

"How do you intend to help me?" Irie asked.

"Cautiously," Kaukatsu said. His steel eyes focused on her. "After all, it is not my place to decide the fate of an Imperial heir. What are your thoughts regarding the Four Winds? Whom do you favor to take the throne?"

Irie shrugged. "I never thought about it," she replied. "I do not know the Four Winds very well."

"I see," Kaukatsu said. "Then rely upon my experience, for I am intimately familiar with all of them. What would you say if I told you that the Winds are all spoiled children? Toturi Tsudao could easily assume the throne with little argument; instead she attends to matters better delegated to others and ignores her inheritance. Akodo Kaneka beats his chest and grants titles to himself, stirring up discord so that he can heap glory upon his name. Toturi Sezaru wanders aimlessly, hunting monsters and frightening the people with unseemly displays of magic. Hantei Naseru claims that he desires a unified Empire, and yet he will not set his own self-ish claim aside and support one of his siblings. I have little respect for any of the Four Winds."

"A dangerous statement for the Imperial Chancellor to make," she said.

"So tell someone I said it," Kaukatsu said with an amused grin. "Your status as ronin gives you certain advantages, but it also presents distinct obstacles. I can speak to you freely because no one will believe you. Please do not take this as an insult; it is merely the truth, and in this case, it is an advantage. Now what are your thoughts on this matter? Which Wind would make the best Emperor?"

"I do not know," Irie said truthfully. She chose her words carefully, hoping the Imperial Chancellor would not notice the disdain she was building for him.

"Guess," the chancellor prompted with an insincere smile.

The chancellor radiated power and confidence, the certainty that any move against him would be met with terrible reprisal despite the fact that he posed no physical threat. Irie was not used to dealing with such opponents. She suspected that as unsettling as the chancellor was, it would be far worse when she finally encountered Hantei Naseru. When that happened, she would make certain it was on her own terms.

"To guess would waste your time, as I have no experience in politics," Irie said. "You are Imperial Chancellor. I would bow to your superior wisdom."

"You respect my wisdom so much?" Kaukatsu asked in a mild voice. "Then heed it now. I fear that the Empire will never know peace so long as the Four Winds continue to compete. Otosan Uchi has already paid the price for their arrogance. While I do not share your vendetta against Naseru, neither do I have any special loyalty toward him. I believe it may be time to thin the herd. Unfortunately, I cannot help you act against any of the Four Winds directly. My position would be compromised."

"I did not ask for your aid, Kaukatsu-sama," Irie said.

"Which makes you a particularly useful associate," the Scorpion said with a smile. "It is your very independence that allows me to aid you indirectly without attracting suspicion. I can offer you useful advice and information, Yotsu Irie."

"Such as?" Irie replied, still hesitant to trust the Scorpion's words.

"You will never find your vengeance if you attack Naseru directly," Kaukatsu said. "The City of Lies protects him."

"The city?" Irie replied.

"Let me explain," Kaukatsu said. "Ryoko Owari has been a Scorpion city for centuries. It has been conquered a handful of times, but none have ever held it for long. The people of the city know quite well that the luxuries they enjoy here would be impossible under other leadership. Any other clan would frown upon the business they conduct. Each time the city has been taken, its invaders faced resistance not only from without, but also from within, as their soldiers slowly succumbed to the seductive pleasures of the city. And yet, nine months ago, the Khan's army invaded the City of Lies, forcing Scorpion Champion Bayushi Yojiro to withdraw his forces. Most Scorpion expected the Unicorn to withdraw from the city before long, but that has not happened. The Unicorn Khan has proven himself cannier than we expected.

With the exception of the governor and his magistrates, the Khan's troops are stationed outside the city, far from the sake, geisha, and gambling houses. Otherwise, the businesses here are still operated by the same Scorpion bushi who always ran them, but now they must pay a substantial tax to the Khan. All Scorpion operatives are forbidden to carry weapons or armor other than the daisho within the walls."

"Churai and his men had spears," Irie said.

"The law is defined by exceptions," Kaukatsu said with a thin smile. "I am the Imperial Chancellor and they are my personal guard. They serve not as Scorpion, but as Imperial Legionnaires."

"I see," Irie said. "What does this have to do with Naseru?"

"The City of Lies is like a string of Dragon firecrackers waiting for a spark to light the fires of revolution," Kaukatsu replied. "The Scorpion are unhappy with the Khan's rule, but we remember what happened last time we faced his soldiers. The Unicorn are bitter at the compromise they have made and begin to wonder if they truly need the Scorpion to rule Ryoko Owari. I do not desire a war with the Unicorn. Given time, I could return the city to Scorpion rule via careful negotiation, but the death of a Wind would be just the sort of chaotic event that would doom the city. Both sides would blame the other, and war would ensue. So long as Hantei Naseru remains in the city, the Unicorn and Scorpion who desire peace will both protect him. The governor's magistrates, Naseru's bodyguards, and even my own agents would move to stop you if you attacked him here."

"Convenient for the Anvil," Irie said with a grimace.

Kaukatsu chuckled. "You think his choice of a new home was a coincidence?" the chancellor said. "Always choose your battlefield. Any general will give you that advice. Hantei Naseru is a samurai just as you are, Yotsu Irie. He merely prefers a different style of combat."

"So what do I do?" Irie asked.

"When in doubt, wait," Kaukatsu said. "Eventually, the Anvil will stray from the protective walls of Ryoko Owari, and then it will be your time to strike. You will still have to deal with his bodyguards, but I have faith that the Sword of Yotsu would not have granted you fealty if you were not talented and resourceful."

Irie was quiet for several moments. The chancellor's words rang with guile and duplicity, but she could not deny that his offer seemed logical. "So how will I know when to strike?" she asked. "Do you expect me to spy upon Naseru like a common criminal?"

"Of course not," Kaukatsu said, feigning disgust quite believably. "That is why I retain agents such as Vile Seiji. Simply remain in Ryoko Owari, and when the time is right, I will find you."

Irie said nothing. She only stared into the depths of the fine teacup Kaukatsu had given her.

"Speak up, girl," Kaukatsu said sharply. "Are my terms acceptable or not?"

"I suppose so," she said. "Did I really have a choice?"

"Of course not," Kaukatsu said smugly, "but that was your final test. Ability to accept one's fate is another useful talent in Ryoko Owari. You are learning quickly, Yotsu Irie. Churai will show you to the door."

11 | LIFE AFTER DEATH

Kinji sighed, sat back on his heels, and slammed the furnace door. Taking a deep breath, he wiped the sweat from his ash-stained face. With a sour look he studied the long tables that filled the room. Six were covered with white shrouds, each covering a dead body.

"Only six?" Kinji called out in a disappointed voice.

"Don't complain," growled Masu. The fat old man knelt at the neighboring furnace and sifted the bones out of the ashes with a short rake. "It's still early in the season. Business will pick up."

"I hope so," Kinji said mournfully. He took a small urn from a shelf above and handed it down to Masu. "Shigi is pregnant again. We'll need extra money."

Masu grinned at his fellow cremator, broadly displaying several gaps in his teeth. "You didn't tell me that! How many children is that now? Five?"

"Seven," Kinji replied slyly.

"Benten must be watching your marriage," Masu said. He looked down at the urn in his hand. "And may Benten watch over you as well, whoever you were." He unceremoniously dumped a handful of ashes in the urn and slapped the lid shut.

"If it's Benten's fault I have such a full house then maybe I can pray to her to leave us alone," Kinji said. "Any more children and I won't be able to feed us all."

Masu stood, clapping the ashes off his hands. "Well, it's still early spring. With any luck one of the firemen gangs will start a turf war or something, and we'll have plenty of business."

"You think that might happen?" Kinji asked hopefully. The younger cremator plucked up the urn and carried it to the shelf at the far end where the family would collect it later. "A turf war would be really lucky. Well, except for the firemen, I mean."

"Naturally," Masu agreed. The fat man rooted around in his nose with one thick finger. "Anyway, complaining about not having enough work is pretty stupid when we haven't even finished what we have." He moved to the foot of the nearest table. "Kinji, take a look at this."

Kinji hurried to Masu's side. The burial shroud that lay before them had a massive red stain in the center. It also sank in the middle. The body looked as if it had been cut into two pieces at the waist.

"Osema's magistrates dropped him off earlier today," Masu said. "What do you think? Pickpocket?"

"I don't think so," Kinji pointed at the kanji on the shroud. "It says he's a samurai from the Shosuro family."

"Really?" Masu blinked stupidly, finger still in his nose. "That explains the mess. Samurai aren't dainty when they kill each other. Been a while since samurai cut each other in half in Ryoko Owari. Reminds me of the old days." Masu sighed and pulled out his finger, wiping it on the burial shroud. "Oh well. I'll get his legs."

Masu tucked one arm under the body's legs and hoisted. Kinji remained by the table, staring at the covered body. He had never seen a dead samurai before. On impulse, he pulled the shroud away.

"I've never seen a samurai's face before," Kinji said. Eta were beneath the notice of samurai. They were expected to prostrate themselves in the presence of such individuals. To make eye contact was an offense punishable by death if the samurai wished; most eta did not take the risk and kept their eyes on the ground.

"Pretty strange, huh?" Masu said, shoving the dead Scorpion's legs into the furnace. "They look just like us."

Kinji did not reply, fascinated by the dead samurai. A pale face stared back at him, covered with a blue velvet fox mask stained with blood from a deep wound on the man's forehead. Kinji wondered how much that mask was worth. He knew a few good shops in the Merchant Quarter where he might get a good price for it once it was properly cleaned. Masu frowned on that sort of thing, but he was busy right now. He didn't have to know. The young cremator grabbed the mask and quickly yanked it off.

The dead body's eyes moved, fixing Kinji with a soulless stare. The eta cried out in alarm, but was cut off when the dead man seized him by the throat with one hand.

Masu looked up from where he had just finished shoving the Scorpion's legs into one of the furnaces. The old gravedigger's mouth hung open.

"Help!" Kinji choked, the word barely audible.

Masu had lived a long time in Ryoko Owari. Life wasn't easy in the City of Lies, especially when you were an eta so lowborn that no one cared if you lived or died. Masu was one of the oldest eta in the city. He had survived the War of Spirits, the Scorpion Coup, the War against the Darkness, the Clan War, three opium cartel wars, and countless fireman turf wars. He would survive today, too.

Masu screamed and ran for his life, leaving Kinji to his fate. He hardly even noticed the komuso standing outside. The monk ducked to admit his basket hat through the small doorway and calmly made his way to the table where Shosuro Soshu's upper half lay. The Scorpion was still strangling Kinji with one hand. The eta was trying to pry the dead samurai's fingers from his throat, with no luck.

"Now Soshu-san, is this any way to behave?" the komuso asked, leaning his flute against the wall. "I brought you back to talk to me, not to abuse harmless eta. Now let him go."

Soshu's fingers opened and Kinji fell to the floor. Gasping for breath, the eta crawled as far from the table as he could and huddled fearfully in the corner. "Very good," the komuso said, circling the table. He turned, looking down at Kinji from inside his basket. "I shall speak with you in a moment."

Kinji said nothing. He had never been so terrified in his life.

Shosuro Soshu was now sitting up on his table as much as he could. The bisected Scorpion was staring down at where his lower body should be, his mouth working wordlessly. "My legs," he finally croaked, his voice a crackling whisper. "Where are my legs?"

The komuso sniffed the air. "I think they're in the oven," he said. "Now speak to me, Soshu. I gave you three days to find something for me. That time is now elapsed. Do you have it?"

"I . . . died," the Scorpion whispered, eyes glazed as he continued to stare at the end of the table.

"That much is obvious," the komuso snapped irritably. "Do you remember how you died?"

"I . . ." Soshu shook his head stiffly. "It is so hard to think. . . ."

"Not surprising," the komuso said. "It looks like someone put a knife in your head. What do you remember?"

"I broke in through the passageway in the ceiling," Soshu said. He touched his face with one hand. "Where is my mask?"

"The gravedigger stole it," the komuso said, gesturing at Kinji. Soshu looked blankly at Kinji. The eta stared back, unable to look away. Under his breath, he mumbled a short prayer over and over—a blessing against evil spirits. It didn't seem to be working.

"Soshu," the monk said, snapping his fingers in the dead

man's face. "Forget your mask and pay attention. This magic does not last along. Did you make it into Naseru's chamber?"

"Yes," Soshu said. "I thought for a moment that I could escape, but he tricked me. His yojimbo and a Scorpion woman came at me. I saw nothing else."

"I see," the komuso replied, "and what about the opium I gave you? Were you carrying it when you were killed?"

Soshu said nothing, eyes downcast.

"Were you carrying it?" the komuso repeated.

"Yes," the Scorpion replied. "I am sorry. I failed you. Give me another chance."

The komuso laughed. "You're hardly in any shape to face the Anvil now," he said. "You have served your purpose well enough, Shosuro Soshu."

Soshu stared looked at the monk, puzzled. "But I failed to steal the dagger."

"Yes, you did," the monk said with a chuckle. "Well done, Soshu."

Shosuro Soshu opened his mouth to reply, but no words came. The komuso gestured with one hand and Soshu fell back on his table, lifeless once more. The komuso drew the burial shroud over Soshu's face and began to chant a sutra of blessing. Halfway through he trailed off into laughter. "I can't remember the words," he said looking at the eta. "Do you suppose it matters? It isn't as if Soshu is going to the realm of the blessed ancestors, is it?" The monk patted the dead Scorpion on the forehead and moved to retrieve his flute. When he rounded the table again, he found Kinji kneeling before him.

"Please," Kinji begged, grabbing the hem of the monk's robe. "Spare me. I have a wife, children. Let me live, I beg you. I will return the mask."

A low growl emanated from within the komuso's basket hat. "You would dare touch me, gravedigger?" he snarled. "Get out of my way, fool."

The komuso struck Kinji across the side of the face with his long flute. The eta yelped in pain and scurried away. The komuso continued walking, ignoring Kinji completely. Pausing at the door, the komuso placed one hand atop a clay jug of lamp oil and pushed it over, spilling the liquid across the floor. Stepping outside, he played a short trill on his flute.

Behind him, the building burst into flames.

12 THE UNICORN

The House of Foreign Stories was unique in Ryoko Owari. Once it had been a shining gem of the Licensed Quarter, catering to the most exotic tastes of the city. Owned by the Unicorn, it was popular even among their Scorpion rivals. Travelers who visited the city made a point of sampling its unusual foreign cuisine and watching the strange female dancers the Moto brought back from the lands across the Burning Sands. Despite the normal Rokugani aversion to gaijin, there was something about the captive beauty of the House of Foreign Stories that aroused the curiosity of the City of Lies.

Twenty-seven years ago the return of Lady Shinjo, Kami founder of the Unicorn Clan, had changed all of that. When she discovered that Unicorn daimyo Shinjo Yokatsu was secretly a mastermind of the shadowy criminal syndicate known as the Kolat, her wrath was terrible. At her command, the Utaku Battle Maidens galloped across the face of Rokugan, hunting Kolat agents wherever they were found. The House of Foreign Stories, an establishment owned by

Yokatsu's agents, was discovered to be a den of Kolat spies. All who worked there were interrogated and imprisoned. All who had visited were suspected of Kolat affiliation and interrogated by tireless Unicorn magistrates. The stigma of ever having been an employee or a patron was such that soon few would admit even knowing the House's name. The gaijin tapestries and sculptures were destroyed. The dancers were taken away in chains and exiled to the desert. Though the Utaku wished to burn the house as well, the Scorpion magistrates would not allow it. The risk of fire spreading in a city as cramped and populated as Ryoko Owari was too high. Instead, the gaily colored building was painted dead black. The windows and doors were boarded over.

For twenty-five years the House of Foreign Stories stood vacant, a dead weed in the bright garden of the Licensed Quarter. Even squatters and homeless eta avoided the building for fear that they might somehow be implicated in the crimes that took place there. Two years ago, a man had come to Ryoko Owari, taken one look at the House of Foreign Stories, and decided it was time for it to live again. Hated and despised among his own clan, he had very little to lose.

Besides, he already owned the place.

Within a month, the House of Foreign Stories was open again. The building was still drab and black but full of life. It had become a sake and gambling house, catering to the roughest crowd of the Licensed Quarter.

"Pass the dice, Izo," the Unicorn advised. "You're pushing your luck."

His weathered lips creased into a pleasant grin beneath his low-slung jingasa helmet. His face, or what was visible of it, was the sort that was well used to smiling. He was quite delighted by the bowl of rice he was enjoying—or perhaps from watching the Mantis sailor lose money repeatedly.

"Sorry, mate, I didn't catch your name," Izo said, sneering at the Unicorn.

"Good thing you didn't," the Unicorn said with a laugh. "You would have bet it and lost it by now." He took another load of rice onto his chopsticks and chewed merrily.

"Bah," Moshi Izo said, taking another drink from his sake bottle. Izo was not the sort who was ever pleasant or cheerful, and his face looked like it had been chiseled out of a scrap of driftwood. Three equally unpleasant fellows stood behind him, watching the game intently. Wiping his unshaven face with the back of his arm, Izo dropped another three silver coins on the table in the broad central area in front of him. "And three for Lord Moon," he said, dropping an equal amount behind them. The Mantis scooped the five dice in a cup and began rattling them loudly.

"Are all bets in?" prompted Yuya, a short, cherubic peasant girl in a pure white kimono. She looked to the two players expectantly.

"Daikoku's Hunger," the Unicorn said, tossing a copper coin onto the table to Izo's left.

Izo glanced at the coin and glared at the Unicorn. "You're betting a zeni that I'll lose?"

"Oh," the Unicorn said, looking at the coin. "You're right. That was very thoughtless of me." He carefully set down his bowl of rice, reached into his belt, drew out a gold coin, and tossed it beside the copper. "Daikoku's Hunger," he repeated, "and this is for the bank, because she's so pretty." He threw a gold coin to the table in front of Yuya, who smiled demurely.

The three burly sailors standing behind Izo crowded the table, as if trying to appear even larger than they already were. The Unicorn assumed it was their subtle way of requesting that he reconsider. He took no notice. The smallest of the four was already twice his size, so the extra effort at intimidation didn't make much difference.

"All bets are in?" asked Yuya.

"Are you going to roll or not?" the Unicorn asked.

Izo growled deeply, gave the dice a final shake, and tossed them onto the table. They came to a halt, revealing the North Wind, the South Wind, Fire, the Fortunes, and the Fish. Each die represented one of the five elemental rings of enlightenment revealed in Shinsei's Tao. The object of the game was to roll the Four Winds and the Fortunes. The shooter chose to keep or re-roll each die three times until he won, until he ended his turn fruitlessly and lost his bet, or until the Void die (which was re-rolled every time) revealed Lord Moon's Smile—an instant loss of both the shooter's bet and the equal amount set aside for Lord Moon. The game was very simple to learn, but complex in practice. As in all popular games of chance, the odds were geared highly in favor of the house. More fortunes were lost than won playing Fortunes and Winds. The Mantis chuckled and scooped Fire, the Fortunes, and the Fish back into his cup.

"No win, no loss," Yuya said. "Second roll."

"You're sure about this?" the Unicorn said as Izo prepared for his second roll. "I mean I normally don't allow people to back out of the game once it's started, but you really do look like you need the money. I'm sure Yuya would make an exception for you. She's a sweet girl." The Unicorn flashed another smile at the young banker and reached for his rice.

Izo continued to growl as he dumped the dice out a second time. This time they revealed the West Wind, the Void, and the Fish.

"No win, no loss," Yuya repeated. "Final roll."

"Nearly a win," Izo gloated, plucking up the Void and the Fish and dropping them back in the cup.

"Nearly a loss," the Unicorn said, chewing. "Every roll in this game is nearly a loss. The house has it all rigged. That's why I rarely play."

"Bah!" Izo snapped again. He dumped the dice on the table. The Water die stopped immediately, revealing the East Wind. The Void die stopped a moment later, revealing Lord Moon.

"Shooter loses all," Yuya said. "Daikoku's Hunger wins." She pushed several silver coins toward the Unicorn and then reached for Izo's bets with a slim bamboo rake.

Izo stared at the table blankly, as if he had just lost all the money in the world.

"I warned you," the Unicorn said. He set his bowl and chopsticks down carefully and collected his winnings from Yuya. "Some people should stick to honest work."

"No," Izo said, snatching the rake out of Yuya's hands. "That shouldn't count. This imbecile distracted me." He jammed a thumb toward the Unicorn.

"Imbecile?" the Unicorn said with a chuckle. "That's a surprising word coming from one with your limited education. I find it almost ironic that—"

The Unicorn's sentence ended abruptly as Izo's fist collided with his face. He fell out of his chair, flat on his back.

"And these," Izo said, standing up and lifting his chair and wielding it in one hand. "These barbaric Shinjo toys. Sitting on them is like sitting on a tree! Everything here is designed to distract me! This place is as crooked as the Bayushi said."

"Really, sir," the Unicorn said. He crawled to one knee and peered over the edge of the table. "You should calm down. The chair is not your enemy."

Izo smashed the chair over the Unicorn's head. He vanished again. The other three Mantis sailors laughed. A hush had fallen over the House of Fallen Stories. The other gamblers and dealers were watching the table warily. A few of the wiser ones were picking up their money and heading for the door. The Unicorn staggered to his feet again but now leaned heavily over the table, face down.

"Sir," Yuya said. Her voice was now terse and angry. "You lost your bet. Now surrender your winnings."

Izo slapped Yuya hard across the face and reached for his money. The Unicorn snatched his chopsticks from the bowl and buried them through the center of Izo's hand and into the table. Izo screamed.

The Unicorn stood straight now, looking much taller than he had before. His jingasa had fallen away, revealing long black hair and a narrow, weathered face. His left eye glowed with a pale green light.

"Are you sure about this?" the Unicorn asked, his gaze scanning the four Mantis. "I usually don't allow people to back out once the game is begun, but you look like you could use the pity."

Izo screamed again as he tore the chopsticks from his hand and swung at the Unicorn with a thick fist. The Unicorn darted to one side nimbly, pushing the Mantis's arm aside with his left hand. Balling his fist, he used Izo's momentum to fire a swift uppercut into the man's jaw. Izo stumbled, fell forward, and lay still.

"Get your friend out of here and don't ever come back," the Unicorn hissed to the remaining Mantis. "Try your luck a third time, and I take it all. The house has this game rigged, too." He pushed his long cloak to one side, revealing the katana and wakizashi on his belt.

The three Mantis mumbled fearful apologies and stooped to gather up their fallen friend. The four men staggered back out into the streets. The Unicorn watched them leave, righted his chair, and plucked his lost chopsticks and jingasa from the floor. As he sat back down, the other patrons returned to their gambling and carousing.

"Are you all right, Yuya?" he asked, balancing the wide hat on his head again.

"Fine now, thank you," she said, instantly her usual cheerful self again. She frowned at the bloodstained table and left to find something to clean it with.

A second Unicorn samurai quietly sat nearby. His wide face was humorless as he sipped from a cup of tea.

"Talk about unlucky, Huang," the first Unicorn moaned, displaying his broken and bloody chopsticks to the newcomer. "Don't I even get to finish my rice?"

"Truly a tragedy," Huang agreed. "You should know better than to provoke them, though."

"I did not provoke him," the first Unicorn said. "Much."

Huang laughed. The two Unicorn stood, clasped each other's right hand in the way of their clan, and clapped one another on the shoulder fondly.

"What would the Khan say if he knew that you were in Ryoko Owari starting fights, Lord Shono?" Huang asked, still chuckling.

"I think Chagatai-sama would approve," Shono said. "It's really not much different from what he and the Shogun are doing to the Crane Clan."

"Good point."

"I had not realized you were in Ryoko Owari," Shono said, glancing sidelong at his friend as he sat down. "Are you avoiding me?"

"I think it is you who are avoiding Osema," Huang answered, sitting down beside Shono. "I announced myself at his mansion, expecting to find you there. He only admitted you were here after two days of pestering. I take it the two of you are fighting again."

"I am not fighting with Osema," Shono said.

"No?" Huang replied.

"Of course not," Shono said. "If we fought, he would win. His armor is far too bright and shiny. It hurts my eyes to look at him."

"Osema is an honorable man," Huang said. "He has done much for the Shinjo family."

Shono shrugged. "I buried my father a long time ago," he said. "It's men like Osema who keep his ghost alive."

Yuya returned to the table with a bucket of water and a small scrub brush. She passed Shono a new pair of chopsticks and began scrubbing the blood from the table.

"Thank you, Yuya-chan," Shono said gratefully. He caught her gaze, eyes fixed on the door.

Glancing carefully over his shoulder, Shono saw the figure of a lithe samurai-ko highlighted in the afternoon sun. She wore a black kimono with dark red trim, the mon of the Bayushi family emblazoned over her heart. Though she wore no mask, her face was painted white. Shono groaned under his breath. Noting his friend's change of mood, Huang glanced back as well.

"A Scorpion," Huang said. "You know her?"

"Bayushi Sunetra," Shono replied. "She's dangerous."

"Of course she is," Huang replied. "I could tell that by looking at her. Maybe she just came to gamble."

"Not likely," Shono said. "She probably wants me to repay the favor I owe her."

Huang gave Shono a sympathetic look. "You asked for a favor from a Scorpion?" he asked.

Shono shrugged. "It seemed like a good idea at the time."

"She's coming this way," Huang said. "I will leave you two alone."

Shono gave Huang a pained look. "Have you no loyalty to your daimyo?" he asked.

"I live to serve," Huang said. "In this case, I think I can serve my lord best by letting him learn from his own mistakes. Carry the Fortunes, Shono-sama." Huang quickly rose and disappeared into the crowd.

Sunetra sat in the chair Huang had left vacant. Shono tipped his hat low, leaning as far forward as he could to hide his face. The Scorpion glanced at the bloody stain Yuya was cleaning with a curious expression.

"Rough game?" she asked.

"I am sorry, but this table is closed until the table is cleaned," Yuya said meekly. "Please try your luck at another."

"I'm not here to gamble," she said. "You can stop hiding, Shono, I know it's you."

Shono sighed and pushed his hat back again. "Hello, Sunetra," he said. "What are you doing in Ryoko Owari?"

"Well I can't exactly live in Otosan Uchi anymore, can I?" she asked.

"I really don't know," Shono said thoughtfully. "You could try."

"Funny," she said.

"Are you still working for the Anvil?" he asked.

"Why don't you ask him?" she asked. "He just walked in."

Shono looked back at the door. Two men had just entered and seated themselves at a table at the far end of the room. One was tall with broad shoulders and the eyes of a seasoned warrior. The other was thin with a weathered face and a black patch over one eye. Both were dressed in rough, simple clothing. With their scars, they did not look completely out of place in the House of Foreign Stories.

"What is he doing here?" he asked.

"He's trying not to draw attention," she said. "So try not to stare."

Shono shrugged and turned back to face Sunetra. "Why did he send you?" he asked. "If he wants the Shinjo family to support his bid for the throne you can tell him I stay out of politics."

"That's not what I want," she said. She reached into her belt, drew out a misshapen cube of black paper, and set it in front of Shono. "I need information about this."

Shono looked at the cube, then at Sunetra. "Opium?" he said. "I don't deal in opium."

"The writing on the paper is foreign," she said. "I know you run Chagatai's secret trade caravans with the gaijin."

Shono scowled. "I sell weapons, silk, spices. Not this." He pushed the cube away with an offended look. "It saps at the will, weakens the mind. I don't deal in that."

"I never said you did," Sunetra said. "I just want you to read the writing on the inside." She pushed the cube back toward him.

Shono sighed, took the cube, and peeled back one section. He squinted and studied the paper. "Where did you find this?"

"A man named Shosuro Soshu broke into Shinjo Osema's palace the other night," she said. "He was carrying two cubes like this. I found two more in his home."

Shono whistled.

"So what does the writing say?" she asked.

"I can't read it," he said, not meeting her eyes.

"You're lying," she said.

"Could be," he said, lacing his fingers in front of him. "I'm an untrustworthy sort of person."

Sunetra was silent for a moment. "You owe me, Unicorn," she said.

Shono merely shrugged and remained silent.

"Shono, if this is about money . . ." she said, but cut off when he fixed her with a sharp look.

"I don't know what it says," he said. "Now get out of here."

"I don't think so," she snarled. "You owe me, Unicorn. Now you will give me the information I require."

"Is that so?" Shono looked at her calmly.

Sunetra gave him a final disdainful look, collected the cube, stood, and turned to leave. Shono picked up his bowl of rice again. With a sudden jerk, his face smashed into the bowl and the table. A moment later, he was staring at the ceiling. It wasn't until he saw Sunetra's katana pointed at his throat that he realized she had kicked his chair out from under him. His swords were tangled behind his back at too awkward an angle to draw easily.

"Sunetra," he said with a good-natured laugh. "You're making a big mistake."

"Idiot," Sunetra said. "I'm the one with the sword."

"Granted," Shono said. "But you're a bit outnumbered."

A series of mechanical clicks echoed around Sunetra. She looked up to see a half dozen men pointing crossbows at her—gaijin mechanical bows the Unicorn were fond of using. Six more had drawn katanas from hidden sheaths beneath the gambling tables. All were dressed in simple brown clothing; Sunetra had assumed they were peasants before.

"Shinjo bushi, every one," Shono said. "They don't wear their colors, and they hide their daisho while they're working, but that's just good business. Too many swords in a room scares away the sort of clientele the House favors."

"Stay back or your daimyo dies," Sunetra hissed at the crowd.

"Kill him and you will see Shinsei smile," Huang said coldly, his own crossbow held tight against his shoulder. He aimed directly at Sunetra's face.

Shono sighed. "I don't think you're exactly winning them over, Sunetra. Perhaps you had best try putting down the sword. They might kill you anyway, but it's worth a shot, right?" Shono leaned back on his elbows and folded his hands across his chest.

Sunetra paused, uncertain. Her eyes flicked across the samurai who surrounded her. Shono knew that look; he had seen it often enough before—the look of a trapped animal trying to decide exactly how much damage it can do before it dies.

With a swift movement, Shono slapped Sunetra's katana to one side. Pivoting on one hand, he threw a wicked kick at her face. The Scorpion stumbled. Shono rolled forward into a crouch and tackled her, slamming her back into the wall. Sunetra kneed him hard in the groin; her hand darted to the knife hidden in her kimono.

"Don't be stupid," Shono grunted through the pain. "I'm trying to save your life, Sunetra. Stop fighting!"

Sunetra responded with a sharp chop to Shono's jaw. The Unicorn stumbled backward into the table, his jingasa falling back onto the floor. He looked up just as she drew her knife. He reached for his sword, but it had fallen from his belt in the struggle.

"Sunetra!" said a commanding voice. "Stop this at once."

Hantei Naseru stepped forward from the crowd; even the Unicorn crossbowmen made way for his commanding presence. The Anvil's face was livid. At his side, his yojimbo was utterly emotionless, though his sword was drawn one inch from its saya. Sunetra gave Shono a final angry glance and put her knife back in her kimono.

"Who are you?" Shinjo Huang demanded, pointing his crossbow at Naseru.

"An honored guest with exceptional timing," Shono replied, stooping to pick up his hat again. "Put down your weapons, everyone. Yuya doesn't want to mop up any more blood today."

Sunetra collected her blade from the floor and sat at a table in the corner. Naseru's yojimbo took up a post near her. Shono returned to his seat. He wondered if the yojimbo intended to protect Sunetra from the Unicorn guards or vice versa. To the Unicorn's surprise, Hantei Naseru sat beside him.

"Sake, please," the Anvil said, nodding at Yuya as he produced a cup from his robes. After the cup was filled, he sipped from it slowly and turned to Shono. "Did Sunetra tell you who I am?" he asked.

"She did," Shono answered. "Should I be impressed?"

"That is your prerogative," Naseru replied. "I merely wondered if I needed to introduce myself."

"I thought you would be older," Shono said.

"Strange, I assumed you would be younger."

"Then we're even."

"Strange that we've never met, don't you think?" Naseru asked.

"Not so strange," Shono said. "The last time I was invited to Winter Court, three Matsu bushi challenged me to duels. I think Matsu Nimuro asked your father to stop inviting me after I won all three."

"You killed three Matsu?" Naseru asked.

"They started it," Shono said with a shrug. "What can I do for you, Hantei Naseru?"

"I was attacked in my quarters the other night," Naseru said. "Quarters that were protected, in theory, by a Shinjo governor."

"Should I feel some responsibility?" Shono laughed and turned to face Naseru. "If I spent all my time trying to make up for all the mistakes my family made, my work would never be done."

"You are the daimyo of the Shinjo," Naseru said.

"That's not my fault either," Shono said. "I try to stay out of politics," The Unicorn's left eye shone a faint green as he grinned at the Anvil.

The Anvil paused and sipped his sake.

"What?" Shono asked. "Aren't you going to ask me about my eye? Go on. Ask. Everyone does."

"Actually," Naseru said. "I was wondering if this was a Winds and Fortunes table." He ran one hand over the betting pools painted on the table's surface.

Shono gave the Anvil an appraising look. "That it is," he said. "Do you play?"

"I only played once," Naseru said. "I wonder if I still recall the rules. Three rolls, five dice, keep or re-roll each but the die of Void, correct?"

"That's basically it," Shono said.

Naseru reached into his kimono and drew out several coins. He placed two of them on the betting area in front of him, then two more just behind them, for Lord Moon. Each time he set them down firmly enough that the chink of gold could be heard. Each was branded with Imperial kanji, worth two hundred koku. A frugal man could feed a village for two years with that much gold.

"Is that a suitable wager?" the Anvil asked.

Shono's eyes were fixed on the gold. "Get this man some dice," he ordered. Shooing Yuya aside, Shono took her place as banker. Shono looked sharply at Huang, who caught his meaning and nodded. A line of Unicorn bushi silently formed between Naseru's table and the rest of the room, protecting the Anvil's game from any undue attention. The dice were brought. Naseru dropped them in the cup and rolled them. They showed Fire, the East Wind, Rice, the South Wind, and Lord Moon.

"Lord Moon," Shono said with a small shake of his head. "Shooter loses."

Naseru pushed his money across the table and picked up the dice again. Shono collected his money with a satisfied smile. Naseru weighed the dice in his hand before dropping them in the cup.

"You don't trust me?" Shono asked.

"Should I?" Naseru asked.

"Probably not," the Unicorn said. "Might set a strange precedent. Play again?"

"Of course," Naseru said.

Huang quietly stepped forward and placed several silver coins on Daikoku's Hunger, then bowed to Naseru. "No offense intended, my lord," he said.

"None taken," Naseru said. He drew out eight more coins like the others and placed them as his bet, then set eight more just behind them.

Shono whistled. Behind Naseru, Huang shook his head. Shono frowned. Every instinct screamed to say no, to back down, to refuse the Anvil's insane bet, but with the money on that table Shono could fund three caravans to the Burning Sands. Shono squinted. His crystal eye gleamed a bit more brightly. To Shono's vision, Naseru, Huang, and everyone else in the house were surrounded with swirling energy. Shono saw none of the normal disturbances evident when someone was lying or bluffing. Perhaps Naseru really was as bad at this game as he said.

"I'm not sure the house can cover that sort of bet," Shono said.

"Then stake something as collateral," Naseru said. "Whatever you feel is appropriate."

"Fine," Shono said. "I'll stake my crystal eye. I'm told it's priceless, and you look like you could use an eye."

Naseru smirked, scooped up the dice, and rolled. They came to a halt on Earth, Fire, Water, the South Wind, and the Lady Sun.

"No win, no loss," Shono said with some relief. "Second roll."

Naseru scooped up all five dice and returned them to the cup.

Shono blinked. "Er . . . if you had kept Earth, Fire, and Water—"

"I may have rolled Air and won a small bet," Naseru replied with a curt nod. "Not worth my time." He rolled the dice again. This time they revealed the West Wind, Water, the Bird, Rice, and the Void. Huang snickered at the worthless roll.

"No win, no loss," Shono said. "Final roll."

Naseru set the West Wind aside. "That one has always been lucky for me," he said, rolling the other four dice again.

The dice showed the East Wind, West Wind, South Wind, North Wind, and the Fortunes.

"Fortunes and Winds," Shono said, eyes wide as he stared at the best possible roll in the game. "House pays four to one."

Naseru smiled, plucked up a die, and rolled it across the backs of his fingers in a maneuver only an expert gambler could perform.

"I thought you said you only played this game once," Shono said.

"Only once, at Winter Court six years ago," Naseru said. "I played it against Scorpion Champion Bayushi Yojiro when I was fourteen. The game lasted seven weeks. I lost, in the end, but I learned much. Now. I believe you owe me your eye."

"Well, that's the funny thing," Shono said with a nervous laugh. "It really doesn't come out."

"Fine," Naseru said. "I understand. Give me my sixty-four hundred koku."

"Heh," Shono scratched his ear and drummed his fingers on the table. "I don't have that sort of money. The house usually only takes small bets. We're not used to having high rollers in here."

"Then you should not have accepted my wager," Naseru said firmly.

"That's a good point," Shono said. "I can arrange payment once I send word to Shiro Shinjo. They won't like it, but they'll deliver if I tell them to. Shall I have it sent to your quarters in the governor's mansion?"

"What reason do I have to believe you will deliver?" Naseru asked. "You already promised me your eye and broke the deal. Your family has a . . . certain reputation."

Shono's left eye glowed a bright green; an angry vein stood out on his temple. "Choose your words carefully, Naseru," Shono said. "Remember you're surrounded by my Unicorn bushi."

"I am not an enemy you wish to make, Shinjo Shono," Naseru said, steepling his fingers.

"I am not a man you wish to insult," Shono snapped. "If you will not trust me, what choice do I have?"

"You have two choices, as I see them," Naseru said, leaning back in his chair. "Your first choice is to kill me. Unfortunately for you, my servant in the governor's mansion knows exactly where I am. If I do not return, he has orders to report directly to Shinjo Osema and Bayushi Kaukatsu. Now rest assured, while I have no delusions that the chancellor holds my safety in any high regard, I am aware that he has been waiting for a chance to drive a wedge beneath the Unicorn Clan's power base in this city. If Bayushi Kaukatsu reveals that an Imperial heir has died in Ryoko Owari, ostensibly under the protection of a Unicorn governor, he will seize the opportunity to declare your clan unfit to rule the city. Open warfare will erupt between Scorpion and Unicorn interests in the city. Forced with a choice between supporting the Shogun and maintaining his grip on the Empire's largest city, the Unicorn Khan will be forced to withdraw his troops from the Yasuki provinces to put down the civil disturbance. Without the support of the Unicorn armies, the Shogun will cease relying so heavily on Unicorn troops. Chagatai will lose the Khan's favor, a seat at the future Emperor's right hand. Someone must be held accountable for such a loss. Perhaps the dishonored son of a Kolat Master? I hear Kolat make excellent scapegoats. Lady Shinjo thought so."

Naseru's voice remained calm and even, as if he were telling a story rather than predicting his own death. When he finished speaking, he picked up his sake cup with two fingers and drank it down.

"Shinsei once said that a mighty avalanche begins with a small pebble," Shono said. "You look like a pebble right now. What is my other option?"

"Prove to me that you can be trusted," Naseru said. "Give me the information Bayushi Sunetra requested."

"All right," he said. "The language on the opium paper is Moto."

Naseru looked puzzled. "As in the family of the Khan? They have their own language?"

Shono nodded. "The Moto were not originally Rokugani. Their ancestors were the Ujik-hai, a race of barbarians we encountered in our travels. Though they merged with our clan after the Lady Shinjo conquered their leaders, the Moto continued to speak the Ujik-hai language. These days nobody remembers it but the Unicorn who live in the borderlands or guard the caravans to the Burning Sands. It's rare, but I know a few Unicorn who don't speak anything but Moto."

"What does the paper say?" Naseru asked.

"Nothing much," Shono said. "A blessing of good fortune from the Shi-Tien Yen-Wang. Obscure old Ujik-hai gods. The content isn't important. The fact that the writing is Moto means that a Unicorn caravan delivered it. That means there's a very good chance that your Shosuro friend was paid by a Unicorn to break into Osema's palace. Throw you into the mix and it's pretty clear that someone in the Unicorn Clan is out to get you. I don't know why. Like I said, I stay out of politics. Leave me out of it."

"If your eye is any indication, you are already a part of it," Naseru said, scratching the back of one hand as he digested the information

"Why is that?" Shono asked.

Naseru leaned across the table toward Shono. With a quick snap of his wrist, he clutched an amethyst dagger in his hand. The tip hovered inches below Shono's nose.

Shono's eyes widened. "Fortunes, why is everyone drawing weapons on me today?" he said.

"Obviously some sort of deeply ingrained character flaw on your part," Naseru said dryly. The knife flipped in his hand, handle pointed toward Shono.

"You're quick for a politician," Shono observed. He accepted the dagger and studied it carefully.

"A parlor trick I learned from my father's Mantis friends," Naseru said. "What can you tell me about this knife? It seems to be made of the same material as your eye."

"Night crystal," Shono said, leaning forward to study the dagger. His left eye began to burn with a pale green light. The same light was reflected in the heart of the dagger. "Where did you get this?"

"A gift from Ide Tadaji," Naseru said. "I assume from the glow that it is magical."

Shono nodded vigorously. "To say the least."

"What power does it have?" Naseru asked.

"I saw a lot of artifacts made of night crystal while I was in the Seikitsu Pass, and all of them did different things," Shono said. "Some night crystal I saw didn't seem to do anything. Some pieces, when you hold them, speak in a language that isn't Rokugani, Moto, Naga, or anything else I've ever heard. Some of them"—he tapped his left temple— "let you see things no one else can see. That's why I was so sure you would lose earlier. The eye is usually pretty good about picking up when people are bluffing me. How did you do that? Do you have some sort of talisman that protects you from magic?"

"Merely discipline and self-control," Naseru said. "My brother is one of the most talented shugenja in the Empire. When we were children he made a game out of using his magic to find out my secrets. After a while, he stopped winning. Even magic can be conquered by one who is properly prepared."

"Interesting," Shono said. He toyed with the dagger, flipping it in one hand. It fell out of his palm onto the table, cutting a die in half. A burst of sparks erupted from the blade.

"Be careful with that," Naseru warned.

"Quite sharp," Shono said, eyes wide. "Why did Tadaji give this to you?"

"I once expressed an interest in the Way of Night because I believed it was the grave site of my ancestor, Akodo," Naseru said. "When I discovered I was wrong, I had no further interest. I think Tadaji hopes I will go to the Way of Night and convince Moto Vordu to cease his research."

Shono gave Naseru a wary look. "Is that your plan?" he asked.

"What do you think?" Naseru said.

"I think you should take my advice and stay away from Vordu," Shono said, pushing the dagger back across the table toward Naseru. "Tadaji is right. Vordu *is* dangerous."

"How so?" Naseru asked.

"It's personal. Maybe if I liked you, I'd tell you the story, Naseru-sama." Shono smirked at the Anvil.

"I am saddened I have found such disfavor in your . . . eye," Naseru said. "And I was prepared to offer you an opportunity to cancel the debt you owe me."

Shono chuckled.

Naseru was not smiling.

"I'm listening," Shono said soberly. He picked up the sake bottle and poured himself a cup.

"Two conditions," Naseru said, "First, I want a ten percent share in all future profits of this gambling house."

"That's easy," Shono said. "This isn't the most profitable business on Teardrop Island."

"It could be," Naseru said, peering around. "The structure has great potential. The location is perfect. Once it is cleaned and redecorated, I think it may become quite popular."

"I like it the way it is," Shono said, drinking his cup in one gulp and grimacing.

"Blackened and broken, but still alive," Naseru said. "Like your family?"

Shono's grimace deepened. "And I suppose you plan to plant some of your own agents among the staff so that you can spy on my clientele?"

"Is that a problem?"

"Just being clear," Shono said. "Fine. It's a deal."

"Excellent," Naseru replied.

"And your second condition?" Shono asked, pouring himself another cup.

"You will take me to the City of Night," he said.

Shono's hand shook, spilling a bit of sake on the table. He set the bottle aside. "Why are you going there?" he asked in hoarse voice.

"The opium I showed you was found on a thief killed in my quarters," Naseru said. "The thief attempted to steal my dagger and asked where he could find more items like it. That implies he was sent by someone associated with Moto Vordu."

"Or that someone wants you to think so," Shono said.

"Precisely," Naseru said. "In either case, my best bet at solving of this puzzle lies in the City of Night."

"That's funny," Shono said. "When I sense a trap I try to go around it, not into it."

"I prefer to meet my challenges directly," Naseru said. "However, I take great risk by venturing into Unicorn lands. Your Khan is a sworn ally of my rival, Akodo Kaneka. I should travel incognito. I need a guide who is discreet, trustworthy, and knows the land."

"And you think I'm trustworthy just because I owe you money?"

"No. Sunetra says you keep your word, when given."

"I have not given it," Shono said.

"Do so now, and consider your debt cancelled," Naseru said.

Shono frowned. His crystal eye burned with a smoldering light.

"Besides," Naseru continued. "I get the feeling that you have unfinished business with Moto Vordu. Perhaps we can both find the answers we seek."

Shono brooded quietly. "Fine," he said. "I will guide you there and back, Hantei Naseru. I can't promise you will not die for being so foolish, but I'll do my best to keep you alive."

"That is all I ask, Lord Shinjo," Naseru said.

"Fine." Shono extended his right hand toward the Anvil. "I give you my word."

"It is an honor to have you by my side," Naseru said seriously.

The Anvil shook hands with Shono, showing no distaste at the strange Unicorn custom.

"How soon do we leave?" Shono asked.

"Tonight. Meet us at the governor's mansion." Naseru picked up the dagger and tucked it back into his sleeve. He rose from his seat and bowed. "Is that too soon?"

"Not at all." Shono rose and returned Naseru's bow. "The good thing about being from a clan of nomads is that you're always ready to leave."

"Excellent," Naseru said. With that, he turned and left. Sunetra and his yojimbo followed close behind.

As soon as they were gone, Shono collapsed into his chair. Huang stood nearby, still staring at the door. "What was that all about, Shono-sama?" he asked.

"That," Shono said, pointing at the door, "is why I hate politics."

"Funny." Huang sat across from his daimyo. "It almost seems like he sent Sunetra, knowing she would cause a fight just so he could get on your good side by stopping it."

Shono folded his arms on the table and buried his face in them as he thought about the journey ahead. "Careful,

Huang," Shono said. "You're accusing an Imperial heir of swindling us."

Huang nodded. "Well, he did a fine job of it. I think you could learn a few things from Hantei Naseru, Shono-sama."

"Huang?" Shono said, looking up at his friend.

"Yes?"

"Shut up."

13 | HEROES

Yotsu Irie hurried through the streets of the Fisherman's Quarter, her sandals squelching in the thick mud as she pushed through the crowd. She paid no mind to the shrieking fish vendors or the gruff-looking budoka peasant warriors that crowded the narrow streets. Her mind was focused on reaching the small shack that had been her home since her arrival in Ryoko Owari. She hoped she was not too late to catch the Anvil's trail.

The note was still crumpled in her hand. Only ten minutes ago, she had been in a fish market selecting her lunch for the day when an anonymous stranger pressed it into her hand. The contents were simple.

Your quarry vanished from the Governor's Quarters not one hour ago. I hope you are enjoying the teacup.

— A friend

There was no signature, no seal, and no chop. Kaukatsu

was far too canny to leave any such evidence pointing to his involvement. Irie was on her own now. If she was swift enough, she could saddle up her pony and hurry to each of the outer gates of the city. Even if Hantei Naseru had left in disguise, someone might have seen something that could lead her in the right direction. Someone might have seen—

Fire.

Glancing back over one shoulder as a large man shoved her out of the way, Irie saw several plumes of smoke rising above the southwestern end of the city. Irie stopped where she was, staring at the inky black columns.

Cities feared fire. Most structures in Rokugan were wooden, and a small blaze could quickly level an entire neighborhood. Though the small settlement surrounding Kyuden Tonbo had never caught fire during the time Irie lived there, her father had taught her what to do. When you saw smoke, you stopped what you were doing and ran to help put out the blaze. Most large settlements paid gangs of peasant firemen to protect against just such a crisis; peasant or no, even a samurai did not bar the path of a charging fireman.

Knowing this, it seemed very strange to Irie that the people of Ryoko Owari seemed so unconcerned by the smoke. A few paused to comment on it, but that was the extent of their interest. Nearby, three ronin sat around a small table at the side of the road. The largest was laughing and drinking from a black clay bottle. Another was intently focused on some sort of meat on a stick that he was currently chewing. The third sat cross-legged on the ground, staring blankly at the table. Confused, Irie strode up to the trio.

"What are you doing?" she demanded. She noticed out of the corner of her eye that several peasants turned around and found more interesting things to do elsewhere once she raised her voice.

The largest man stared up at her. His eyes were clouded with drink. "Having a bit of shochu," he slurred. "Who're you?"

"It doesn't matter who I am!" she shouted. "Do you not see the smoke?" She pointed to the southeast.

"We see it just fine," said the man on the ground, sneering up at her. The other man had stopped chewing and now watched Irie quietly.

"Do you plan to do anything about it?" Irie demanded when it was clear that none of the men intended to move.

The largest man laughed out loud. "That's a joke, right?" he said with a broad smile. "That's the Leatherworker Quarter, outside the wall. Dogs put out their own fires."

Irie scowled at the three men. With a swift kick, she upended their table, spilling the bottle and meat into the dust. The three ronin shouted out in collective dismay, but Irie was already gone, running to the north, toward her shack. She had to hurry if she still hoped to catch Naseru.

As this thought passed through her mind she came to a dead stop again. She looked over her shoulder at the plume of smoke. She wondered if any samurai had seen the smoke from Kyuden Tonbo on the day the Lion burned it. Did they have better things to do as well?

"Damn!" Irie swore as she turned and ran toward the smoke.

Soon enough she passed through the southern walls of the Fisherman's Quarter. The fire was not in the city itself, but in a small village of tightly packed wooden huts a good distance from the walls. The surrounding land was broad and flat. No wonder the others had been so reluctant to help; there was little chance a fire there would spread to the rest of the city. She guessed it was probably an eta village. Regardless, Irie could not stand by and do nothing.

The fire appeared to be coming from a large stone building at the western end. A squad of men and women dashed madly from the stone building to the river, hauling buckets of precious water to the blaze and hurrying to refill them. Each wore thick rags over their mouths and noses. A small crowd of pregnant women, children, and elderly had escaped and gathered to watch from a safe distance. Every able-bodied man and woman was helping to put out the fire that was spreading swiftly through the village. Irie ran past the onlookers, not even noticing when they fell prostrate at the sight of her daisho. She skidded to a halt by the nearest burning building and looked about for any extra buckets.

A large, soot-stained eta carrying four buckets of water stopped in his tracks. His eyes were wide as he stared at the swords on Irie's hip. "S-sama," he stuttered in terror. Eta were expected to prostrate themselves to all samurai on pain of death. This one was clearly uncertain whether ignoring the fire or the samurai posed greater risk.

Irie shook her head at the man. "Today, I am just a person, the same as you," she said. "Now save your village!"

The man nodded in dumb gratitude and kept running. Irie looked around for any buckets or barrels she could use to fetch water. As she searched, she heard a shrill scream from the nearest building. The large shack was so consumed in flames that the firemen could not get close. Two men stopped next to Irie, staring at the house in shock as they heard the child's scream again.

"Kaomi!" one of the men cried. "I thought she had escaped!"

Irie remembered the day when she had come home to Kyuden Tonbo. The ruins had been burned to the ground, skeletons everywhere. No one had been there to save her father, her brothers. Irie grabbed the shoulder of her kimono, tore off her left sleeve, and tied it around her mouth and nose.

"Dump your water on me," she said, turning to the two eta. "Do it!" she shouted when they hesitated.

The two men nodded quickly and upended their water buckets on her, dousing her hair and clothing. Taking as deep a breath as she could hold, she charged at the door of the burning house. With a swift kick she split the door in half and ran into the inferno. The home was large for an eta's, with three doors leading into other rooms. The fire surrounded her on all sides, roaring like a thing alive. Her soaked hair and clothing kept her from burning to a cinder, but she could feel the heat blistering her flesh.

"Where are you?" Irie shouted as loud as she was able. "Shout so I can hear you!"

Another terrified cry echoed to the left. A wall of fire covered the door. Irie covered her face with her arms and ran at the door. The burning paper and thin wood crumbled as she dove through. Behind her, something heavy hit the floor, but Irie ignored it. She ran into the room and glanced around quickly. The fire had not yet spread to the far end of the room. There, huddled in the corner, was an eta girl no more than six years old. Irie ran to her side and scooped her up in one arm. Turning back the way she had come, she saw that the ceiling had collapsed. Swearing, Irie searched for any other way out.

She looked down at the swords on her belt, then at the nearest wall. Eta homes were not known for the quality of their construction. She set the girl down and drew her katana, holding the hilt firmly in both hands. With a loud kiai shout she buried the sword in the wall. The result was not as dramatic as Irie had hoped. Only two of the thin wooden planks had cracked under the blow. Reaching down, Irie pried the broken wood away, opening a hole just large enough for the child.

"Go!" she shouted, looking back at the girl.

The little girl nodded and crawled through on her hands and knees. Irie let go and the wood pulled back with a snap. Irie tried to lift her sword once more, but her arms sagged with exhaustion. The smoke had crept into her lungs despite the protective rag, sapping her strength. Irie fell to her knees, sword tumbling from her hands. She could hear the roar of the fire growing closer. She could hear her own heartbeat drumming in her ears.

"Father," she whispered, closing her eyes. "I'm sorry."

To Irie's surprise, the sound of her heart grew louder, more erratic. Opening her eyes, she realized the sound wasn't her heartbeat at all. The steady pounding was coming from outside. After a moment, there was a loud crack and a section of the wall fell away. Three large eta, including the two Irie had seen in the street, stood outside wielding sledges. The little girl sat on the ground behind them, watching fearfully.

"There she is!" one of the men yelled, pointing.

Everything went dark.

* * * * *

The next Irie knew, she was lying on her back in a field outside the village. The worried faces of the eta surrounded her. One was washing her face with a damp cloth.

"She is alive!" the man shouted. A chorus of cheers echoed in reply.

Irie sat up groggily. Her throat felt like sandpaper and her skin was covered in blisters. When she sat up she saw her katana lying on the grass nearby. It was unsheathed, its blade blackened with soot. The eta grew silent.

"I am the one who carried your sword, sama," said one, an old man. His voice was grave. He knelt before Irie, touching his forehead to the dirt. "Take my life. I have no excuse."

Imperial law forbade any but a samurai to touch a katana. Any peasants or eta that dared do such a thing dishonored the samurai who owned the sword. The other eta huddled nearby. They also knelt, though they did not bow as deeply as the shamed man.

Irie stood and lifted her sword from the grass. Sheathing it, she looked down at the doomed eta. They were only a short distance outside the village. The fire no longer raged.

"You doused the fire?" she asked.

The eta looked up, extremely confused that he was still alive. "Yes, sama," he replied, nodding rapidly.

"Did the little girl survive?" she asked.

The eta nodded again. "She is my daughter," he said, bowing his head again. "Thank you, sama."

"You saved my life," Irie said. "Now I spare yours. I thank you for not leaving my sword to burn."

The eta looked up at Irie, though he did not meet her eyes. His face was frozen shock, so surprised by her mercy that he could not express his gratitude. He only nodded and bowed his head again.

Turning away from the groveling eta, Irie headed back toward the city. The sound of rapidly moving footsteps behind her gave her pause. She looked back to find the old eta prostrate on the ground behind her again.

"Yes?" she asked sharply. "What is it?"

"Sama," he said, his voice shaking with relief. "I do not wish to waste more of your time, but I thought you should know something about the fire today."

"Go on," she said.

"The fire began in the crematorium," he said. "I fled shortly before it began."

"So?" she asked.

"The crematorium is a stone building, sama," he said. "Naturally, it was constructed to be fire-proof."

"So how did it burn?" she asked.

"Maho, sama," he said.

"Black magic?" she asked.

The old eta hesitated, clearly uncertain whether he should say any more. "I work there. I saw a dead Scorpion rise from his slab, and then I fled in terror."

"A dead man?" she asked. "Are you certain he was dead?"

"Very certain," the old eta nodded rapidly. "He had been cut in two. I ran away just as a strange komuso arrived. I saw him leave again only seconds before the fire began."

"Strange," she said. "But why tell me? Are there not magistrates to whom you should report this?"

"With all respect, sama, the magistrates do not listen to eta. But I saw the mark on your kimono." He pointed at the mon of Yotsu, the kanji for ten thousand. "We eta know the mark of your Order. The Yotsu are more than samurai. They are heroes."

"You are wrong, old man," Irie said, remembering how she had hesitated when first seeing the smoke. "Not all the Yotsu are heroes."

Irie turned and kept walking toward the city, leaving the old man kneeling in the dirt. She wondered how far ahead of her Hantei Naseru was now.

14   AMBUSHED

In his role as Imperial heir and primary bureaucrat of Otosan Uchi, Hantei Naseru had had little opportunity to visit the back roads of the Empire. Though he had traveled extensively, most of his destinations were either the palatial homes of important samurai or specially prepared way stations featuring every luxury. When he traveled incognito, as he did now, he suffered the lack of luxury without complaint but took no joy in the hardship of the open road as his father did. He looked upon the small villages of the Empire with much the same disjointed sense of wonder that he viewed the musty magical scrolls of the Seppun Libraries—interesting, occasionally educational, far too dusty, and ultimately better left for other people to deal with.

The lands of the Unicorn were an entirely new experience for him. There were few real roads, as the clan was nomadic by nature and tended to roam wherever it wished. The only major cities were trade cities. Villages merely served as defensible walled camps for the wandering clan.

Most Unicorn palaces had few permanent residents but existed mostly for the purposes of receiving and housing guests from other clans. The lands were mostly flat, broad plains carpeted with thick grass and the occasional tree. The notable exception to this rule now stood before them, stretching from one horizon to the other like a great stone wall.

"The Seikitsu Mountains," Naseru said, reining in his horse as he admired the view. The Anvil was dressed in plain clothing and light armor. The black silken eye patch had been replaced with a rough bandage over his right eye.

"Still half a day away," Shono said, riding up beside the Anvil. "The mountains are just that big."

Shono now looked more like a true samurai than he had in the House of Foreign Stories. He wore a suit of dark purple armor and a quiver of arrows on his back. A daikyu, the long horse-bow favored by his family, was strapped across the back of his saddle.

Naseru glanced back the way they had come. Isei, Sunetra, and Bakin were a short distance behind them. Their mounts were standard Rokugani ponies—short, squat, shaggy, and ill-tempered. Naseru and Shono rode long-legged Shinjo horses—swift, proud animals that were well adapted to the open plains of the Unicorn homeland. The Shinjo guarded their steeds jealously; it was rare that anyone outside their clan was granted one of their mounts. Naseru's horse had been a gift from the Unicorn to the Imperial Families several years ago. Though it was a gelding, it was still far swifter than any pony. Shono's black stallion was the finest horse Naseru had ever seen, one of the few luxuries the Shinjo daimyo allowed himself.

"Thank the Fortunes," Sunetra said as she joined them. The Scorpion wore only a plain black kimono and light armored plates over her chest and forearms. Her customary white makeup was gone. She looked tired and irritable.

Shono looked back at Sunetra. "You have only been riding for two days," he said. "Surely your journey to Ryoko Owari from Otosan Uchi was much longer than this."

"Much longer but more interesting," Sunetra said. "I'm

beginning to think that you Unicorn intentionally make your lands dull as a defense against Scorpion invasion."

Shono laughed. "You've been spoiled by the city, girl," he said. "If you can't appreciate the beauty in a wild plain, the wonder in finding out what lies behind the next hill, you can never understand what it means to be a Unicorn."

"That's a relief," Sunetra replied. "I do not want to understand you, old man."

"Fair enough."

"Let's keep riding," she said. "We can be in the pass tonight, and this cursed journey will be over."

"That may not be the best idea."

"Why is that?" Naseru asked, looking at the Unicorn.

"The pass is guarded by Unicorn bushi, but Moto Vordu and his shugenja are the true power there," Shono said. "Unicorn shugenja are extremely paranoid and secretive. If we appear at night we might look suspicious."

"Why are they so paranoid?" Sunetra asked.

"Not sure." Shono grinned at Sunetra. "Sharing a border with the Scorpion for three centuries probably has something to do with it."

Sunetra ignored the jab. "So we sleep on the dirt again tonight?" she asked with a sigh.

"Perhaps not," Naseru said. "What is that over there?" He pointed to the west. A herd of dark shapes could be seen moving across the horizon. A figure on horseback followed them as they wandered across the plains.

"Cattle," Shono said. "There should be a village nearby. That horseman can probably give us directions."

"Do you know this village?" Isei asked. The yojimbo wore a heavy suit of black armor without any symbols of rank or family.

"One Unicorn village is much like any other," Shono said. "This entire area is protected by the Junghar, the Unicorn Army of the East. I doubt we'll run into any trouble, so long as we don't make any." Shono gave Sunetra a sidelong look.

"Then let us rest there for the night," Naseru said. "Perhaps we can . . ." He trailed off, looking down in confusion. A faint green light pulsated behind his belt. Drawing out the crystal dagger, he saw that its blade was suffused in bright light. "What does this mean?" he asked, looking at Shono.

Shono's face was pale. His left eye had begun to glow brightly as well. "That means trouble," he said. The Unicorn drew his bow and looked about in all directions. Isei's sword was instantly in his hand. The yojimbo moved his steed between Shono and Naseru.

"Over there," Naseru said, pointing. A quartet of dark shapes was moving across the plains toward them.

"More riders?" Sunetra said, squinting for a better look. "They don't look right for riders."

As the shapes grew closer and more distinct, Naseru saw that they were humanoid creatures. They ran hunched on the ground, loping along with one hand and clutching a curved black sword in the other. Their heads were crowned by massive horns.

"Those aren't riders," Shono said. "Those are Tsuno."

"I fought them in Otosan Uchi," Isei said. "Have you faced them before, Unicorn?"

"A few times up north," Shono said. "I'm not eager to repeat the experience."

"I thought you said these lands were safe," Sunetra said.

"They used to be."

"Do we fight or flee?" Naseru asked. The Anvil's own sword was in his hand.

"Against four Tsuno?" Shono said. "I think we have a slim chance."

The Unicorn drew back his bow and fired. The lead Tsuno of the group reared and batted the arrow from the air with his heavy sword. Four more Tsuno rose up out of the earth behind the first group and joined them.

"They were waiting in ambush," Sunetra whispered.

"But they did not attack him," Naseru said, peering over one shoulder at the horseman tending his cattle. "They are hunting *us*."

Shono frowned. "We should retreat."

Naseru nodded and gave a sharp cry. His horse broke into

a gallop and the others fell into line behind him. A metallic roar rose from the Tsuno pack as they gave chase. Beside him, Shono had turned halfway in his saddle. The Unicorn drew another arrow and fired with practiced skill, the galloping motion of his horse hardly affecting his aim. The arrow struck one of the Tsuno in the eye. The creature fell in a cloud of dust.

Peering back, Naseru saw that the Tsuno were gaining ground. They were nearly as swift as his Unicorn steed. In the rear, old Bakin's eyes were wide with terror. The old servant released the pack mule and pushed his own old pony into a gallop. The terrified mule ran in pathetic circles. The lead Tsuno leaped over the creature in a single bound. The next roared and cleaved the beast in half with its sword without losing speed. The lead Tsuno lashed out with its weapon and Bakin's horse went down. The old man tumbled from his saddle like a rag doll. Shono drew another arrow and fired, striking the creature in the chest. It screamed and retreated.

"Run, Lord Naseru!" Isei shouted. "I will cover your escape!" The yojimbo wheeled his pony around and charged the Tsuno. His steed crashed into one of the beasts as it attempted to finish off Bakin.

Sunetra had also stopped, realizing that her pony's stubby legs could never outrun the Tsuno. She drew several small knives from her kimono and held them between the fingers of one hand, waiting for the Tsuno to come into range.

Naseru had seen enough Tsuno in Otosan Uchi to know how deadly the creatures were. It was very likely that Isei, Sunetra, and Bakin were doomed. Outnumbered, they stood little chance.

"An Emperor must think only of himself, Naseru-san," the Steel Chrysanthemum whispered in his mind. "Never of others. Nothing else matters."

It made sense, Naseru realized bitterly. Isei and Sunetra knew they could not win; they only intended to delay the Tsuno while he escaped. Shono, his guide, was the only person truly necessary for him to find his way home safely.

With his Shinjo steed, Shono could escape any time he wished. Staying here and fighting would be a pointless sacrifice.

Naseru looked at the plains ahead. The herds of cattle milled about, oblivious to the combat. The horseman, jaw slack in terror, was staring at the combat. Somewhere beyond lay a fortified Unicorn village. He would be safe there.

There was only one option. That much was obvious.

Hantei Naseru kicked his horse into a gallop, leaving the others behind.

"Naseru?" Shono called out. The Unicorn fired another arrow at the Tsuno, then faced forward in his saddle and galloped after Naseru. "Are we abandoning them?"

Naseru said nothing, only galloped straight ahead.

"Naseru!" Shono shouted again. "We can't just leave them to die!"

Naseru kept riding, steering his horse directly into the herd. The cows mooed and ambled clumsily out of his path.

"Naseru!" Shono shouted angrily.

Naseru ignored him. "You!" he shouted to the horseman. "Stop staring and get out of here! This herd is not worth your life!"

The horseman nodded, wheeled his steed around, and galloped away.

Charging to the far end of the herd, Naseru pulled his horse to a halt and vaulted to the ground. Shono rode up beside him. Green energy boiled from his left eye as he glared at Naseru. "Damn you, what are you doing?" Shono demanded. "Your friends are dying back there!" He pointed with his long, curved bow.

Naseru said nothing. He ran toward a tree standing near the rear of the herd and slashed at it with his crystal dagger. A small shower of sparks erupted from the blade. The cattle danced away with wide eyes.

"What in Jigoku are you doing?" Shono asked, trotting up next to him. "Are you insane?"

The Anvil looked up at Shono a fierce grimace. "I am

trying to save them, you fool!" he snapped. "Do you intend to help me or not?" He turned and stabbed the tree again, producing another flash of bright light and a tremendous shower of sparks.

Shono blinked in surprise, then looked at the herd. Their eyes rolled fearfully each time Naseru stabbed the tree, each time a new explosion of green fire erupted. Realizing the Anvil's plan, Shono drew another arrow and fired it into the haunches of a nearby cow. He shouted, driving the herd. The Anvil attacked the tree trunk again. This time, a loud snap echoed along with the sparks and the tree fell with a crash. That was all it took for the entire herd to break into a thunderous stampede, directly toward the Tsuno.

"Your friends are in the herd's path, too," Shono said as he watched the herd gallop away.

"An acceptable risk," Naseru said as he climbed back into his saddle. "They are smaller than the Tsuno, and I have faith in their ability to avoid danger."

The two men followed the wake of the herd, looking for any sign of the others. Shono pointed to the left, and Naseru looked a moment too late. A Tsuno burst out of the herd, slashing at the Anvil with one outstretched claw. Naseru grunted and rolled with the attack, falling out of his saddle and landing solidly on his back as the creature leaped over him. It turned and charged back just as Isei galloped out of the cloud of dust, Bakin cringing in the saddle behind him. Isei swung his no-dachi in a broad stroke, knocking the creature's head from its shoulders before it could return to finish off Naseru. A second Tsuno emerged behind Isei but fell with one of Shono's arrows lodged in its forehead.

The herd galloped onward. When the dust cleared, two more of the Tsuno lay limp upon the ground, trampled. Sunetra's pony also lay unmoving. The remaining three Tsuno were bloody and battered. One had lost its sword. Sunetra crouched in the high grass, katana held low to one side as she waited for them to advance. The Tsuno shifted uneasily as they gauged the strength of their foes.

Naseru rose to his feet, clutching his bleeding left shoulder with one hand. "Your master has underestimated us again!" Naseru shouted. Even from this distance, he could see that their eyes were red-gold, just as they had appeared in his dream. "Return and tell the one you serve that you have failed."

The lead Tsuno glared at Naseru with open hatred. "You have not escaped us, son of the Slayer," it said with a hiss.

"If this is the best you can muster I have no fear," Naseru retorted. He gestured at the claw marks on his chest.

The Tsuno leader roared in impotent fury. Naseru watched him coolly. With a spiteful hiss, each of the Tsuno slung one of their fallen brethren over one shoulder and loped back the way they had come.

When they were gone, Naseru staggered weakly and sat on the ground. Bakin quickly hurried to tend his master's wounds.

"They always carry away their dead," Shono said. "We should leave before they return for the others."

"I agree," Naseru nodded, tying one torn sleeve over his shoulder. "I am fine for now, Bakin. We can tend my wounds more thoroughly when we reach the village."

Sunetra looked at Naseru with a curious expression.

"Yes?" Naseru asked, looking back at her as he stood and climbed into his saddle.

"You told them to return to their master," she said. "Who is their master?"

Naseru shrugged, then winced as he tightened his bandage. "I have no idea, but it's obvious that *someone* sent them to ambush us. Now the Tsuno believe I know who they work for. They will wonder how much more I know. They will be more cautious before they make another attempt." Naseru held one hand out for Sunetra, helping her climb into the saddle behind him.

"I thought it was strange that they attacked us in the light," Shono said. "Those beasts can see in the darkness, so they usually use that to their advantage. They must have wanted to catch us before we reached the village." Shono shook his head slowly.

"Whoever sent them will no doubt try again," Naseru said. Bakin climbed up behind him. "Are you regretting that you came, Shono?"

Shono laughed. "Regret is for old men and cowards. I am glad I came. This is the most fun I have had in some time."

"I am glad you are enjoying yourself, Shono," Naseru remarked dryly. "Now perhaps we can find this village you spoke of before the Tsuno return to amuse us further."

"Follow me, Naseru-sama," Shono said. Giving an exaggerated bow from his saddle, the Unicorn turned and galloped off across the plains.

15 WAR STORIES

Shinjo Shono strolled deeper into the darkened sake house, looking for someplace where he could sit undisturbed and spend the evening consuming the bottle of sake he had just acquired. Fortunately, no one in the village of Katai had recognized them or had even cared when they arrived. Most of the citizens of Katai were peasants, and peasants minded their own business where dangerous-looking samurai were concerned. Shono appreciated that. It was nice to be recognized, but sometimes it was much nicer to be nobody at all.

Shono chose a dark table in the corner and seated himself. It took him a moment before his crystal eye picked out a figure sitting in the darkness across from him.

"Ah, I'm sorry," Shono said, starting to rise again. "I did not realize this table was occupied."

"No, it's all right," said a gruff voice. "Sit."

"Isei-san?" Shono said, recognizing the voice of Naseru's yojimbo. He sat back down. "What are you doing here?"

"Naseru is upstairs in his room, consulting with Sunetra,"

Isei said. "He sent me down here to look for any possible threats."

Shono nodded. He noticed that Isei was seated quite strategically. While the yojimbo had a clear view of the entire sake house, he himself could barely be seen.

"How is his injury?" Shono asked.

"Not serious. He lost some blood, but he still plans to leave tomorrow. He is stronger than most give him credit for. Most days, I find it hard to keep pace with him."

"Care to have a drink?" Shono offered his bottle over the empty cup in front of Isei.

Isei placed his hand over the cup. "No, thank you," he replied, gray eyes flicking at the bottle with disapproval.

"Suit yourself." Shono shrugged. He took a drink directly from the bottle.

Isei looked at Shono for a long moment, his face as grave as stone. The yojimbo returned his attention to the three other patrons in the tavern.

"So which one do you think is the threat?" Shono asked. "The old blind man or the fat woman petting the cat?"

"Everyone is a threat," Isei said, looking meaningfully at Shono.

"Ah," Shono said, taking another drink. "Present company included, I assume."

"Almost," Isei said. "When you drew your sword, before the rest of us could see the Tsuno, I thought you were about to attack Lord Naseru. I was wrong. You could have fled, but you did not. I trust you."

"You don't really know me."

"Battle is the truest test of character, Shinjo Shono," Isei said. "Those who judge you for your father's crimes are wrong. You are a true samurai."

Shono was silent for a moment, uncertain what to say. "Thank you, Isei-san," he said.

Isei nodded, returning his attention to the room. "Tell me about the City of Night," he said.

"What do you want to know?"

"Whatever you can tell me. Naseru has told me very little.

I prefer not to walk into unknown territory unprepared."

"Good policy," Shono said. "Well, first of all there are two passes through the mountains, each on either side of a series of craters Lord Sun made in the Seikitsu. The Sun's Arc Way is to the east. It's the only pass in Rokugan large enough to accommodate an army since Beiden was destroyed, so it's a major strategic holding for the clan. The Way of Night is to the west. It's an underground passage that was discovered soon after the pass was formed. The ruins we call the City of Night lie deep in the caverns."

"How well is the Way of Night guarded?" Isei asked.

"Relatively lightly. If Vordu ever runs into any real trouble, the Sun's Arc and the thousands of Unicorn camped there are only an hour away. Vordu has a small personal guard and his apprentices. Mostly he's guarded by reputation and the fact that the Way of Night is nearly impossible to find unless you know what you're looking for. It's very secluded. If Vordu wanted to, he could quietly kill us all and hide our bodies in the cave, and no one would know that we had ever been there. I hope for our sake that things go somewhat better than that."

"So you have been there?" Isei asked.

"Only once," Shono said in a quiet voice.

"Is that where you found your eye?" Isei asked.

"In a way," Shono said. "Four years ago, I made a deal with Vordu. He promised he would use his magic to help me hunt the Kolat. All he asked in return was that I aid him in one of his experiments. When I woke up he had carved out one of my eyes and replaced it with this." He gestured at his face.

"Did Vordu keep his end of the deal?"

Shono laughed. "Are you kidding? I didn't keep *my* end. Vordu wanted to replace the other eye too. I got out of the City of Night as quickly as I could and never turned back. Since then I've made it a point to avoid the Way of Night. There are other passes through the mountains, you know. They're small and they're dangerous, but I'm used to taking my chances."

"What does it do?" Isei asked, glancing at Shono's jewel eye.

"It lets me see in the dark and sometimes it tells me when trouble is coming." Shono said. "Most of the time it just gives me headaches and nightmares."

Isei nodded, returning his attention to the room.

"How long have you served Naseru?"

"Eight years," Isei said. "I have protected him since his first visit to the house of the Steel Chrysanthemum, by order of Toturi himself. Before that, I served in the Imperial Guard for nearly two decades."

"How did you get that scar?" Shono asked.

"This?" Isei asked, pointing at the jagged line that bisected his face.

Shono nodded.

"An oni buried its sword in my skull during the Battle of Oblivion's Gate," Isei said.

"Incredible," Shono said. "How did you survive that?"

"I didn't," Isei said. "One minute I was charging into the battle with the Legion of the Wolf under the command of General Saigorei; the next I found myself riding with Toturi's spirit armies on the other side of the Gate. I was only sixteen. I had only passed my gempukku three weeks before. I died in my first real battle."

"You're a spirit?" Shono asked, surprised. "I thought the returned spirits had a glowing aura, like Toturi."

Isei shook his head. "I, like the other spirits who chose to follow Toturi, underwent a Phoenix ritual that removed the powers Oblivion's Gate gave the returned spirits. I am a normal man again."

"Well, look at it this way," Shono said with a chuckle. "Lots of people sit around worrying about when they're going to die. At least you got it out of the way early."

Isei scowled. "I'm glad my death amused you."

"I find it best not to treat death too seriously," Shono said. "If you don't mind me asking, what was it like? Dying, I mean. I suppose once you've died once there isn't much to fear from it any more."

"I suppose," Isei said.

"What did you see?" Shono asked.

"It was strange," Isei said. "For a short time, I stood on the fields of Yomi. I saw the Realm of the Blessed Ancestors and the wonders that lay there. I saw the faces of the great heroes who have gone before and the wondrous palaces they have built. It was the most beautiful thing I have ever seen." Isei's gaze grew distant as he remembered. "Rokugan is nothing in comparison."

"Here's to Yomi," Shono said, lifting his bottle again. "May we meet one another there someday."

Isei looked at Shono sharply. "You will not see me there," he said.

Shono tipped the bottle away from his mouth. "Why's that?"

"The first time I died, I went to Yomi because I died with honor. Now I know the rewards that await a life well lived. I wonder if I now serve so loyally because I truly revere bushido, or merely because I know what awards wait for me. If the latter, Yomi will see through my selfishness. A samurai should not do his duty with any thought of reward."

"You're putting too much thought into this, Isei," Shono said. "I would think that catching a glimpse of the afterlife would give you more faith, not less."

"There is a difference between faith and certainty, Shono," Isei said. "The truest test of a samurai is whether he is willing to die for his lord. I died once already, but it was a fluke. I was unprepared, unaware that I was in danger. Now when the time comes for me to die again it will mean nothing. I serve without fear, but my bravery means nothing. How can I prove my courage when I have nothing left to risk? The question has consumed me for twenty-seven years."

Shono pondered Isei's words, then shook his head. "I remember hearing somewhere that courage isn't the lack of fear, but the ability to deal with your fear."

"What is your point?"

"I'm not really sure," Shono said. "It just seemed pithy."

Isei's dour face twisted into a grin, and a rare laugh escaped his lips.

"Now that's the spirit. Relax, Isei-san. Have a drink and

forget about death for ten minutes." Shono poured some of his sake into Isei's cup. "We'll have plenty of time to die tomorrow."

"I must maintain my vigil," Isei said.

"Your master is in good hands," Shono said. "I've known Sunetra for a long time. She may be a snoop, but she's loyal to her friends. The trick is getting her to consider you a friend, but I think Naseru has that covered."

Isei looked at the cup for a long moment, sighed, and drank it down. The grim yojimbo's shoulders relaxed slightly, and he offered his cup for more. Shono refilled the cup and held the bottle high.

"So what about you, Shono?" Isei asked. "How did the daimyo of the Shinjo family come to work in a gambling house in Ryoko Owari?"

"I don't run it. I own it," Shono refilled Isei's cup. "I just like sitting at the tables. Watching other people lose their money reminds me of how much less fortunate I could be."

"How so?" Isei asked, sipping his sake more slowly this time.

"Don't tell me you haven't heard my story."

Isei shook his head. "Should I have?"

"Hm," Shono said, looking somewhat forlorn. "I don't know whether to be disappointed or relieved that you don't know about my father."

"I know your father was the Champion of the Unicorn until he was revealed to be some sort of criminal," Isei said. "Lord Naseru said you are often judged for his crimes."

Shono snickered. "That's quite an understatement. My father was a Kolat Master, one of the leaders of a secret conspiracy against the Emperor. When my clan discovered his secret, he was cast out. Everyone who followed him was purged, including most of my family. When the Moto family took over the clan, the Khan gave me one chance to prove my loyalty. He sent me to hunt down my father."

Shono was silent for a long time. Isei said nothing, content to let the Unicorn tell the tale if he wished or let it end there.

"Huang and I hunted him for seven years," Shono said,

drinking his sake. "I was so angry for all the shame he had brought our clan. When we found him . . . he was just a frightened old man."

"What did you do?"

"We killed him," Shono said bleakly. "He was a criminal, after all, a conspirator against the throne. It was my duty. It was justice. Or so they said. For me, it felt more like killing my father. I know what he did. I know he was guilty. Still, it's hard to forget."

Isei refilled Shono's cup.

"You have much in common with Lord Naseru," Isei said. "Both of you have made difficult choices. Both of you are resented for it, when you should be heroes."

Shono raised an eyebrow and drank his sake. "Hard for me to imagine Naseru as a hero."

"You do not know him as I do."

"I'll take your word for it. To think, in a different world, I might have been the lord of the Unicorn Clan and your master might be Emperor."

"That day may yet come, Shinjo Shono," Isei said.

Shono laughed and poured Isei some sake, holding his own cup high. "To Emperor Hantei Naseru, then," the Unicorn said with a small grin. "May his reign be long and just."

"I will drink to that," Isei said, lifting his own cup. Both men drank.

"What sort of Emperor do you think he'll make, Isei?" Shono asked.

"He will never be Emperor."

Shono looked confused.

"He knows more about law, politics, and government than all of his siblings combined, but all the people see is the Steel Chrysanthemum's student. Because he is a politician, not a warrior, the clans see him as weak. They do not realize that he has the same warrior spirit as Tsudao and Kaneka, but that he prefers the way of peace. He was raised by a conqueror and wishes to avoid becoming one. He is more like his father than the Empire knows."

"Peaceful and honorable?" Shono said. "With all due

respect, are we talking about the same man who hustled me in Winds and Fortunes and then blackmailed me into joining this adventure?"

Isei laughed and drank from his cup. "Naseru-sama always takes the most efficient route," he said, choosing his words carefully. "Sometimes he favors efficiency over compassion."

"So he is flawed like the rest of us," Shono said. "I like him more by the minute. I just wonder . . ."

"Yes?" Isei replied.

"For a moment, when the Tsuno were attacking, it seemed as if Naseru was about to abandon us," Shono said. "I wonder, if he had not found a better way, if he would have left us all behind."

"I do not know," Isei replied soberly. "He is not a normal man. He is the son of an Emperor. Some day, I think, he will leave us all behind."

16   KYUDEN VORDU

There it is," Shono said, gesturing at the mountains ahead. A narrow pass was barely discernible through the jagged Seikitsu Mountains.

"Most anticlimactic," Naseru said, grinning slightly as he looked down at the mountains. He had discarded his earlier disguise for his fine kimono and eye-patch. "After all the trouble we've gone through to get here, I hoped it might look a bit more impressive."

"Funny," Shono said with a small laugh. "If you'd like I could pray to the Fortunes. Maybe they can arrange a dramatic thundercloud or something."

The grizzled daimyo's face was bland, but Naseru could tell from the quaver in his voice that Shono was nervous at the sight of the Way of Night.

"I see none of the guards you mentioned," Naseru said.

"They're there. We won't see them unless they reveal themselves. Vordu chose his guards for discretion and subtlety, not power. I wouldn't be surprised if I trained a few of them myself."

"What shall we do, my lord?" Isei asked, studying the pass with the cautious eye of a career soldier. "We cannot approach much closer without betraying our presence to the guards."

"I have no intent of hiding," Naseru said. "I intend to ride into the pass and pay Vordu-san my respects."

"What if Vordu sends for the Khan's warriors, my lord?"

"I do not think he will," Naseru said. "Vordu is an explorer, a seeker of mysteries. My presence here will spark enough curiosity in him that he will at least hesitate before sending for angry Moto soldiers to do away with us."

"Or he might be so suspicious that he'll kill you himself," Shono said, "knowing that the Khan would support him fully."

Naseru shrugged. "Possibly, but curiosity is a form of greed, and I have always found that greed is quite a reliable motivational factor. It is an acceptable risk."

"Maybe." Shono sounded uncertain. "But you're not going to learn much by announcing yourself. Vordu is a very secretive man."

"I am counting on that as well," Naseru said. "Bakin, ride ahead and announce our arrival. Tell Vordu-sama that he can expect the three of us to arrive at sunset."

"Yes, my lord." The servant bowed from his saddle and galloped off toward the pass. At the mouth of the pass, they saw four horsemen appear seemingly from nowhere to escort Bakin into the Way of Night.

"Three?" Shono glanced around behind them.

"Hm?" Naseru said.

"You said there were only three of us," Shono looked around. "Where did Sunetra go?"

"Is she gone?" Naseru asked, feigning surprise. "I had not noticed. Perhaps she had pressing business elsewhere. I am certain she will reveal herself in good time."

"Very well." Shono dismounted. "I suppose we should take the chance to rest, then."

Naseru looked down at Shono. "We can rest once we have arrived in Vordu's castle."

Shono frowned. "You told Bakin we would arrive at sunset. That is several hours, yet."

"When your enemy expects you to wait," Isei said, "make him hurry. When he expects you to hurry, make him wait."

"Sun Tao?" Shono said, questioning the source of the quote.

Naseru nodded. "You would be surprised how many of the legendary general's teachings apply to the court, Shono. We will let Vordu think he has hours to prepare. Instead, we will give him minutes. Now lead the way, Shono-san."

Shono glanced at Isei. The yojimbo shrugged, well used to Naseru's unpredictable behavior. Shono climbed back into his saddle and led them toward the pass.

The three samurai rode at a leisurely pace so as not to upset the hidden guards. As they neared the mouth of the pass, three more horsemen emerged from hiding. All wore the same purple armor Shono favored and had long bows strapped across their saddles. Naseru's eye searched the rocks on either side of the pass. He counted at least three figures moving in the shadows. He wondered how many arrows were trained on him at this very moment.

"Hold there, samurai!" shouted the leader of the three Unicorn. "State your business!"

"I am Hantei Naseru, son of Toturi the First," Naseru said, his deep voice carrying across the pass. "I ride with Taisa Captain Seppun Isei, defender of the Imperial Family, and Shinjo Shono, daimyo of the Shinjo family. Were you not told to expect us?" Naseru let the barest hint of impatience creep into his voice.

"We were told not to expect you for hours," the lead samurai said. He adjusted his helmet with one hand, clearly uncertain how to deal with this situation.

"What of it?" Isei demanded in a booming voice. "The Anvil keeps his own schedule. He does not bow to your whim!"

The Seppun rode several paces closer, one hand resting on the hilt of his huge sword. Though they outnumbered him three to one, not counting the archers in the shadows, the three samurai were taken aback by the outburst.

"Isei-san, please," Naseru said in a soothing voice. "These men are not to blame. It is this silly Shinjo steed my father gave me. Every time I expect a journey to take seven hours, instead I arrive in one. I suppose I am too used to riding the clumsy oversized dogs the Crab generals breed." Naseru patted the side of his horse's neck fondly.

The three Unicorn laughed at the joke. Isei laughed as well, returning to his place. The tension was broken. Naseru could tell from the guards' smiles and relaxed posture that they no longer considered him a threat. The guards were at ease with him now. It was a simple enough tactic that Naseru had used many times in the past—threaten a potential foe with Isei's blade, then turn that blade away and gain a friend. Naseru smiled as the guards stood aside to allow them entry into the pass. One galloped ahead to alert Vordu to their arrival.

"Do you require an escort, Naseru-sama?" one man asked.

"That's all right," Shono replied. "I can show him the way."

"Shono-sama, it is good to see you again," one of the men said as they passed.

Shono turned, surprised. He said nothing, only nodded at the man in return.

"One of your students?" Naseru asked.

"My cousin's youngest son," Shono said. "The last I saw him he was seven years old. Now he is a samurai."

"Mourning your old age?" Naseru asked with a chuckle.

"I am not old."

Naseru shrugged. "I just find it ironic," he said. "I often mourn my youth. If I were older my opponents would take me more seriously. If I were older my claim on the throne would be viewed with more respect. People mistake age for wisdom and youth for foolishness."

"Maybe it's not that," Shono said. "Maybe it's that you consider everyone an enemy or an opponent that puts people off."

Naseru chuckled. "With the exceptions of Isei and Bakin, everyone I have met has eventually proven themselves unworthy of trust. I have learned to give my trust warily, if at all."

"Did the Steel Chrysanthemum teach you that?"

"Actually no," Naseru said. "It was a lesson I learned from my father, when he gave me into the keeping of a monster. I loved my father, and I know he did what he did for the good of the Empire, but I find I cannot forgive him. I think that part of my soul has been burned away."

"I know the feeling, Naseru-sama," Shono said. "It's a strange world. If it were not for our fathers, today you might be Emperor and I might be Khan of the Unicorn."

"And we might have four eyes between us instead of two."

Even Isei laughed at that, though the dour yojimbo quickly regained his composure and returned his attention to searching for any sign of ambush. The three samurai rode deeper into the pass. In places the surface had been melted when Lord Sun had created the pass, and then cooled into smooth, black rock. Some of the rock was much lighter in color and jagged in shape. This tended to be arranged in large piles on either side of the pass.

"The cave that holds the City of Night was half collapsed when we discovered it," Shono said. "We had to hire workers to excavate. It took us four years."

"Where are the workers now?" Naseru said.

"Vordu sent them away when he discovered the Temple. That's what he calls it, at any rate. It's a place of great magical power in the deepest part of the city, where the most powerful night crystal artifacts were found. Since the excavation Vordu and his apprentices have worked down there without peasant labor, using only their magic."

"Four years," Naseru said. "That was when he gave you the eye, is it not?"

Shono only nodded. His face had broken out in a damp sheen of sweat. Naseru could tell that the Shinjo daimyo was clearly unwilling to return to the City of Night but was not about to turn away or voice his fear.

"Strange," Shono said. "The place has changed much since I was here last. After the peasant laborers left, there were still apprentice shugenja everywhere. This is a perfect time of the day for meditation. I would have thought at least a few of them would be out here. I do not see any."

"Intriguing," Naseru said. "Perhaps we can ask Vordu what became of them."

"You ask. The less I talk to him the better."

The trio rounded a sharp bend in the pass, circling to their right. Before them, a great pit gaped in the side of a mountain like an open wound. Within the cave stood a small castle, hewn from the stone of the surrounding mountains. Pale violet lights burned in the castle's windows. Just looking at it, Naseru thought the stone looked a bit too smooth, the pagodas too perfect. The entire place smacked of magical construction.

"A castle inside a cave," Naseru said. "Must be a dreadful sort of place to live."

"Moto Vordu is a dreadful sort of person," Shono said wryly. "I told you that already."

As Naseru rode deeper into the pass, it was not the strange castle that occupied his attention. He stared at the walls of the pass, a familiar feeling consuming him. He had been here before. Though much time had passed and rubble now choked the pass, this was the same pass he had seen in his dream. The place where the great cavern yawned in the mountainside was in the same place where the Tsuno had burrowed so fervently. Either the komuso had planned his illusion well, or this truly was the place where Akodo died.

"Is something wrong, my lord?" Isei asked, noting the pensive look on his master's face.

"Just a memory," Naseru said, returning to reality. He rubbed his bandaged shoulder with one hand. "Ah. I see our host has prepared for our arrival." He nodded toward the small castle.

The gates opened as they approached. A mounted Unicorn samurai rode out to flank each side of the gate, lance raised in salute. A small man emerged between them, dressed in a fur hat and thick fur robes, both dyed dark purple. A long moustache dangled from his upper lip, and he had the squat, weathered features of many Unicorn, making it impossible to discern his age. The many gold and crystal amulets that dangled from his robes proclaimed him a master of mei-shodo, the strange magic of the Unicorn shugenja. The shugenja bowed deeply as the three guests approached and dismounted. Shono and Isei bowed in return. Naseru barely nodded.

"Lord Hantei-sama," the little man said, eyes wide as he looked upon his visitors. "Lord Shinjo-sama. Taisa Seppun-san. I am Horiuchi Shem-Zhe, apprentice of Moto Vordu."

"May we come inside?" Naseru asked pertly.

"Of course," the shugenja said, bowing again before he scampered into the castle. He stood to one side, waiting for Naseru and the others.

Naseru took his time entering and walked as slowly as he could through the halls, studying every wall, peering out every window. He took no joy in tormenting the shugenja, who was clearly intimidated by visitors of such high standing. However, he knew that somewhere in the castle Moto Vordu awaited. Having hurried to arrange a suitable greeting for his visitors, he had now been interrupted with news that they had arrived. When your enemy expects you to hurry, make him wait. . . .

In the meantime, Naseru observed, the castle was every bit as dreadful as he had expected it to be. It was dark and cold. The stone walls sweated moisture in places. Dark gray mold crawled across the ceiling. Naseru wondered how any man could live in a place like this.

"I apologize for the lack of formal welcome," the shugenja said in his excited, eager voice. "Vordu-sama does not receive many visitors."

"Oh?" Naseru replied, leaving control of the conversation in the hands of the uncomfortable shugenja.

"This castle is rather remote," Shem-Zhe said with a cautious smile.

"One day away from a major trade route," Naseru countered. "Not so remote, I think."

"My master has never been a particularly sociable person."

"Is that so?" Naseru asked, feigning surprise. "My old friend Asako Misao visited this place just last summer. He

RICH WULF

enjoyed his stay considerably. He raved about it."

The shugenja tripped over his robes but quickly gathered his composure again. "The incident with the cartographer was regrettable," he said in a quiet voice. "The dangers of the caverns are great. Vordu-sama warned the Phoenix that he studied the magic of the city at his own risk."

"Your master sounds like a very considerate man," Naseru said. "I am certain that Misao's injuries were not his fault."

"Vordu-sama carries the favor of the Khan for good reason," the shugenja replied.

Naseru found the Shem-Zhe's reaction interesting. He had not agreed with Naseru's implied accusation, but neither had he defended Vordu. Such relatively open contempt among underlings usually happened only in two cases—with masters who were totally incompetent or with those so driven that they cared little for the feelings of those beneath them. With luck, Naseru could discern what sort of person this Moto Vordu was well before their meeting.

"Your name, the Horiuchi," Naseru said in a bored voice, "who are they?"

Shem-Zhe's face fell in disappointment. "We are a rather small family."

"I am sure you must have heard of them in the courts, Naseru-sama," Shono said.

"Perhaps I may have heard them mentioned," Naseru said, glancing about at the architecture. "I probably just forgot."

"Your honorable father granted us our family name," Shem-Zhe said, his voice growing more heated.

"My father did many things," Naseru said, peeling up the corner of a silk painting and frowning at the artist's chop.

"He did so to honor our mother, Shoan, guardian of the Four Temples," Shem-Zhe said. His face was now beginning to grow red. "Surely you have heard of the Four Temples of Kyuden Seppun?"

Naseru chuckled. He folded his arms behind his back and turned, meeting Shem-Zhe's gaze directly. The offended shugenja did not look away from the Anvil's gaze. "Shem-Zhe-san," he said in a friendly voice, "I confess that I have been trifling with you. I know your family well. I have prayed at the temples many times with Shoan-sama. When I hear the pride in her voice when she speaks of you and her other adopted children, I must confess I wish there was as much love and unity in my own family. Is it true that your sister, Suyin, is to be married in three months?"

Shem-Zhe's mouth hung open. "Th-that is true," he stuttered after a moment. "I arranged for her to be married to the son of the Hare daimyo, Usagi Kashira."

"Congratulations to them both," Naseru said warmly. "I hope it would not be too presumptuous if I were to send them a gift?"

"Not at all, Naseru-sama," Shem-Zhe said, eyes growing wider by the moment. The shugenja's face was still flushed, now with pride rather than embarrassment. "We would be honored!"

Naseru nodded graciously. Beaming with pleasure, Shem-Zhe led them toward their meeting with Moto Vordu. Meanwhile, Naseru reflected. This Shem-Zhe was not as weak-willed as he appeared. He was not the sort of person to follow an incompetent master.

"How long have you been here, Shem-Zhe-san?" Naseru asked, interrupting the silence again.

"Two years. I offered my services once I heard that Vordu was seeking a competent assistant."

"Was this before or after Vordu dismissed the apprentices?" Naseru asked. He had no idea if Vordu had dismissed the apprentices or not, but it did no harm to guess.

"After," Shem-Zhe said. "He believed that their limited talents had become more a hindrance than an aid, given the advanced magical constructs he had been discovering. There were a few accidents." Shem-Zhe looked at his feet uncomfortably. "A few of them died."

"Died?"

"Some parts of the ruins are haunted by unquiet spirits," Shem-Zhe said. "For one who is unprepared, they can be deadly."

"I see," Naseru said. He worried for Sunetra for a moment.

He hoped she could take care of herself. "So the ruins are dangerous?"

"Not terribly so," Shem-Zhe said. "It was not merely because of the spirits that the apprentices were sent away. Our research became more complex. Vordu-sama deemed the presence of such unskilled aides unnecessary. After working here for so long, I tend to agree. At times, even I have trouble understanding many of the items in the Temple, and I consider myself something of an expert regarding nemuranai." The shugenja looked at Naseru. "Nemuranai are items with awakened spirits within them," he explained. "Items of magic."

"I know what nemuranai are," Naseru said with a small laugh. "My brother is quite a talented shugenja."

"Of course," Shem-Zhe said. He paused at a large door, waiting for the others to catch up. "Please wait here. I will tell Vordu-sama that you have arrived." He bowed a final time and slipped through the door.

"I have not seen a single servant since we entered," Isei said in a low voice.

"I noticed," Naseru said.

"What sort of man sends a family daimyo to answer the door for him?"

"We shall see, I suppose."

Shono said nothing. The Shinjo folded his arms across his chest. His left eye glowed a faint green.

Misao had called Moto Vordu a fiend. Tadaji considered him untrustworthy. Shono had called him dangerous. Even Shem-Zhe did not seem to fully approve of his master. Indeed, what sort of man *was* Moto Vordu?

The door opened, and Hantei Naseru met the master of the Way of Night.

17 | THE OLD MASTER

Yotsu Irie reined in her pony and swore. The trail had gone cold again. With a resigned frown, she leaned back and dug around in her saddlebag for something to eat. Finding a rice cake and a chunk of dried fish, she considered her next move as she chewed.

Given the circumstances, she had been lucky to make it this far. Kaukatsu's letter said that Naseru had vanished. That meant he had either been kidnapped or had left in disguise. The former was too much to hope for, so Irie had gambled on the latter. She had studied her quarry well, and knew that the Anvil favored riding a black gelding given to her father by the Shinjo family. It was easy to disguise a man, but not so easy to disguise a horse. She had made her rounds at all the gates of the city, inquiring if any of the guards had seen a man riding a black Shinjo steed that was not a Unicorn.

Fortunately, the guards of the city were Unicorn bushi, and Unicorn noticed things like horses. The guards at the northern gate had pointed her in the right direction. She had learned that Naseru traveled with four others, three on ponies and one on another Shinjo horse. The leader had identified himself as Shinjo Shono, the eccentric daimyo of the Shinjo family. The others had remained anonymous. With their number and types of steeds known, it was easy for Irie to find their tracks. From there, it had only been a matter of keeping up with them. The Shinjo steeds were faster than her horse, but they had to wait for the ponies that rode with them. With luck, Irie had hoped that the size of their group would slow them and she would be able to catch up.

She had not stopped to wonder what the Shinjo daimyo would be doing with a disguised Hantei Naseru. She had not yet considered what she would do when she found them. She focused on the chase. A plan would come in time.

Or not, as the case may be. The trail became more difficult to follow after the five riders left the road to cut across the plains. Last night she had lost them entirely. Now she had been roaming randomly for hours without any sign. She was not prepared to give up, but she had to admit she had little recourse. She only hoped that she could find her way back to Ryoko Owari, if it came to that.

The deep bass sound of cattle mooing rolled across the plains. Irie knew that the Unicorn Clan sometimes kept cattle, using them as a source of meat and leather. She kicked her horse into a swift trot. Perhaps if she followed the sound, she might find someone who could help her find her way.

"Fortunes," Yotsu Irie swore as she crested the hill.

A small village lay before her, utterly ravaged. The bodies of Unicorn samurai lay in the streets near peasant warriors with spears or staffs in hand. A battle had taken place here, and none of the residents had survived.

"Who did this?" Irie whispered.

"Tsuno," said a voice from the tree above her.

Irie wheeled her horse and drew her sword. Looking up into the tree she saw a hunched little man in dark robes. His face was that of a crow, covered with dark feathers and split with a long black beak. He wore a katana across his back. He was, in fact, no man at all.

"Kenku!" she said, surprised. She quickly sheathed her katana and bowed deeply from her saddle.

"You have heard of us?" The raven-man looked surprised.

"My father told me many legends of the kenku. He said that when the founder of the Dragonfly Clan was killed in a duel, it was a kenku who taught his son the techniques that he used to gain his vengeance."

"Not vengeance," the kenku replied. "Justice. We do not teach vengeance."

"What is the difference?"

The kenku's feathers ruffled indignantly. "There is a world of difference," he said in a sad voice. "The Dragonfly Clan knew that."

"There are no more Dragonfly," Irie replied.

"The Dragonfly will die when their children forget what they stood for."

Irie looked away, toward the village. "Why did the Tsuno attack this village?"

"They hunt Hantei Naseru, just as you do," the kenku said. "They tracked him to this village after he killed several of their number. They missed him by mere hours and took out their anger on these innocents. Now follow me. We must hurry from here in case any of the pack remain."

The kenku leaped from his perch, falling nearly to the earth before broad black wings snapped open from beneath his bulky robes. The creature soared low over the tall grass, peering back only once to see if Irie was following. Irie kicked her pony into a gallop, struggling to keep up with the kenku's swift flight. They soared over the broad plains for a while before they reached a small stand of trees. The kenku alighted easily on a branch that looked far too thin to support a creature his size. The broad wings vanished beneath his clothing once more. Irie reined in her horse and vaulted to the ground, walking to the base of the kenku's tree.

"How did you know I hunt Hantei Naseru?" asked Irie, eyes narrowing.

"I know all there is to know about you, Irie-chan," the

kenku said. "I have watched you since you were a young girl. Had you not ended your warrior pilgrimage early to attend to the tragedy of Kyuden Tonbo, I had intended to reveal myself and teach you the way of the sword, as I taught your father and grandfather. Many of the greatest swordsmen of the Dragonfly Clan were my students."

"If you are such a great swordsman, where were you when Kyuden Tonbo burned?" Irie asked.

The kenku's beak clicked sharply. "Show some respect, girl. None wept more than I on the day the Tonbo died. I would have helped them if I could, but even my sword cannot turn aside an army of Lion. If you had been there during the attack, you would have died as well."

"If you cared for my clan, then join me," Irie said fiercely. "If Hantei Naseru gains the throne others will suffer like the Dragonfly. Help me kill the Anvil and lay the spirits of my family to rest."

"Your guilt and pain have blinded you. Your actions will bring shame to the Dragonfly Clan."

"What does it matter? The Dragonfly are dead."

"They died with honor," the kenku replied. "Would you taint their legacy with murder?"

Irie did not answer. She looked down, unwilling to meet the kenku's eyes.

"You know that this is wrong, Yotsu Irie."

Irie closed her eyes. "Is it better that I do nothing?"

"I never said that," the kenku said.

Irie looked back at the kenku. "Then what must I do?" she demanded.

"I do not know," the kenku said with a mocking chuckle. It scratched its fluffy cheek feathers with a clawed hind foot. "Destiny can be fickle, but after a while you begin to sense the patterns. There is a certain symmetry to your hunt for Hantei Naseru. I see that you will be tested soon, Irie-chan. The place where you are headed has long been a focal point for great events."

"You speak in riddles and prophecy," Irie said. "You sound like a Dragon."

The kenku fluffed its feathers indignantly. "I am insulted," it said. "We kenku perfected the art of sounding vague and incomprehensible when Togashi was still a babe in Amaterasu's arms. If anything, the Dragon sound like *us*."

Irie laughed despite herself.

"Ah," the kenku exclaimed, pointing at her with one long finger. "There. Laughter. I knew there was more to you than rage and self-pity."

"I am sorry," Irie said with a frown, "but I cannot set aside my quest, little master."

"I never asked you to. As I said, I know you. You are a stubborn human, but you are also an honorable one. I believe that when the time comes you will reflect upon what I have said and you will make the right decision. Wisdom will replace rage, and the Dragonfly will be reborn."

"We shall see," Irie said. "In the end, it may make little difference. I have lost the Anvil's trail. By the time I find him, he may be safe in the City of Lies again."

"Perhaps not," the kenku said. "I can tell you where he is."

"Why should I believe you? You might lie, hoping to turn me in the wrong direction."

"I would not do that." The kenku shook its head slowly. "Your fate is entwined with the Anvil's. Even if you choose not to kill him, you must face him."

"Then tell me where he is."

"First you must accept a gift from me."

Irie shrugged. "Fine," she said. It was not as if she had much choice. If she did not find Naseru soon, he would slip beyond her grasp.

The kenku reached into its robes and drew out a katana in a fine lacquered scabbard. Leaning forward on its branch, it carefully handed the weapon down to Irie. She accepted it in both hands with a graceful nod.

"I thank you, little master," Irie said.

"Do not thank me," the kenku said. "It is a burden as well as a gift. You must be worthy of the blade."

Irie nodded. She drew the blade. Her eyes widened in astonishment. The blade was pure purple crystal. As it moved through the air, it left sparkling green motes of light in its wake.

"This is extraordinary!" Irie exclaimed, looking up at the kenku.

Shrugging, the kenku scratched its other cheek.

Irie took several more practice swings with the blade. It was perfectly balanced, almost weightless in her hands. The blade left spiraling trails as she moved through a simple kenjutsu kata. She drew the image of a dragonfly in the air. Its wings seemed to vibrate as if in flight, making her laugh in delight. She wondered if the crystal was as strong as steel or as soft as glass. Testing the edge with one finger, she found that it was quite sharp. She was unwilling to test the blade against anything solid, lest it turn out to be true crystal after all and shatter.

"Why did you give me this sword, little master?" she asked, looking back up in the tree.

The kenku was gone. Irie glanced around but saw no sign of him. Shrugging, she strapped the fine crystal blade across her back and returned to her horse. It was only as she began to ride from the clearing that she realized the kenku had never told her which way to go.

18 | SHADOWS AND GHOSTS

Bayushi Sunetra clung to the shadows, using the rough mountain terrain to her advantage. Her formal kimono and daisho had been left with her horse in a copse of trees a mile away. She now wore a formfitting costume dyed in streaks of dark gray and black, designed to blend in with the rocks. Her face was covered in a mask of the same colors, leaving only her pale blue eyes visible. A belt of short throwing knives hung about her waist. Leather bandages with sharp metal claws designed for climbing were strapped to her palms and the soles of her feet.

She looked, for all practical purposes, like a ninja straight out of legend. There was no such thing as a ninja, of course. Scorpion samurai—such as Sunetra—would be the first to correct any who mentioned the topic.

Sunetra smiled behind her mask as she darted through the shadows, expertly avoiding the eyes of the Unicorn sentries. She moved within sixty feet of the mouth of the pass, ducking behind a boulder just as a mounted Unicorn bushi appeared. The man opened his mouth in a wide yawn, glanced around, and proceeded to scratch his backside. The horse, equally bored, neighed and kicked one hoof in the dust.

"Move on, stupid!" Sunetra cursed in her head. She wished she had picked a darker place to hide. If the Unicorn happened to turn around, he might notice her.

Instead of moving along, to her horror, the Unicorn slowly dismounted from his horse. The man started looking around nervously. Had he heard something? Sunetra drew a short knife from her belt and held it ready to throw.

The man turned, looked at the place where Sunetra was hiding, and began to walk directly toward her. He continued to glance in either direction, and now had begun fumbling with the lacings his trousers.

Sunetra sighed. Of all the times and places he had to answer a call of nature. She rolled onto her back and flicked her wrist, letting the knife fly.

The blade landed at the opposite side of the pass with a loud metallic ping.

"Huh?" the sentry said, and turned to look in that direction. He quickly tied the drawstrings of his pants and ran over to see what had happened.

Sunetra ducked out from behind the boulder and ran right past the man, not making a sound. By the time the Unicorn lost interest in chasing phantoms, Sunetra had vanished around the bend. The terrain was more rugged here, with more hiding places to offer. Sunetra moved more quickly, jogging toward the enormous cave at the end of the pass. She avoided the castle, cleaving to the opposite end of the path.

There were no guards outside the castle, no sentry towers. That was the amazing thing about shugenja. Most thieves and spies feared magic. The power of the kami could weave wards too subtle for mundane eyes to locate and provide defenses that ordinary men could not hope to pierce. As a result, most shugenja did not bother with mundane defenses, trusting in their spells and hiring only a token honor guard to protect their holdings.

Sunetra did not fear magic. Though she did not fully understand the power shugenja wielded, she viewed it with the cold logic of a Scorpion. The kami offered great power, but ultimately it was the minds of ordinary humans who commanded them, and humans were fallible. Thus, it stood to reason that magical security was no better than mundane security for a spy who was properly prepared. It was all a matter of understanding one's opponent.

Fortunately, Sunetra's adopted Scorpion mother had a close friend in the Yogo family, the Empire's premier masters of ward magic. Sunetra had always made it a point to stay on good terms with the old man, visiting and presenting gifts whenever she had the chance. In return, the old shugenja had developed quite a fancy for the pretty young samurai-ko. When she had expressed, quite innocently, an interest in the arts of magic, the old Yogo had been more than happy to discuss them with her. When she had pouted and cried over never being able to see the wonderful energies the old man wielded, he had taken it as a challenge. He gave Sunetra a ring made of purest Phoenix silver, awakened with the power of her magic. When she wore the ring, she could see the dancing magical auras of the kami. With practice, she learned how to sort through the confusing jumble of colors and auras and see the specific spirits that created magical wards.

As she moved quietly past the castle, Sunetra drew the silver ring from a pouch and slipped it onto her finger. The world shifted, solid shapes replaced with the playful, dancing auras of elemental spirits. Deeper in the cavern, she saw a crisscrossing pattern of dancing water spirits woven into a powerful ward. Sunetra did not know what would happen if they were disturbed. The spirits might simply frighten her away—or they might freeze the blood in her veins. Either way, she did not intend to find out. Dropping to her hands and knees, she crawled through a narrow gap in the wards. Looking back to confirm no one in the castle had noticed her entrance, she ran deeper into the cave.

Once she was out of sight of the castle, Sunetra drew a

small lamp covered with an iron hood from the satchel on her back. Kneeling and striking a shard of flint and steel as quietly as she could, she lit the small wick within and attached the lamp to her belt. The tool was an invention of the Shosuro, the Scorpion family that had raised espionage and infiltration to a high art form. The lantern had been specially designed to keep its oil reservoir upright and not spill even if she tumbled or fell. She could close the hood if necessary, covering the light without dousing the flame.

A large crystal gate, carved with the figures of strange and fantastic creatures, reflected the light of Sunetra's tiny lantern. She had never seen such a huge piece of crystal in her life. The gate stood open, and just beyond it Sunetra could see a complex web of elemental spirits. The entire area beyond the gate was covered with one enormous ward.

Sunetra paused, staring helplessly. She had never seen any wards of quite this level of power. They filled the whole cavern beyond. She could not imagine what sort of shugenja could create such a defense. She could see no path, no easy way through.

On the other hand, she knew that the spirits that created wards were very intelligent and somewhat picky. They were trained to react to specific stimuli. Wards that specifically targeted creatures of the Shadowlands protected many holy temples. Her Yogo friend had bragged that he once wove a ward that reacted only to shugenja who had trained in the halls of Shiro Soshi, a rival school of the Yogo family.

Perhaps, if she were lucky, this ward did not concern her at all.

Sunetra stuck her right hand directly into the ward. Nothing happened.

Sunetra breathed a sigh of relief, but it was tinged with fear. If this ward was not intended to keep out intruders, then what was its purpose? She would save that mystery for later. Sunetra removed the ring as she stepped into the ruins. The minor nemuranai had its uses, but it was far too difficult to see normally while she was wearing it.

She gasped in shock as her light flooded into the caverns.

She had heard the somewhat limited tales Asako Misao and Shinjo Shono told of the City of the Night, but she was unprepared for this. Scattered amid the rubble of the cave were domed buildings and columns made entirely of pale violet crystal. The light of her small lantern caught and reflected in the crystal structures, illuminating them with a pale green witchfire. The light spread across the entire cavern, trailing off into numerous side caverns, revealing a broken city of glowing stone. Pools of pure, clear water lay here and there among the ruins. As a girl, she had once visited the ruins of the Naga city, Siksa. The ruins here looked even older than that timeless city. Sunetra felt that she could sense the weight of the ages on the City of Night. This city was something older than mankind, perhaps something that was not meant to be found.

Sunetra noticed that a path had been cleared from the cavern entrance. It wound among the buildings. A white silken ribbon bordered either side of the path one foot above the ground, supported here and there by pitons driven into the earth. Sunetra quickly donned her ring to make certain the ribbon did not represent another ward of some sort. Amid the magical weaves that protected the entire cavern, she could sense that the ribbon radiated a faint but distinct magic. She recognized it as a common sort of blessing used to protect against spirits. Could the creatures that once built this city now haunt it?

Sunetra had little experience with spirits, but she did not fear them. Kneeling, she stripped away a section of the ribbon and tied it about one wrist. She hoped that would be enough to frighten away any curious ghosts. Even if it wasn't, she could learn little more here. Satisfied with her precautions, Sunetra stepped off the path toward the nearest building. The door's frame was huge, built for a creature much taller than herself. She reached out and touched one side of the door. The frame was cool to the touch, like ice. The green light danced down her fingers, swirling around her arm like fireflies. Sunetra looked at her hand, watching as the glow faded over the course of several seconds. She stepped inside.

The floor was littered with shards of oddly shaped white stone. Crouching to take a closer look, Sunetra realized that they were not stones at all, but bleached bones. Sunetra crouched to examine the nearest—the skeleton of a large humanoid lying on its back. Its skull was like a man's, but larger. The jaw was more pronounced, with sharp tusks jutting up on either side. It looked something like a troll. Near it stood a high stone platform table surrounded by heavy chairs. Another skeleton slumped in one of the chairs, the bones of the skull and right arm scattered across the table. The skull was broad and flat, like the head of a giant reptile.

Stepping back outside, Sunetra continued her exploration of the city. She moved from building to building. She saw more scenes like the first. Skeletal forms lay scattered about on crystal furniture. Some were large like the troll. Others were stunted and dwarflike with large, flat, reptilian skulls. Others, near the pools, were slender with willowy bones and a thin tail in place of legs. Lying in the middle of one path she found a skeleton with broad wings and a beaked skull.

"A kenku," Sunetra whispered, reaching out to touch the beak with the tips of her fingers. The bone was cool to the touch, like stone.

What was this place? Though the architecture was admittedly unusual, it did not resemble a tomb or mausoleum. The bodies lay about randomly, haphazardly. Some of the remains looked almost as if they had been working, reading, eating, or even playing with children when they perished. There were no signs of weapons or any sort of attack. It was as if every creature in the city had been stripped to bare bones in a single instant.

Sunetra stepped back over the white ribbon onto the path. The path led deeper into the caves, and she continued further into the City of Night. She soon arrived at an enormous central building made entirely of faintly glowing night crystal. It was the largest building she had seen yet, and it was no surprise that the path leading to it was well traveled, free of dust and obstructions.

When the path looked obvious, find another. That was part of a Scorpion bushi's basic training.

Holding up her small lantern, Sunetra drew back the hood that covered the flame. The light flickered slightly, blown by some unseen draft. Turning in that direction, she knelt and studied the ground, holding her light high. A wide, darkened tunnel led upward, unlit by the crystal. The path leading up, like the path leading to the Temple, had been cleared by frequent travel. Studying the ribbon path, she found it to be slightly scuffed, as if someone had kicked it in haste to see whatever waited above.

The signs were subtle, but Sunetra could not ignore them. Someone was using this tunnel frequently but had not moved the ribbons or extended the path to ward this area as well. That suggested that whoever was using this tunnel was doing it secretly. Why bother with secrecy? This entire area was already off limits to all but a few. Sunetra put the silver ring on her finger again. She saw that the wards that protected the caverns ended just a few feet beyond the path. This strange side tunnel was not protected.

Secrets within secrets. Sunetra's curiosity was piqued.

She stole up the tunnel, though she was not quite certain why she bothered. No one in the castle would hear her so deep in the caves. Still, her instincts told her to maintain her stealthy approach.

At first, Sunetra feared she might simply find a secret chamber where the apprentices slept when they were supposed to be working or, worse yet, a lavatory. When the tunnel continued on for several minutes, she knew she was unlikely to find either. The walls were unnatural, gouged in the earth by sharp tools of some sort. Sunetra had been trained in the arts of sabotage. To her eye, these walls looked newer and less stable than the others. The tunnel led sharply upward, and the draft became stronger. The light of the crystal city receded, but a faint ambient light from above began to fill the tunnel. Sunetra closed her lantern so that the tiny light would not reveal her and stalked onward. Eventually, she could see the end of the tunnel; the moon shone bright in the sky above. By her estimation, this cavern was miles away from any known entrance to the Way of Night. Why was it kept secret?

The clank of metal on metal made Sunetra duck behind a large boulder and freeze. She could hear heavy footsteps moving about above. It was most likely a Unicorn guardsman out on patrol. Cautiously, Sunetra peered out to see who approached.

The figure that stood silhouetted in the mouth of the cave was far too large to be a Unicorn. Enormous horns curved from its brow. A curved black blade was clutched lazily in one clawed hand. Its eyes shone red-gold in the darkness, scanning the tunnel for any sign of movement.

Tsuno.

Sunetra resisted the urge to duck back behind the stone. Shono said that the Tsuno could see in the dark, and any such motion would be detected. Instead, she held perfectly still, trusting her camouflage to conceal her. After a few tense seconds, the Tsuno gave a satisfied grunt and lumbered away.

With a sigh of relief, Sunetra turned and fled back the way she had come. She did not dare open her lantern again for fear the Tsuno would see the light. She darted through the darkness, one hand outstretched to prevent a high-speed collision with a cavern wall. After a minute she opened the lantern and skidded to a halt. Reaching into her satchel again she drew out a small clay jar filled with densely packed black powder. Explosives were illegal in Rokugan, and for good reason. In an expert's hands, a few well-placed charges of black powder could quickly reduce a proud castle to rubble.

Sunetra's hands were an expert's hands.

Wedging the clay pot where she thought it would do the most damage, Sunetra lit the cloth wick and ran. Twenty seconds later she heard the soft thud of the pot exploding, followed by the thunderous roar of the tunnel collapsing behind her. Sunetra increased her pace, grinning in satisfaction behind her mask. She would have to find a place to hide before the noise drew attention.

She was relieved to see her lantern's feeble radiance

reflected in the crystal walls of the City of Night, and ran faster. Ten feet from the ribbon-marked path, she slipped and fell hard, hitting her chin on the stone floor. With a grunt of pain, Sunetra looked back to see what she had tripped over. A group of ethereal figures hovered in the air, looking down at Sunetra with outstretched arms. Sunetra scrambled for the path, but the spirits were swifter. One brushed her cheek with its long fingers, and her body went rigid.

A mournful moan filled the tunnels as the restless dead swarmed over Bayushi Sunetra.

19 | MOTO VORDU

"Greetings, Hantei Naseru."

Moto Vordu's voice was dry and crisp, the hiss of a serpent. The voice fit the speaker well. The old Moto's face was withered with age. His scalp was completely bald, though a thick beard fell from his chin. His black eyes, sharp with intelligence, flicked from one visitor to the next like the gaze of a bird of prey. Like Shem-Zhe, Vordu wore a thick fur cloak that dangled with meishodo amulets; it covered the pronounced hunch in the old man's back. Vordu's amulets were exclusively crafted of pale amethyst crystal—night crystal. As Shono stepped into the room, some of Vordu's crystals began to sparkle gently with green light.

The shugenja bowed sharply, his agile movements belying his age.

"Greetings, Moto Vordu-san," Naseru replied, bowing not quite as deeply to Vordu. "I am pleased to finally meet a shugenja of your notable reputation."

"Oh?" Vordu tilted his head. "I was not aware I had any

reputation. Unless you have been speaking to Shono-sama."

Vordu's eyes moved to the Shinjo. Shono only scowled.

"Please sit," Vordu said. He gestured to a long table surrounded by the high-backed wooden chairs the Unicorn
Clan favored, adjacent to a roaring fire. Naseru noticed
Bakin waiting in the shadows, watching his master expectantly. No doubt Vordu had been prying the servant for the
true reason behind their visit. Bakin had survived far worse
than Moto Vordu.

Naseru, Shono, Isei, and Shem-Zhe took seats around the
large table. Vordu sat at one end of the table, leaving the
opposite chair open for Naseru. The table was covered in
large plates of steaming beef and noodles.

"I know that those outside my clan do not share our taste
for red meat," Vordu said with a feral grin. "I pray that you
do not take insult, Naseru-sama, but this is the finest fare I
have to offer. As Shem-Zhe has no doubt informed you, I am
not used to entertaining guests."

"Of course," Naseru said. "If anything the fault is mine for
dropping by unexpectedly. I hope you are not insulted by
this surprise visit."

"Insulted?" Vordu smiled. "I am honored to have the
youngest brother of the Shogun in my presence. I wish only
that the Khan were here so that he could share in my honor."

"That would make for an interesting visit, I think," Naseru
said, refusing to rise to the shugenja's barb. He took up his
chopsticks and ate a large mouthful of beef. The taste was
vile to Naseru's cultured palate, but he would not show
weakness in front of the Moto.

"Speaking of interesting," Vordu said, looking at Shono. "I
must admit that I am doubly surprised to see the esteemed
daimyo of the Shinjo in your party. Your return fills me with
joy, Shono-sama. My friend." Vordu's voice remained dry
and toneless, implying none of the joy or friendship of
which he spoke.

"Good to be back," Shono said with a tight smile. He did
not look at Vordu. His crystal eye flickered gently with the
same pulsating rhythm as Vordu's amulets.

"I see you still have the eye," Vordu asked. "Has it treated you well?"

"The eye is fine," Shono said.

"Do you still hear voices in your sleep?" Vordu asked.

"The eye is fine," Shono said in a more forceful voice. "I do not wish to discuss it." He still did not look at Vordu.

"Shono's eye is a most intriguing nemuranai," Naseru said, returning the shugenja's attention to him. "He tells me there is an entire ruined city of such artifacts in these caverns."

"Ah, yes," Vordu replied. "The City of Night. I assume the night crystal is what drew you here, Naseru-sama."

"What do you mean?" Naseru replied, as if such a thing had never occurred to him.

"By your reputation, you are a man who lusts for power," Vordu said. "The City of Night seethes with power. That is why we must keep it secret. Otherwise, ambitious men would swarm about the Seikitsu like ravenous insects. The purity of my research here must remain intact."

"An associate of mine, Asako Misao, called your work blasphemous," Naseru said flatly.

"Asako Misao is a fool," Vordu replied. "He could not appreciate what I have learned here."

"Misao is an Imperial cartographer and a priest of the kami. You would call such man a fool?"

Vordu frowned. "Pardon me if I have insulted your friend, Naseru-sama, but we Unicorn do not believe in dancing around the truth for the sake of saving face. If it were up to Misao-san, he would have buried the City of Night rather than face an uncomfortable truth. The wonders I have discovered would be lost forever."

"Wonders?" Naseru said. "Is that not a bit arrogant, to call your own work a wonder?"

"Shinsei defines arrogance as misplaced pride," Vordu said. "My pride is not misplaced. Since we have begun to explore the mysteries of the City of Night, the fields of the Unicorn have become more fertile. Our steel is sharper. The magical artifacts I have discovered can grant a samurai extraordinary martial prowess. No doubt you have seen the extraordinary abilities Shono-sama displays due to his eye. In addition to the potent magical items we have found simply lying about in the ruins, Shem-Zhe and I have only just begun to master the art of crafting new nemuranai out of raw night crystal. With what we have discovered, the possibilities are quite limitless."

"And what of this 'uncomfortable truth' you mentioned?" Naseru said. "What was it that you discovered here that Misao found so disturbing?"

Vordu gave a thin smile. "Are you certain you are prepared to hear the answer to that question, Anvil?"

"If you are trying to impress me with your air of mystery, you have failed," Naseru said, sipping from his cup. "I am merely curious. Either tell me or do not."

"You might not understand," Vordu said with a sigh. He looked at the Anvil sharply. "What do you know of the kami, Naseru-sama?"

"They are spirits of great power. There are two types—the greater Kami who fell from the heavens and founded the Great Clans, and the lesser kami, spirits that dwell within every thing that exists. These lesser kami are the minor deities that shugenja call upon to work their magic."

"Precisely," Vordu said. "We know that the greater Kami were born of the union of the Sun and Moon, but none ever wonder at the origins of the lesser kami." The old shugenja's voice grew excited, his eyes more intense. "As far as the Phoenix Council of Masters is concerned, the kami have always existed and always will. But I believe that I have discovered their true origins. I believe that the first kami were born here, in the Way of Night."

"How is that possible?" Naseru asked. "If I understand correctly, the kami are not merely spirits that inhabit nature. They *are* nature. If there were no kami at one time, then what existed before?"

"The mortal realm did not exist as we know it," Vordu said. "It was a half-formed realm of chaos, peppered with small pockets of random order. In these pockets, there came into being the Five Races, five societies of intelligent creatures, each of whom had mastered some form of control over the turmoil by focusing their will. Unfortunately, none of them could hold back the tides of destruction for long. Not alone. So they combined their powers. Together, they created a focus, harnessed their spiritual energy within it, and created the mortal realm as we now recognize it. Each of them severed a portion of their own soul, releasing the most powerful parts of themselves to hold and stabilize the new environment. Each of the Five Races embodied a particular sort of spirit. The clever kenku were air, the fickle ningyo were water, the doughty zokujin were earth, the fierce trolls were fire, and the wise kitsu were void. And thus was our world created."

"An interesting theory, but what of it?" Naseru said. "The Ashalan and the Naga have theories regarding the creation of the world that do not match our own. The people of the Burning Sands have beliefs that are almost diametrically opposed to our own, but are no less true by their perceptions. Create a religion and you will create a new way to create the world. Why should I believe this story is more valid than my own beliefs?"

"It is not a belief," Vordu said, an excited edge to his voice. "It is truth. The City of Night houses the focus that the Five Races used to create the first kami. I have seen that focus—a sphere of crystal so pure and bright that it hurts my soul to look upon it. This cavern is the womb of all creation!"

"If you have found an artifact of such limitless power, then why have you not used it yet?"

"There are complications. The sphere requires more study before it can be used safely."

"You seem very certain," Naseru said, "yet all of the races you mentioned are either obscure or dead. The zokujin are slaves. The ningyo are barely sentient. The trolls have fallen to the Taint. The kitsu are extinct and the kenku nearly so. If they were all so wise and powerful, how could such a fate have befallen them?"

"The wise are seldom invincible," Vordu said with a rueful chuckle. "Once the Five Races brought order to this realm, their power diminished. In time, the world they had created drew the attention of the dark powers of Jigoku, the Realm of Evil. Nameless ravening beasts issued forth into the mortal realm, seeking to corrupt and destroy everything they touched. In many ways it was like our own Day of Thunder."

"Intriguing," Naseru said, chewing a mouth full of noodles. He gave no appearance of paying any special attention to Vordu's story, though he listened intently.

"The Five Races could not agree upon how to deal with this threat. Some wished to fight the hordes. Some felt they should simply flee into another Spirit Realm and let Jigoku have the world they had made. The kitsu, traditionally the strongest of the Five Races, saw it as their duty to lead the rest. Soli Xiaomin, a kitsu mystic who had aided in creating the City of Night, felt that only by unifying the Five Races could they hope to stand against Jigoku. Kishenku, the general of a militant group that referred to themselves as the Soultwisters, disagreed. He felt they did not require the aid of the other races—all that they required was the City of Night. Xiaomin forbade the general from using the City of Night as a weapon, and Kishenku obeyed."

"Only to gather his troops and take the city by force once Xiaomin was distracted," Naseru said.

"Very good," Vordu said with a respectful nod. "You have the mind of a true villain, Hantei Naseru."

"So I have been told. Pray continue."

"Of course," Vordu said. "Kishenku's forces killed Xiaomin, slaughtered the city's guards and seized control of the crystal sphere. The traitor discovered, to his sorrow, that the City of Night would not be controlled so easily. Kishenku could not master the sphere. A shockwave of destructive magical energy erupted from the city. I find it interesting to note that according to the histories I have found in the ruins, the city was not always crystal. The night crystal was formed, it seems, in reaction to Kishenku's attempt to dominate the city. It is a substance that naturally absorbs magical energies, but also conducts them under the appropriate circumstances. The crystal was formed as an attempt to buffer the destructive power Kishenku summoned, but even that remarkable transmutation could only do so much. The hordes of Jigoku were destroyed, but the civilization of the Five Races was also left in ruins. The survivors hunted down the Soultwister and his former followers and cast them into the Realm of Slaughter. Over the centuries, their bodies were twisted by the murderous nature of that realm, until they no longer resembled their leonine kitsu cousins."

"They became Tsuno," Naseru said.

"Most impressive." Vordu looked at Naseru shrewdly. "The order of Tsuno was the militant arm of the kitsu race. How did you know that?"

"Just a guess," Naseru said, sipping his tea. "Tell me, Vordu, how do you know so much about the city's history?"

"There are records. I have translated them with some difficulty."

"Records of its creation, perhaps," Naseru said, "but why would a city record its own destruction? It seems unlikely."

"Well," Vordu said, smiling tightly as he considered his reply. "It is something of a mixed blessing that the ruins are not entirely uninhabited. There are many restless spirits there, ghosts of the inhuman architects of the city. Sometimes, they can be encouraged to communicate."

"Though more often they are dangerous," Shem-Zhe added. Vordu cast the apprentice an unreadable look.

"Dangerous how?" Naseru asked.

"There were some incidents," Vordu said. "Some of the apprentices, including Shem-Zhe's own cousin Liyun, were killed. I sent the others away so that such a thing would not occur again."

"Shem-Zhe mentioned something to that effect," Naseru said with a nod. "I am sorry for your loss."

Vordu grunted noncommittally. "So is that what truly drew you here, then? You hunt the mysteries of the Tsuno?"

"If the Tsuno knew of this City of Night, then why have they not attempted to gain access to it before?" Naseru asked, ignoring Vordu's question.

"They cannot enter the city," Vordu said. "Xiaomin's son

placed wards upon the ruins shortly before he buried them. Members of the order of Tsuno cannot pass through its gateway. The sphere itself has been rendered inert until Xiaomin's heir returns to the city."

"We think that they may have attempted to gain access at some point in the past," Shem-Zhe added quickly. "We discovered many Tsuno skeletons in the rubble just beyond the gates of the city. They had been there for some time."

Naseru remembered his dream of the Seikitsu. He remembered the Tsuno who struggled to open the tunnel leading to the City of Night. He remembered the Tsuno that had attacked him on the journey here.

"With the City of Night here, you must have a lot of trouble with Tsuno attacks," Naseru said. "If the magic of these ruins is as powerful as you claim, then they must eager to reclaim it."

"Actually we have had very few problems with Tsuno," Vordu answered. "A little over a year ago, when the creatures first began to appear following Emperor Toturi's death, there were a few packs in the mountains. The soldiers of the Khan hounded them relentlessly. Fast the Tsuno may be, but the steeds of the Unicorn are faster. Those who escaped passed the word to others. Now the Tsuno know that they are not safe in our lands."

"Is that so?" Shono asked. "Strange that we ran into a pack of them not a day's ride from here."

A decidedly uncomfortable look crossed Vordu's face for a brief instant before the old man composed himself. "That is quite impossible," the old shugenja said. "There are no Tsuno in Unicorn lands."

"We ran into fourteen," Shono said, leaping on the chance to brag.

"Fourteen?" Vordu exclaimed in shock.

"Eight, actually," Naseru corrected him. "I have a wound to prove it."

"How bizarre," Vordu said in a distracted voice. "The appearance of such a large pack suggests there may be more. I must send word to Commander Chen to mobilize his scouts at once." The shugenja rose, absently toppling his teacup with one flowing sleeve. "If you will excuse me, Shem-Zhe will attend your needs."

Vordu shuffled out of the chamber, closing the shoji screen behind him.

"Quite an eccentric person," Naseru said, turning to Shem-Zhe.

"Yes," the younger shugenja said with a forced laugh. "Vordu-sama is an acquired taste, I think."

"If you say so, Shem-Zhe-san," Naseru said with a polite smile.

They continued eating in silence for some time. Naseru noticed Shem-Zhe frequently casting nervous glances at his guests. The shugenja's social skills had clearly deteriorated during his time in the ruins.

"Incidentally," Naseru said, breaking the silence after nearly ten minutes, "I do not suppose it would be possible for us to explore the ruins while we are here, would it? I would very much like to see this omnipotent crystal sphere of which your master spoke. Would that be located in the place you call the Temple?"

"Heh." Shem-Zhe fidgeted. "No one enters the Temple except for Vordu-sama and myself. Our research is very delicate. Even the Khan respects the privacy of the Temple. I am surprised that Vordu even mentioned the sphere. It is a matter of utmost secrecy. Not even the Khan knows of it."

"It must be my naturally trustworthy air that leads people to reveal such things," Naseru said with a small laugh. "Forget that I asked. It would be rude for me to demand entrance to such a place, and I apologize for my temerity. Would it be possible for us to see the rest? The parts Misao saw when he came here?"

"Of course," Shem-Zhe said. "I could speak to Vordu-sama. I am certain we could arrange a visit. Perhaps tomorrow evening?"

"Excellent," Naseru replied.

A low rumble suddenly filled the chamber, causing the plates to rattle on the table. The sound continued for several seconds, causing the diners to look at one another warily.

"Earthquakes are very common in Otosan Uchi," Naseru said. "I was not aware that you had them here."

"We do not," Shem-Zhe said, scratching his short beard with one hand. "This is most unusual. I must commune with the earth kami tonight and determine what has happened."

"I will not keep you from your duty," Naseru said, pushing his plate aside. "At any rate, I think I have consumed enough dead flesh for one night. Could you please show us to our rooms?" Naseru stood.

"Right away," Shem-Zhe said, quickly rising from his chair.

Shono looked at Naseru dubiously, chopsticks halfway to his mouth. The Shinjo daimyo was clearly not finished eating. Naseru gave him a pointed look. Isei rose without comment, setting his empty bowl aside. A career as a warrior had taught Isei to eat rapidly when he had a chance. Shono took several large mouthfuls, choosing the choicest bits of meat as quickly as he could, then set down his chopsticks, wiped his hands on his pants, and rose.

The little shugenja led them to a series of rooms on the second floor, then quickly vanished again. Naseru's quarters were small but lavishly decorated in the rather rustic style of the Unicorn Clan. Fur carpets covered the floors. Gaudy paintings with ugly wooden frames hung from the walls. Naseru ignored the decorations, studying the window instead. His room offered a perfect view of the darkened pass outside.

After nearly a minute, the screen slid open behind him. Isei, Shono, and Bakin entered.

"What did you think of that 'earthquake,' Naseru-sama?" Isei asked quietly.

"I think Sunetra works quickly," Naseru said with a small smile. "That sounded like her work. I, for one, cannot wait to find out what she destroyed."

"Fantastic," Shono said, sitting on a small stool in the corner. "So when do we leave?"

"Leave?" Naseru looked back at the Shinjo daimyo. "I have no intention of leaving. This visit has only begun to pique my interest."

"Vordu said that he planned to send word to Moto Chen about the Tsuno," Isei replied. "Chen is one of the Khan's most trusted officers. If the Khan finds out you are here . . ."

"Vordu will do no such thing," Naseru said. "He was lying about sending word to Commander Chen. It was painfully obvious, which surprises me. The old man had been quite talented at masking his reactions up until that point in the conversation. He has something to hide."

"That may be the biggest understatement I've heard in some time," Shono said. "Whatever Vordu's secrets are, I don't *want* to know them. Of course he's creepy, secretive, and insane, but he's also the Khan's pet shugenja. If we're irritating him, he has no reason not to summon Chen's Junghar crack troops to do away with us." Shono paused briefly. "Well, to do away with *you*, anyway. They won't hurt me. I just don't want to be here."

"Look out the window, Shono-san," Naseru said, gesturing as he stepped to one side. "In particular, look at the dust in the road."

Shono rose and walked to the window. He squinted as he peered out into the darkness, then looked at Naseru. "There aren't any new tracks leading from the castle."

"Moto Vordu left in a hurry, but he dispatched no messenger," Naseru said.

"Then where did Vordu go?" Isei asked.

"I do not know," Naseru said, "but this is an opportunity we cannot miss."

"Opportunity?" Shono asked.

"Vordu became agitated when you mentioned the Tsuno," Naseru said. "Agitated men hurry, and men who hurry make mistakes. This is the perfect time to learn what the Moto is doing in these caves. The time has come to change the rules of this game. Bakin, I wish to send a message to Commander Chen."

"Moto Chen," Shono said, folding his arms. "I assume you have some ulterior motive here and don't really want the Commander of the Junghar to come destroy you."

"All a matter of distraction," Naseru said. "Something

about the way Vordu reacted when he said he planned to send word to Chen struck me as false. Now I know that he plans to do no such thing. He only threatened to send word to Chen to distract us."

"From what?" Isei asked.

Naseru shrugged. "We may well find out when we call Vordu's bluff. Or we may discover that he has sent word to Chen after all, in which case we shall soon have opportunity to discover just how fast our horses can ride."

20 | UNQUIET SPIRITS

Moto Vordu stalked through the tunnels leading to the City of Night, a furious look painted on his wrinkled features. The amulets woven in his cloak shimmered as he walked, casting the cavern in a sickly green light. Vordu moved quickly over the uneven terrain. He knew every slope and trench in these caves better than his childhood home. This *was* his home now.

"Come out," Vordu whispered as he glanced about the empty tunnels. "I know you are here."

The trill of a flute echoed in reply. A komuso, complete with basket hat, stepped out of a shadow far too small to conceal a man his size. He held a shakuhachi flute tucked under one arm. The monk watched Moto Vordu silently.

"You!" Vordu raged, grabbing the hem of the monk's cloak in one fist. "You and your allies sought to betray me!"

"Did we?" the monk asked mildly. "When did we do that?"

"Your Tsuno attacked Naseru during his journey to the pass. That was not part of our arrangement."

"They are hardly *my* Tsuno," the komuso said with a small laugh. "I wish I had the power to control them, but I do not. These are the chances we take when we make deals with such creatures. Now let us be serious, Vordu-sama. Do not pretend as if you have no plans to betray the Tsuno."

Vordu scowled. "You promised to aid me, creature. Together, we will both be free."

"As long as we are clear," the komuso said he tucked the tip of his flute into his basket and began playing softly.

"If the Tsuno think they can use Hantei Naseru without me, they are mistaken," Vordu said in a low voice. "They cannot even enter the city with the wards in place!"

"I am sure . . . you are . . . correct," the komuso said between notes.

"I will not be manipulated," Vordu said.

"Of course not." The komuso stopped his music.

"I will not be denied!"

"Perish the thought," the komuso said, clearly amused by the shugenja's frayed temper. "In that case, I think it should be your priority to deal with the spy skulking about in the ruins."

"Spy?" Vordu said, shocked.

The cough of a small explosion echoed from deeper in the tunnels, followed by a low rumble that shook the entire cavern.

"That would be her now," the komuso said. "She has collapsed the secondary tunnel. You may wish to stop her before she does further damage."

"Damn!" Vordu's face twisting in annoyance. "Where is she?"

The komuso laughed. "If I gave you all the answers, where would you find challenge in life? Find her yourself, Vordu-sama." The komuso gave a final trill on his shakuhachi and vanished into shadow.

"Wretched, useless creature!" Vordu grumbled as he shuffled deeper into the caves.

He passed through the gates and into the ruins. Sure enough, he could see green energy rippling through the crystal ruins—a sure sign that someone was carrying their own light source somewhere within. The old Unicorn whispered a short prayer to the kami, summoning an invisible air spirit that concealed the sound of his footsteps and the crystal chink of his cloak.

Silenced by magic, Vordu moved hurriedly down the ribbon-marked path. He ignored the whispers and moans that echoed through the ruins as he passed. The spirits that haunted the city had come to know him during his time here. The wiser spirits had come to fear him. Vordu moved ever deeper into the city, following the ripples of light that would lead him to his intruder. Finally, he arrived at the entrance to the Temple. There, at the edge of the path, a quartet of ephemeral spirits hovered over a limp body.

"Ah," Vordu whispered with a small smile. "There you are."

Three of the ghosts were clearly not human. To Vordu's eye they looked like kitsu. The fourth was a woman in long flowing robes, covered with shimmering amulets similar to Vordu's. The four spirits hunched in a circle around a black-garbed figure lying face down in the road. The spy's left hand rested on a short blade. The weapon would do no good against the spirits. However, the scrap of blessed ribbon the spy wore around her wrist was preventing the curious spirits from doing her further harm.

Moto Vordu sighed and plucked a shimmering amulet from the shoulder of his cloak. He held it forth as he chanted words of magic. A shimmering aura surrounded the body of the fallen spy, repelling the undead. The four spirits looked up in alarm.

"Defiler," the ghostly woman moaned, pointing at Vordu. "Traitor!"

"I warned you not to stray from the ribbon-marked path, Liyun," Vordu said with a bored sigh, "but the student always knows better than the teacher, yes?"

"Fool!" the spirit hissed, advancing toward Vordu. "You know not what you have done here! The power you intend to release cannot be chained! It cannot be controlled!"

The spectral kitsu prowled forward at her side, claws

extended toward Moto Vordu. The quartet stopped at the border of the ribbon-marked path, growling in impotent fury as they found themselves unable to cross the threshold.

Vordu shook his head in quiet pity. "Liyun, when will it end? We have had this discussion so many times before. Must I kill you again?"

The spectral woman screamed even more fiercely. Her kitsu companions charged the invisible wall repeatedly, to no avail. Vordu calmly grasped another amulet hanging from his robe and chanted a brief prayer. The four spirits, shrieking in pain, disappeared in a burst of green flame.

Vordu shuffled to the edge of the path and stepped over the ribbon. He knelt by the fallen spy. "Hello?" he said. "Can you hear me?"

"Cannot ... move ..." Bayushi Sunetra whispered, her eyes wide with fear and pain.

"The paralysis should pass shortly," Vordu said. "You have blue eyes. Are you a Crane?"

"Scorpion," she whispered.

"Even worse," Vordu said with an irritated frown.

"Thank you ... saving my life," she said.

"You misunderstand me," Vordu said with a scowl. "It is not your life that concerns me but rather your soul. Had you died outside the boundaries of the path, your restless spirit would haunt these halls for eternity. Liyun is difficult enough to explain as it is. I can hardly afford for Naseru to arrive and find the ghost of his own spy wandering these ruins."

Vordu seized Sunetra's feet and dragged her back to the path, pausing to untie the ribbon and replace it once she was within the boundary. Then, with a sigh, Vordu reached into his robes and drew out a wicked knife.

Sunetra's eyes narrowed, but there was no fear. "Make it ... quick."

"Of course," Vordu said with a merciful smile. "I take no joy in the suffering of others." He leaned close with his knife and pressed it against Sunetra's throat.

Vordu could not bring himself to drive the blade home.

Even after all that he had done, murder did not come easily. A vexed look crossed the old shugenja's face. His hand tightened on the blade as he struggled for the courage to kill the spy.

"Vordu-sama!" a voice echoed through the caverns behind him. "Vordu-sama, are you here? I can see your light."

Moto Vordu frowned, his eyes still fixed on Sunetra's. He could not kill her now. Shem-Zhe would fail to understand, and things would become unnecessarily complex. If Naseru discovered that one of his spies had died in the caverns, he might become suspicious and take flight. That was unacceptable. If, on the other hand, he valued this woman enough to wish to keep her alive, she might yet be an effective bargaining chip. Vordu tucked the knife back into his robes.

Sunetra smirked. "You will regret . . . letting me . . . live," she whispered.

"I already do," Vordu said. He removed her mask and unfurled it into a long strip of black cloth. Shem-Zhe stumbled into the caves behind him just as he finished tying the mask around her mouth as a gag.

"Vordu-sama, there you are!" Shem-Zhe said, running into the cavern behind him.

"Yes?" Vordu said, looking over one shoulder. "What is it?"

"Hantei Naseru has a message he wishes you to relay to Moto Chen when you send your courier," Shem-Zhe replied. "I did not see you in the castle so I became worried. You know how dangerous it is to visit the ruins at this time of night. The spirits are restless."

"I am well aware," Vordu replied. "I have already attended to Liyun's deranged ghost."

"What was that sound earlier?" Shem-Zhe asked. "It sounded like an earthquake."

"I do not know," Vordu lied. "Now come give me aid. I have discovered a spy, sent by the Scorpion Clan. Vordu stood and turned to face Shem-Zhe, letting him see the collapsed woman.

Shem-Zhe gasped, one hand covering his mouth. "Is she . . . is she still alive?"

Vordu nodded. "Liyun and some others attacked her. Fortunately, I arrived before they could do much more than paralyze her. Shem-Zhe, you must carry her to the Temple, quickly."

"To the Temple?" Shem-Zhe asked, surprised. "Why not the castle? Would she not be more secure there?"

"I do not wish to disturb our esteemed guest with the presence of a prisoner," Vordu said. "This is a Unicorn problem, and we shall deal with it ourselves. Take her to the small side chamber to the east of the room with the crystal sphere. There are some manacles there. Make sure you search her thoroughly to make sure she has no hidden weapons or tools. Oh, and do not speak to her. She is a Scorpion, and cannot be trusted. You know how her clan has always envied our magic."

"Of course, Vordu-sama," Shem-Zhe said, hurrying to comply. "Oh," he said, stopping short as he remembered something. "I came to give you this. Lord Naseru wishes to include his own message for General Moto Chen along with yours." Shem-Zhe offered a scroll bearing the Hantei's seal, which Vordu accepted with a curious expression.

Vordu stepped back onto the path, not sparing a second glance for Shem-Zhe or the spy. Shem-Zhe, he knew, could be trusted to follow orders. The man was completely honorable and always trusted his superiors implicitly.

That made him predictable.

That made him weak.

21   INTO THE CITY

Good morning, gentlemen," Moto Vordu said.

The old shugenja entered the dining hall in no particular hurry. Even early in the morning, the castle was so dark that the room required illumination from several small lanterns. Some of them shone with the strange green radiance of night crystal.

"I apologize for my tardiness. I am no longer a young man. Some days my bones find it necessary to remind me."

Naseru, Shono, Isei, and Shem-Zhe had already been there for some time. Naseru was not surprised that Vordu had made them wait so long. This was simply another attempt to intimidate them. By making them wait, he kept them from eating. The longer he kept his guests in hunger, the weaker they became. Naseru had seen this tired game many times during his visits to the homes of potentially hostile samurai. He was so accustomed to the tactic that he had eaten a small breakfast of trail rations while he dressed in the morning. Isei had done so as well. The sour expression on Shinjo Shono's face suggested that he had not had similar foresight, or perhaps he was just uncomfortable to be in Vordu's presence again.

While hunger had not been an issue for Naseru, he was nonetheless quite uncomfortable. Sunetra should have reported by now. Surely the defenses of Vordu's castle were not such that the Scorpion could not gain entry and find Naseru's rooms. He wondered if she had been captured, or if she had run into danger in the ruins. The fact that he worried for her safety was even more unsettling. Since the death of the Steel Chrysanthemum, Naseru kept his distance from others. He tried not to forge close attachments. Those he drew close to were inevitably killed or ruined by his presence in their life. Only by remaining cold and distant could he continue to function. But now, when he thought of Sunetra lying dead or captured in the accursed caverns below, he felt a slow rage burning in his heart.

Vordu seated himself at the head of the table. The servants entered bearing steaming plates of small rice cakes and light tea. Naseru ate some of the food to make a show of being polite. The thought crossed Naseru's mind that Vordu might have poisoned the food, but the Anvil pushed it aside. He was still not entirely certain why he had been drawn here, but he did not think that murder was the shugenja's intent.

As they ate breakfast, Naseru engaged Vordu in light conversation. Naseru considered himself a master of the art of conversation—the act of engaging a stranger in extended discourse while neither offending him nor revealing anything of importance. It was another game of the court, and a skill that came quite handy in situations such as these. If nothing else, it was a useful tool for gauging a person's mood. Vordu put on a good display of calm, but he was distracted, paying no attention to details. Shem-Zhe, on the other hand, was unusually quiet and withdrawn.

As the meal concluded, Shono was the first to rise. "I hope you'll excuse me," he said with a brief nod. "I cannot remain in this dank cave any longer. I must feel the wind on my face, or I can no longer call myself Shinjo."

Vordu frowned at Shono, clearly insulted by the comment.

"I am certain he meant no offense, Vordu-sama," Shem-Zhe said with a nervous laugh.

"No, you're wrong, Shem-Zhe," Shono said. "I did mean offense." He looked at Vordu evenly. "But then I outrank you, old man, so there's not much you can do but get angry. Is there? I'm getting out of this pit and going for a ride. Do you have a problem with that, Vordu-san?"

"I knew that you Shinjo were born and bred in barns," Vordu said in a quiet voice, "but I had no idea that your poor manners extended to insulting a host in his own home. Tell me, Shono, do you have any redeeming virtues so that you can call yourself a samurai without shame? Or have you merely accepted shame as a necessary part of your existence?"

"I reserve my respect for those who deserve it, butcher," Shono said. His left eye gleamed to punctuate his comment. Shono turned his back and stalked out of the room.

Vordu's fingers were clasped tightly on the table before him. His lips were a thin line. The man was clearly enraged by Shono's comments and was having difficulty hiding his emotions. Naseru wished he could have thanked Shono for the unexpected assistance without looking boorish as well.

"Ah, Shono," Naseru said with a small smile. "I have known him only briefly, but I have learned that his mind is swifter than a Shinjo steed. He speaks his mind, and like a wild horse sometimes his words lead him into troublesome territory."

"No," Vordu said quietly, folding his hands on the table and staring at them intently. "Do not defend him. Do not defend me. I deserve his hatred."

Naseru raised an eyebrow curiously.

"But that is in the past," Vordu said with a negligent wave. "Shono is right. This castle is too dark. We Unicorn need to feel the light upon our faces from time to time. Some days I wish that my work here was done so that I could roam the Empire as freely as our Shinjo friend."

"But will your work ever be complete?" Naseru asked. "Is not the study of magic a constantly developing art?"

"In a general sense, yes," Vordu said, "but I have a specific goal in mind. I think that I shall take a walk in the ruins. Would you like to accompany me, Naseru-sama?" The shugenja rose from his seat and gestured toward the door.

"Of course," Naseru said, also rising. "I am eager to see this City of Night."

"Shem-Zhe, go on ahead," Vordu said. "See that the Temple is presentable when we arrive."

"You are taking them to the Temple?" the younger shugenja was shocked. "Not even the Khan—"

"Naseru-sama is heir to the throne," Vordu said. "We have no secrets from him."

"Of course, Vordu-sama," Shem-Zhe replied, though he looked dubious. "I will go immediately." Shem-Zhe rose, bowed quickly, and exited the room.

Vordu followed, moving much more slowly. The old man stopped frequently to point out pieces of art hanging on the walls. Naseru assumed Vordu was delaying so that Shem-Zhe would have time to reach the Temple and make whatever preparations Vordu spoke of. As they finally exited the castle and stepped deeper into the caverns, Naseru wondered what truly lay in store for him.

"Oh," Vordu said, looking at the silent shadow that followed them. "Your yojimbo will not be necessary, Hantei-sama."

"You said the ruins were dangerous," Naseru replied.

"You will find a sword of little use against the dangers you will face here. Simply follow my instructions and you will be quite safe."

"Where I go, Isei goes," Naseru said. "On that, I will not compromise."

Vordu looked at the yojimbo, then returned his hawk-like gaze to Naseru. "Very well," he said, sneering in disapproval as he led them into the caves. "Stay close to me, both of you. There are wards everywhere, but they are attuned to the resonance of night crystal. You will not be harmed if you stay near the light radiated by my cloak."

As Vordu spoke, the many amulets hanging from his

fur cloak began to glow softly. Naseru saw the handle of the dagger in his sleeve begin to glow in reply. He tucked the weapon deeper into his clothing so the shugenja would not see.

"The ruins are just through here," Vordu whispered, gesturing at a gigantic crystal gate that stood open on the cavern wall.

"Fortunes," Naseru breathed as he stared up in awe. The front of the gate was carved with the figures of kenku, ningyo, trolls, zokujin, and kitsu dancing about a great spiral. In the center, a single kitsu stood beneath a circle. It was the same gate the komuso had shown him in his dream, but in person it seemed much more magnificent.

"The picture on the gate is a map of the city," Vordu explained, tracing a lower spiral with one long finger. "The circle in the center is the crystal sphere. The kitsu that stands beneath it represents Soli Xiaomin, the legendary kitsu elder. It is said that his son summoned the power of Xiaomin's spirit to guard the city."

Naseru nodded and quietly followed Vordu through the gates, into the City of Night. As Vordu stepped onto the path beyond, the light that shone in his amulets was instantly reflected in the nearby stones. The green light spread out in a wave, illuminating the wreckage of a city fashioned entirely of night crystal. The ruins continued into the distance, curving off into many side tunnels. The sight amazed Naseru. He could sense the magical power radiating from the very walls of this place.

"These gates are a wonder in and of themselves," Vordu said, pointing to the walls behind the massive crystal gates. "The winch mechanism is quite simple. From this side, even a child could operate it. When closed, not even an army could gain entry. The enchantment on the gates renders them nearly indestructible. Even the Kaiu family could learn a thing or two about siege warfare from the Five Races, I think."

"Fascinating," Naseru said, studying the intricately fashioned crystal gears and levers as he stepped past the gates.

"Stay within the ribbon-marked path," Vordu warned, pointing to the white silken ribbons that cut through the ruins. "The ribbons are a special nemuranai Shem-Zhe crafted to ward off spirits. So long as you stay within their area, the ghosts can do you no harm."

"These ruins remind me of Volturnum, the city where Oblivion's Gate stood," Isei said. The yojimbo's usual emotionless glare had also changed to a look of open wonder.

"At one time, the trolls were great craftsmen and architects," Vordu replied. "The wonders they created outshone Kyuden Asako, the spires of Toshi no Inazuma, and even the palace of Otosan Uchi. The buildings here are of troll make, as was Volturnum. The fall of troll society and their corruption by the Shadowlands is one of the great tragedies of all time. Now they are nothing more than lumbering, stupid brutes, hiding in the muck. Perhaps it is just as well. The trolls had accomplished so much. After creating such wonders, what else was left?"

"Some see accomplishment as a reason to keep striving, not an excuse to give up and die," Naseru said.

"Ah, but you are young, Hantei-sama. I am an old man, and as the days get shorter, sometimes I look back on my life and I wonder what difference I have made."

"What of your research here?" Naseru said. "You spoke of the limitless possibilities."

"Possibilities, yes, but what of the applications? I develop magic to keep meat fresh, but rather than use it to feed the hungry, the Khan uses it to produce better rations for his armies. I find a way to temper our steel more efficiently. It is used to make weapons rather than tools. I am a man of vision, Hantei Naseru, but I am only one man. The powerful magic I have developed will be remembered. The armies of the Khan have never been stronger." He looked at Naseru with a sad smile. "But is that how I wish to be remembered?"

"How would you prefer to be remembered?" Naseru asked.

"As a scholar," Vordu said as he shuffled on through the

city. "As a loving husband. As the father of four and grandfather of nine. As someone who lived a life that means something." Vordu laughed bitterly. "Unlikely. Ours is a nation of warriors. How does the saying go? 'Find glory in war or find none at all.'"

"Akodo's *Leadership*," Naseru said. "That quote is taken out of context. Akodo was a man of peace."

"That's what all the killers say."

"Akodo became a warrior only to bring order to Rokugan," Naseru said. "If it were not for him, there would be no Empire."

"I see," Vordu said, looking back at Naseru. "Is that what he said to the kitsu? 'Please step aside. We need to build an Empire on your bones.' What did the kitsu say to that?"

"I do not like your tone, shugenja," Naseru said, folding his arms across his chest.

"I apologize if I have offended, Hantei-sama." Vordu bowed his head. "Once more I blame my age and my solitude. I fear my social skills have deteriorated during my time in the darkness, and I speak my mind more than is proper."

"Indeed," Naseru said sharply. The three men continued to walk in silence.

Isei coughed quietly, drawing the Anvil's attention. Naseru looked at his yojimbo. The old bushi's face was unusually worried. His dark eyes were fixed on Vordu. He spoke with no words, knowing that Naseru could read his lips.

"Stay alert," Isei said. "This is a trap."

Naseru nodded. He could not help but agree, but he could also not deny the power he sensed in these caverns. Vordu was clearly not a sane man, but whether he had been driven insane by the City of Night or had been mad to begin with was anyone's guess. In either case, if the city truly had the power Vordu claimed, it could not be trusted in the shugenja's hands. Naseru had ventured into these ruins knowing that he would face danger. Now that the danger was so close, he could not back out. He could only trust in his own abilities and those of his allies to see him through safely.

"Here we are," Moto Vordu said, a note of pride in his

voice as they turned a corner into a much larger tunnel. "The Temple."

Unlike the rest of the city, the walls of the Temple seemed untouched by the ravages of time. The structure was all tall columns and elegant domes, easily the size of any Great Clan daimyo's palace, buried here deep beneath the earth. The entire building glowed with a pale green radiance, the power of the strange crystal. Above the doors of the Temple five familiar symbols were etched into the stone—fire, water, earth, air, void.

"You have noticed the kanji of the five rings," Vordu said with an eager smile.

"How is that possible?" Naseru said, staring up at the building. "The five rings are a human concept, invented by Shinsei. Those are characters from the Rokugani alphabet."

"Are you so sure?" Vordu asked as he shuffled up the stairs. "Come with me, Anvil. I have much more to show you."

22 | WIND AND STEEL

It was good to feel the wind again.

Shono let out a triumphant whoop as he galloped headlong across the open plains, leaving the Seikitsu behind. The Shinjo daimyo wheeled his horse about and galloped in a random direction for a while, then turned and ran back the other way for no other reason than to enjoy the speed and freedom of the ride. The thought passed through his mind that this was how others often perceived his clan—as a bunch of backwoods hicks who enjoyed nothing so much as a full-speed gallop across an open field.

The stereotype did not bother Shinjo Shono at all. Instead, he felt a mild pity for the other clans that looked down on the Unicorn for their simple pleasures. They didn't know what they were missing.

Shono was so wrapped up in the joy of the moment, in fact, that he nearly ran over the archer.

"Halt where you are, Unicorn!" the samurai shouted, her bow trained upon his chest.

Shono reined in his steed and stared curiously down at the young woman who barred his path. She wore armor of dark brown and emerald green. The kanji for ten thousand was emblazoned on her helm.

"A Yotsu?" Shono asked, looking down at the girl curiously. "You're far from home."

"Yotsu Irie, of the Sword of Yotsu," she said, still keeping the bow trained on Shono. "You know my order?"

"I'm Shinjo Shono," he said with a cocky grin. "I know everything."

"Get off your horse," she said, her voice a low growl.

"That's odd," Shono said in a disappointed voice. "Women are usually impressed when I act arrogant."

He climbed out of his saddle and stood with his hands open to his sides, showing he had no intent to fight.

"What can I do for you, Yotsu-chan?"

"You ride with Hantei Naseru?" she asked.

Shono sighed. "I knew getting involved with a politician was going to get me into trouble."

"Answer the question!" she demanded, drawing her bow-string back sharply.

"Yes, I ride with Naseru," he said. "You don't have to point that at me. I don't mean you any harm."

"But perhaps I mean *you* harm, Unicorn," she said. "What business have you in the Way of Night?"

Shono looked confused. "I'm a Unicorn," he said. "I live here."

"Do not toy with me, Shinjo! Why did you bring Naseru here?"

"A good question," Shono said in a calm voice. "But Hantei Naseru isn't the sort of person who's very forthcoming about things like that. He just says things and expects you do to them. Kind of annoying at times. You know what I mean?"

"You expect me to believe that a daimyo of the Unicorn would bow down to the whim of the Anvil simply because he told you to do so?" Irie said. "You must think I am a fool."

Shono shrugged. "Possibly. But I tend to have a low opinion of people who point weapons at me. Listen, Yotsu-chan. I've faced down oni, Kolat, Tsuno, and Utaku Battle Maidens in my time. If you want to intimidate me, you're going to have to shoot that arrow into my chest. On the other hand, you could put the bow away and just talk to me politely. I'm actually a very friendly person. If I wasn't, I would have run you over with my horse instead of stopping."

Irie grinned slightly but did not put her bow away. "Are you always such a buffoon?"

"Mostly."

Irie opened her mouth to say something else, but the words died in her mouth. She took several steps back, keeping her bow trained at Shono's face as motes of green light boiled out of his left eye. Shono was similarly surprised as the eye began to burn in his skull. There was only one time when the eye did this.

"What in Jigoku is wrong with your eye?" Irie demanded.

Shono looked at Irie sharply, his expression grim. He lunged toward the samurai-ko so swiftly that she barely saw him move. With a surprised shout she released her bow as he lunged. Shono dodged to one side and grunted in pain, then tackled Irie just as the first Tsuno's blade cleaved the air where she had been standing. The creature roared and drew his blade back for another swing. Shono grabbed Irie's shoulders and tumbled to one side just as the curved black sword buried itself in the earth.

Irie and Shono rolled to their feet, back to back. A quartet of Tsuno had appeared from nowhere. Three of the creatures held wickedly curved blades. The fourth simply held a gnarled wooden staff and watched quietly from the shadows. That one worried Shono the most. Tsuno warriors were deadly. Tsuno spellcasters were worse.

"Tsuno!" Irie drew another arrow as the creatures advanced. "If you saw them why did you not simply shout a warning instead of attacking me?"

"Oh, come on, Yotsu-chan," Shono said, tearing a strip of

silk from his sleeve to bind the shallow wound in his fore-arm. "That would be like yelling 'Look behind you! Tsuno!' Would you have believed me?"

"Probably not. I am sorry I shot you."

"No harm done," Shono said. "A small wound. Besides, we'll most likely be dead soon."

Yotsu cursed and fired her arrow, which struck one of the Tsuno squarely in the chest. The creature glanced down at the tiny projectile, looked at Irie, and roared in fury. The three Tsuno charged.

"Scatter!" Shono shouted, pushing off of Irie's back and rolling forward. Irie did the same, discarding her useless bow. Shono drew his katana as he rolled between the legs of the nearest Tsuno, turning as he tumbled and slicing the creature's hamstrings. The Tsuno screamed and fell forward, its legs unable to support its bulky frame.

"Human excrement," a second Tsuno snarled, kicking Shono in the back with an iron-shod foot. Shono bounced like a rag doll, rolled, and sat up groaning.

Irie stood and faced the third Tsuno, wielding a katana in one hand and a wakizashi in the other. The Tsuno strode toward her lazily, his bestial face twisted in amusement. The creature swung its long blade tentatively. Irie brought both swords up to deflect the blow. The creature chuckled and swung his blade again in an identical movement. Irie brought her swords up to defend again, but this time the Tsuno threw and incredible amount of force into the swing. A metallic clang echoed across the field and Irie was thrown onto her back. When she looked down at her hands, she saw that she now held the broken hilts of her swords—the swords Yotsu Seou had given her.

"Human steel is even weaker than the flesh that wields it," the Tsuno said with a sneer.

"End this!" commanded the Tsuno spellcaster as he exam-ined the wounds of his fallen brother. "Kill them both, then bring me the Unicorn's eye. It intrigues me."

Shono laughed. "I bet you say that to all the—ugh!" His quip was interrupted by a fierce kick to the stomach.

Irie's Tsuno turned to laugh at Shono's plight, and in that instant Irie remembered the crystal sword strapped across her back. If it were as soft as the glass it resembled, it would do her little good, but under the circumstances she did not have much other choice. She reached back and drew the blade. The crystal flared, radiating motes of green light like Shono's eye.

All four Tsuno turned to glare at her. Shono took advantage of their distraction and searched for his sword, all the while trying to look unconscious.

"She has a night crystal blade!" cried the Tsuno spellcaster.

Irie's Tsuno chopped at her with its sword again. Again, Irie brought her sword up to deflect. Another metallic clang echoed. The Tsuno stared at its sword, now broken just above the hilt. Irie was just as surprised, but she did not hesitate. She lunged to her feet, buried her blade in the Tsuno's chest, and twisted. The creature fell to its knees and crumpled on its side as Irie pulled the sword free.

The second Tsuno leaped, and Irie met the creature's strike with a slash across the belly. A flash of pain in her shins made her gasp. Irie cursed as she realized the other creature's attack had been nothing more than a distraction. The crippled Tsuno had seized her legs from behind. It gave a sharp tug and she fell forward. The creature scrambled forward onto her back, clutching her throat with a hand larger than her head. Irie brought her sword up blindly, impaling the monstrous beast between the eyes.

The fourth Tsuno shook its head in disapproval as it looked down at Irie, pinned beneath the dead Tsuno. "All for nothing," the creature whispered, spinning its staff in the air as it stood safely out of her reach. Its free hand glowed with a deep blue fire. "Their deaths mean nothing. So long as one of us lives, the others will be reborn. You, my dear, are not so fortunate."

The creature's eyes widened. With a confused look, it fell over dead. Shinjo Shono flicked the blood from his katana and slid it back into its scabbard.

"Looks like he wasn't so fortunate either," Shono said. He

helped roll the dead Tsuno off of Irie's back and pulled her to her feet.

"Where did those creatures come from?" Irie asked. "What did they want from us?"

"They're Tsuno," Shono said. "They don't really need a reason to cause trouble. Where did you find that sword?"

"A kenku gave it to me," Irie said, sheathing the crystal katana over her shoulder.

"Fine," Shono said with a laugh. "Don't tell me the truth. See if I care. Now, weren't you trying to kill me earlier or something?"

Irie's face flushed a deep red. She bowed her head in shame. "I have no words, Shono-sama," she said. "You saved my life when I would have slain you."

"Well, you saved my life one, two, three times," Shono said, counting the Tsuno Irie had killed. "Let's just call it even, neh? Now what did you want? Why were you asking about Naseru?"

"That is my business," Irie said firmly.

"Whatever," Shono said, walking back to his horse. The animal was terrified, but it had waited patiently for its master. He patted the frightened creature's flank soothingly and climbed into the saddle. "I have enough worries. I don't really need to share the Anvil's, too. Next time you have a problem with him, you take it up with him. Not me. Understood?"

Irie said nothing. She simply glared at the Unicorn in silence, gathered her lost bow, and looked around for her pony. It had fled in terror when the Tsuno appeared and likely would not return. Shono watched her, his expression curious. Before he could find the words to ask her the question that was forming in his mind, a metallic roar echoed across the plains.

"More Tsuno?" Irie asked, looking in that direction.

Shono nodded. "Sounds that way."

"It sounds like they are already in combat," Irie said as a chorus of other triumphant roars joined the first. "What are they attacking?"

"The Way of Night," Shono said with a scowl. "They are killing my kinsmen!"

"Take me with you," Irie said impulsively. "I will help."

Shono looked at her suspiciously for a brief moment, then nodded and extended his hand. He pulled her up into the saddle behind him and charged toward the battle.

23 TO FIND THE TRUTH

As breathtaking as the rest of the city had been, the Temple was even more so. What could be seen was larger than Vordu's castle by far, despite the fact that much of it was still submerged beneath rubble.

"Careful, Hantei-sama," Vordu said. "You do not wish to step from the path, especially here. See?"

The shabby little shugenja pointed. Near the edge of the path, Naseru could make out the shapes of a group of figures, as ephemeral as smoke.

"Slayer," one of them hissed, eyes fixed on Naseru. "The son of the Slayer has come."

"Slayer?" Naseru asked, stepping to the edge of the path and looking at the spirit. It looked like a kitsu, but it was so insubstantial it was difficult to tell.

The creature opened its mouth to say something more, but Vordu interrupted with the harsh words of a spell. With a bright flash of white light and a scream of pain, the spirits vanished.

"Try not to talk to them, Hantei-sama," Vordu said, his

voice full of pity. "Therein lies madness. They must come to realize that their part in this world is done."

Naseru grunted noncommittally and followed Vordu down the path toward the Temple. He found it interesting that Vordu himself had claimed to learn much from the spirits, yet forbade him to speak with them. More secrets. Isei shadowed Naseru, watching over one shoulder as if concerned the spirits would return. They followed Vordu through the doors of the Temple. The shugenja led them through the hallways, eagerly pointing out inscriptions on the wall that spoke of the history of the city and the power of those who created it.

"Your thoughts, Hantei-sama?" asked Vordu as they walked. His voice echoed through the halls, taking on a musical tone as the crystal vibrated in response. "I notice that you have been keenly interested in the sculptures and engravings here. I have long felt that this site would have been worth the trouble we have taken to excavate it for the artwork alone."

Naseru nodded as they continued to walk through the halls. "The inscriptions are quite intriguing. The style is far more realistic than traditional Rokugani artwork."

"Yes, quite," Vordu nodded quickly. "More sophisticated."

Naseru gave Vordu a curious look. "Why do you find it more sophisticated to portray something exactly as you see it? I feel quite the opposite. Why endeavor to exactly portray a tree? Your work will never compare to the beauty of nature. Better, I think, for art to be inspired by reality than to be enslaved by it. Otherwise, it means nothing."

"So you are not impressed?" Vordu asked, fixing a disbelieving eye on the Anvil.

"The craftsmanship is impressive, to be sure"—Naseru motioned to a wall carving depicting a group of kenku dancing in some mysterious ritual— "but it is not art. It is merely decoration, perhaps instruction. I think that these carvings are meant to depict historical events and are not purely intended to be enjoyed for the sake of their beauty."

Vordu smiled slightly. "A clever deduction, Hantei-sama,"

he said. "Come this way. This may be of particular interest to you."

The hunchbacked shugenja turned down a side hallway, leading Naseru to a wall carving that depicted a solitary kitsu. It resembled a Lion, though its shoulders were broader and its eyes larger.

"What is it you wish me to see here?" Naseru asked.

"This," Vordu said as he pointed to the portrait, "is Soli Izumo, the only son of Xiaomin. With the aid of the kenku, he created the wards that keep the Tsuno from returning to the city. It was he who became the leader of his people after Kishenku's betrayal shattered their civilization."

"Izumo?" Naseru replied. "The name sounds familiar."

"He was one of the five kitsu who survived after Akodo's culling caused their race to die out," he said. "Izumo became human, a member of the Lion Clan. You may know him as Akodo Izumo. He was the only kitsu to take the Akodo name, after he married Akodo's daughter. He is your ancestor, I believe."

"Is that possible?" Naseru asked. "This city was built before the Naga race even began to flourish. That must have been thousands of years ago. Soli Izumo and Akodo Izumo could not have been one and the same."

"The kitsu were not like other creatures," Vordu said as they began to walk once more. "Before Akodo began to massacre their race, the kitsu magic was very strong. They were virtually immortal. You can see a hint of that immortality in the Tsuno today, albeit in a twisted form. While the kitsu were long-lived, they always felt that the resurrection of the dead was an aberration of the natural order. The Tsuno have no such qualms. That is why they always carry away their dead. So long as a Tsuno body is intact, the Soultwisters can restore it to life. Quite a useful ability to have, don't you think?"

"Resurrection is overrated," Isei said quietly.

"I still find the idea fascinating," Vordu said. "Unfortunately the techniques the kitsu utilized to extend their lives and revive the dead do not function for humans."

"I see," Naseru said. "How do you know?"

"I do not wish to bore you with the specifics of my research, but I think you shall like this."

Stepping ahead of them, Vordu pushed open the door leading to a large central chamber. The floor was emblazoned with the kanji of the five rings, glowing with their own light. A thick pedestal rose from the center of the room, equidistant from the five symbols. It was as tall as man's shoulders and was topped by a clear crystal sphere the size of a melon. Countless racks filled with thick scrolls stood against the walls of the room. Some lay open on the floor, covered with notes scribbled in a messy hand.

"Were these scrolls here when you found the city?" Naseru asked in a wry voice.

Vordu laughed. "No, of course not. These are my accumulated observations—all that I have learned about the City of Night."

As they stepped into the room, a vibrant pattern of purple and green light danced through the walls, rippling out from their footsteps.

"Breathtaking," Naseru said, genuinely impressed as he watched the display of lights. "Does the crystal always shine like this?"

"I have never seen it behave exactly like this," Vordu replied, also watching the lights, "but the city often has a life of its own. Night crystal is quite unpredictable."

"And this, I assume, must be the crystal sphere that you described," Naseru said, walking toward the pedestal. He extended one hand toward the sphere, fingers hovering inches from its surface.

"Yes," Vordu said. "Feel free to touch it if you like."

Naseru looked into the sphere's depths for a long moment, then closed his fist. He looked at Vordu, who was watching him with a strangely eager expression.

"Why do you hesitate, Hantei-sama?" Vordu asked. "I assure you it is quite harmless."

"Actually, I was just thinking about my brother."

Vordu looked baffled. "Kaneka? What does he have to do with this?"

"Not Kaneka," Naseru said. "Sezaru. During his training he was admitted to study among the Kitsu family of the Lion—quite an unprecedented act, for only those of the Kitsu bloodline are granted such an honor. At the time we all thought it was merely because Sezaru was the son of an Emperor. Now I think differently. You mentioned that Soli Xiaomin married into Akodo's family. Akodo was my own ancestor, and now I suspect Xiaomin was as well."

Vordu's face twisted into a scowl.

"If I were a suspicious man, I would think that you were not at all surprised by my arrival here," Naseru said. "That perhaps you somehow arranged for the attacks on my person that led me here."

"Touch the sphere, Naseru," Vordu said. "Do not be foolish."

Naseru ignored Vordu's taunt. "The ghosts called me the son of the Slayer. What were they going to tell me before you silenced them? What will happen when a descendant of Xiaomin touches that sphere? Tell me or I will leave immediately."

"Fine!" Vordu snarled. "The sphere is useless until Xiaomin's heir returns to claim it. It will grant its user omnipotence, but until you break the seal it may as well be worthless glass."

"So you planned to give me limitless power?" Naseru said, looking at the sphere dubiously. "You are very generous."

"Don't be foolish. You do not know how to command the sphere. It requires years of study to master its intricacies. It would have done nothing for you."

"So I was to make you a god?" Naseru asked, fist still hovering near the sphere.

"Only for a time," Vordu said, his voice pleading. "There is only one thing I need to do, one evil I need to correct. Once that is done, I will need it no more. Please, Naseru, I beg you. Touch the sphere, remove the wards, and I will teach you to use the power of the City of Night. What I can give you in return for this small favor could easily place you on your father's throne."

"No." Naseru folded his arms behind his back.

"How can you deny me?" Vordu said, extending a pleading

hand to the Anvil. "I offer you everything you desire!"

"How can I possibly trust you?"

"I will have what I wish!" the shugenja roared. "I do not require your trust!"

Vordu seized an amulet from his cloak and spoke words of power. A bolt of pure white energy erupted from the amulet, streaking toward Naseru. Isei dove into its path, taking the blast on his shoulder. The yojimbo grunted and staggered as the magic robbed him of his strength. Grimacing in determination, the yojimbo charged at Vordu, but struck an invisible wall of force and fell to one knee.

"Foolish samurai," Vordu said, scowling down at Isei as he clasped another amulet.

"Master Vordu!" Horiuchi Shem-Zhe shouted, busting through the door at the far end of the room. "What are you doing?"

"This is not your concern, Shem-Zhe," Vordu growled, keeping his attention on Isei and Naseru. "I told you to remain with the prisoner."

"I did," Shem-Zhe said sadly.

Vordu looked sharply at the Shem-Zhe. Just as he did, Bayushi Sunetra stepped out from behind Vordu's apprentice and hurled something small at Moto Vordu. Vordu grunted in pain as the knife struck him in the shoulder. He reached for the weapon with a shaking hand, whimpered in pain, and collapsed. Seppun Isei quickly staggered toward the Moto, stripped his amulet-studded cloak from his shoulders, and hurled it across the room.

"Is he dead?" Naseru asked as he strode toward the fallen shugenja.

"Only unconscious," Sunetra said, her voice mildly disappointed. "I thought you might have questions for him."

"You have a way with understatement," Naseru said.

"But your timing is impeccable," Isei added, nodding respectfully to the Scorpion.

"My most sincere apologies, Lord Naseru," Shem-Zhe said, approaching the Anvil and bowing deeply. "I had suspected that Vordu-sama had become irrational, but I had no idea how far he had gone. Lady Sunetra told me the truth. Had I known that Vordu-sama was in league with the Tsuno . . ."

"Tsuno?" Naseru raised a curious eyebrow. "Is this true, Sunetra?"

"Yes, Lord Anvil."

"Wake him," Naseru commanded.

Isei and Sunetra searched Vordu, removing the rest of his magical scrolls, fetishes, and amulets, and binding his wrists behind his back. When they were done, Shem-Zhe spoke a minor prayer to the water kami, cleansing the poison from his master's bloodstream. The old shugenja's eyes opened instantly. When he found himself tied helpless without his magical amulets, his face twisted into a grimace.

"You have ruined everything," he said in a defeated voice.

"Explain what is going on here," Naseru said.

"Is it not obvious?"

"I wish to hear it from you. Consider it a confession. All samurai are entitled to one before execution."

Isei drew his blade and held it at Vordu's throat. Vordu looked away, his eyes focused on the crystal sphere. His misshapen shoulders slumped. He seemed unconcerned with Naseru's threats, but spoke nonetheless.

"My wife, three of my children, and most of my grandchildren died after the War of Spirits, killed by the Steel Chrysanthemum's soldiers two weeks after your father signed the treaty to end the war. I thought that once I had seized the sphere, I could use it to make right all that had gone wrong. I have been attempting to lure you here for a very long time, Naseru-sama."

"You were the one who sent Shosuro Soshu?" Naseru asked. He wondered if Vordu was responsible for his dream as well, but was uncertain how to broach the subject. The idea that it had been a dream that had truly led him here still struck him as somewhat illogical behavior, and Naseru did not like to admit when he was behaving illogically.

Vordu shrugged. "I do not know anyone by that name. I left the details of drawing you out of Ryoko Owari to an associate. He did his job well, though I had not counted on your stubborn refusal in the end."

"Why did you choose me? Why not one of the other Winds? They share the same bloodline as myself."

Vordu shrugged. "You are not a great general, a duelist, or a powerful shugenja like your siblings. Of all the Winds, I assumed you would be the least dangerous."

Naseru's expression did not change. "You misjudged me."

Vordu only stared at the ground.

"He's surprisingly cooperative for a prisoner," Sunetra said. "If it were me I do not think I would tell you anything. Do not believe his words, Naseru."

"I speak the truth," Vordu retorted. "What have I to lose?" He looked up at Naseru plaintively. "Manipulation failed. Force failed. Perhaps logic can still triumph. It is not too late, Naseru. Unlock the sphere. I shall show you how to use it!"

Naseru shook his head slowly.

"So what do the Tsuno have to do with this, Vordu-sama?" Shem-Zhe asked. His voice was still edged with terror. "Are you truly working with them as the Scorpion claimed?"

Vordu frowned bitterly. "Yes," he said.

Shem-Zhe's shoulders slumped. Naseru could tell that in that moment the young shugenja had finally lost his last ounce of faith in his master. It was a feeling Naseru knew all too well.

"Why?" Shem-Zhe whispered, his voice cracking.

"I had no choice," Vordu answered. "You remember the early days of the excavation. For the first three years, we learned almost nothing. It was obvious we had uncovered something important, but we knew too little about the culture of the Five Races to understand it. I translated just enough of the writings to know the sphere's significance, but I had no idea of its history or how to operate it. The few living zokujin and ningyo we found were unwilling to aid us. They were afraid of the city. The Khan grew impatient. He heard reports of the restless spirits that wandered the streets and feared that we had uncovered something evil. I was given an ultimatum. If I could not prove my research to be of some use within one year, the cave would be sealed permanently."

"So you sought out the Tsuno?" Naseru asked.

"No," Vordu said. "I was visited by a komuso, a monk who claimed to be a servant of the Tsuno."

"A komuso?" Naseru asked.

Vordu nodded. "The monk taught me a spell he had learned from the Tsuno, a magic that allows communication with the unquiet dead. I used the spell to make contact with the spirit of Tsuno Kishenku, who had haunted this temple since his failed attempt to seize control of the sphere. He offered to teach me how to translate the writings on the walls, to master the power of the night crystal. For one year, the ghost of Tsuno Kishenku taught me. The spells and nemuranai I developed during that time were so powerful that the results were immediate. The Khan never interfered with my research again. What Kishenku asked for in return did not seem like so large a thing."

"And what was that?" Naseru asked, folding his arms as he paced between Vordu and the sphere.

"He asked that I give his remains and the remains of those other Tsuno who died here to the komuso," Vordu said.

Naseru scowled. "So that Kishenku's brethren could restore them to life."

Vordu bowed his head. "I did not realize that was their intent at the time," he said. "I assumed that he merely desired a decent burial. It is not an uncommon wish for the unquiet dead. Kishenku visited me once more, this time in the flesh, six months after I gave his bones to the monk." Vordu looked directly at Naseru, his eyes intense. "This time the Soultwister held Ichiro, my infant grandson. The Tsuno informed me that Ichiro and his mother, my only surviving daughter, were safe in the custody of his pack. The rest of their village had been slaughtered, wiped off the map by Kishenku and his pack." Vordu paused for a long time, still staring at the Anvil. "So long as I continued my research into the Way of Night, they would remain safe."

"How do you know they are still alive?" Naseru asked.

"I have nothing left but hope," Vordu said. "Hisae was my youngest daughter. She looks so much like her mother. Her life means everything to me. It is more important than all of my research here, more important than a lifetime of service to the Khan. I realized that too late, and now all I can do is pray they will return her to me."

"After three and a half years?" Isei said. "You are a fool, Vordu. Your daughter is dead."

"No," Vordu said, his voice a low growl. "I can save her. I can still save them both and make the Tsuno pay. I know how to use the sphere now. If you unlock the ward that protects it, I can still make everything right. I can destroy them all and rescue her, even from the realm of death itself!"

"And what makes you so certain you can control it?" Naseru asked, looking at the sphere.

"I have studied it, using the lessons Kishenku taught me," Vordu said. "I am confident I can control it."

"You trust the creature who destroyed his own civilization using this very same artifact?" Naseru shouted, his voice heated.

"You do not understand," Vordu said, shaking his head rapidly. "After his death, Kishenku's spirit was trapped in the Temple for thousands of years. He has had nothing but time to study the crystal sphere, to learn from his mistake. Using the techniques he taught me, I have been unraveling the wards that protect the sphere until only one remains. He assured me that all that was needed was the touch of a descendant of Xiaomin for the wards to be unlocked permanently. He promised that if I led you here and removed the wards, he would release my family. He does not realize that I, too, have learned how to control the sphere."

"Fool!" Naseru shouted, his voice now seething with anger. "Do you not see it? You have already lost!"

Vordu stared at Naseru, wrinkled face blank with confusion. "What do you mean?" he asked.

"There is no enemy more dangerous than one who has had time to plan," Naseru said. "Kishenku has had thousands of years. Do you truly think he has not foreseen the possibility of your betrayal? Do you not think he has contingencies?"

"Nonsense," Vordu said. "I have taken everything into consideration."

As if on cue, the metallic howls of Tsuno rang through the City of Night.

"That was close by," Isei said, looking up quickly. "They are almost within the city."

"They cannot enter," Vordu said. "The night crystal bars their entrance."

"Perhaps it is not as firm a barrier as you believe," Naseru replied. "Why would they risk attacking the Unicorn if they did not believe they could gain entry?"

Vordu's angry scowl melted, replaced by a look of horror and doubt. "Then you must untie me, Naseru. We must use the crystal sphere! We must stop them!"

"Under the circumstances, I think that touching the sphere would be the worst thing we could do," Naseru said.

"And why is that?" Vordu demanded.

"Because if I were the one setting a trap, *that* would be where I would set it." Naseru pointed at the sphere. "Sunetra, do you have your ring?"

The Scorpion nodded. She quickly slipped the ring over one finger.

"What do you see?" Naseru asked.

"Nothing," she replied, studying the pedestal for a long moment. "No, wait. I see some sort of ward upon the pedestal. It is very subtle, but very powerful."

"No doubt a trap laid by Kishenku," Naseru said.

"I never saw any ward," Vordu snapped.

"Could Kishenku have laid a spell so that it could be activated by some other event, and would remain unnoticed until then?" Naseru asked, looking at Shem-Zhe.

"It is possible," Shem-Zhe replied. "If there was a great release of magical power, a latent spell could draw upon it to activate itself."

"There is more," Sunetra said, frowning in confusion. "When I used the ring earlier, this entire cavern was covered in one large web of magic, the largest I have ever seen. That web is gone now."

"That web must have been what prevented the Tsuno from entering the city," Naseru said, scratching his beard thoughtfully as he paced the chamber, "and what powers the spell that protects the sphere now. But why is the city no longer protected? What has changed?"

"The Tsuno can enter the City of Night?" Vordu said, horrified. "How?"

Naseru looked down, noting the ripples of light that spread through the chamber with each step he took. The same ripples did not follow Isei, Shem-Zhe, Sunetra, or Vordu. "They lied to you, Vordu," Naseru said as he realized the truth. "The sphere is not the key at all. Remember how the chamber reacted when I first entered?"

Shem-Zhe was the first beside Naseru to realize the truth. "The spell that Soli Xiaomin placed upon this city to protect it from the Tsuno was not intended to last forever," the apprentice said in a quavering voice. "Only until his heir returned."

"Because surely his heir could use the sphere to protect the city," Naseru said in a wry voice. "Except here I am, and the sphere is hardly safe."

"And the Tsuno are coming," Vordu whispered.

"With Kishenku at the head of the pack, I would wager."

"We need defenses," Isei added quickly. "We need a way to stop them from reaching this room."

"I destroyed their tunnel," Sunetra offered. "If they wish to enter the city, they will have to enter through the pass, past the Unicorn guards."

"Tsuno are tenacious foes," Isei said. "That will only delay them."

"What if we closed the crystal gates?" Naseru asked. "Would that stop them?"

"If they are not already inside," Shem-Zhe answered.

"We must close the gates," Naseru said, looking to Isei and Sunetra. "With luck, Shono has seen the attack and will ride for help. All we must do is survive until he returns."

"What about me?" Shem-Zhe asked.

"Stay here and guard your errant master," Naseru said, pointing at Vordu.

The old Unicorn said something in acknowledgment, but Naseru did not hear. He was already out the door, rushing to head off the terror coming for them all.

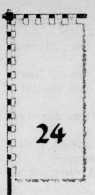

24 BETRAYAL

The Anvil moved purposefully down the ribbon-marked paths of the City of Night. His katana, usually little more than an ornament on his hip, was now held in one hand in a variant of the ancient Kakita techniques the Steel Chrysanthemum had taught him.

"Lord Naseru, it would be best if you returned to the Temple," Isei said as they continued their march. The grizzled samurai had to walk swiftly to keep pace with his master.

"Our best chance to stop the Tsuno lies in closing the gates before the Tsuno arrive," Naseru said, eyes straight ahead as he walked. "The more swords we have to hold the breach, the better."

"This is too much of a risk for you, my lord."

"Too much of a risk for me? And what of you? Have you recovered from Vordu's attack?"

"I am fine. I would be better if you did not risk yourself foolishly, my lord."

Naseru looked back at Isei, never slowing his pace. "I

appreciate your concern, Isei-san, but I risk more if I remain behind."

"You cannot believe that mad wizard's stories," Sunetra broke in. "Do you truly think that sphere holds the sort of power he claims?"

"We can worry about that once the Tsuno have been stopped," Naseru said.

The three samurai followed the path around a sharp corner. All stopped when they saw the crystal gates.

"They are already closed," Sunetra said, surprised. She crouched in the shadow of a fallen pillar.

"They were not designed to be closed from the outside," Isei said, drawing his sword slowly.

"Perhaps the Unicorn guards retreated here?" Naseru said.

"Then where are they?"

A savage howl echoed from the buildings nearby. Two Tsuno charged from either side, black steel blades held high. One leaped for Sunetra, but she rolled and hurled a knife at the creature's throat. The Tsuno roared in pain, glared at Sunetra, and crumpled.

Screaming a defiant battle cry, the other Tsuno lunged at Isei. The yojimbo brought his sword up to meet the larger blade and deflected the weapon with a loud clang and a shower of sparks. The force of the blow knocked Isei to the ground. The creature planted one foot solidly on Isei's sword arm and seized the man's collar. Lifting its sword again, it prepared to bury the weapon in his chest.

"Hold!" Naseru shouted, standing before the Tsuno. "Do you still seek the son of the Slayer?"

"Kishenku will deal with you in time, pitiful creature," the Tsuno said.

"Will he?" Naseru held the blade of his katana to his own throat and glared at the creature defiantly. "I am useless to your master if I am dead. Weigh your options, Tsuno. Release my friend."

"You are not needed any longer."

"Are you so certain? Then why do you hold your blade?"

It was a risk, Naseru knew, gambling on the stupidity of

the Tsuno. Generally the most capable and intelligent warrior wasn't the sort you left behind to guard an impenetrable door. Naseru was hoping that sort of logic carried over to the Tsuno.

"You bluff," the Tsuno said in a mocking tone. "Your kind fears death."

"You know nothing about samurai." The edge of Naseru's blade drew a drop of blood. "Are you prepared to risk everything your master has spent thousands of years planning?"

The Tsuno's red-gold eyes flickered with doubt. It released Isei's collar and grabbed at Naseru. Naseru dodged backward and slashed at the Tsuno's hand. At the same moment, Isei rolled, drew his wakizashi, and stabbed the creature in the stomach. The Tsuno staggered backward, howling in pain. Sunetra buried a long knife in the creature's lower back and dodged aside as its massive body crashed to the earth.

"We are too late," Isei said, rising to his feet with a pained grunt. "The Tsuno are already inside the city."

"Open the gates, then," Naseru said. "If more Unicorn troops arrive I want them to be able to enter."

Isei nodded, quickly moving to the winch and opening the crystal gates.

"What do we do?" Sunetra asked, looking to Naseru.

"We return to the Temple," Naseru said, looking back the way they had come. He began to stride purposefully down the street.

"And fight?" Sunetra asked, shocked. She followed beside him, attempting to slow his pace. "We have been fortunate so far, but we have no idea how many Tsuno are in there. Do you plan to run in there with your sword at your own throat and hope they will all surrender?"

"No," Naseru said, frowning at Sunetra. "Nor do I plan to flee. If the City of Night is as powerful as Vordu claims, then running will accomplish nothing. We must stop Kishenku now or not at all."

"I think 'if' is the important word there," Sunetra said, looking warily down the street. Isei hurried to catch up with them. "Why do you believe anything that mad old Unicorn says? Just because Vordu believes that you are part of his twisted delusion is no reason to risk yourself to save him. You are not behaving logically, Naseru. I said nothing until now because it was not my place, but if you pursue this any further you will die."

Naseru stopped and looked back at Sunetra. He had nothing to say. In fact, he found himself agreeing with her. He could not speak of the strange dream he had had that night in Ryoko Owari. He could not speak of the true reason he had come here; it had simply felt right.

"Your chances are not so bad, you know," said a quiet voice.

A small monk with a basket hat and a shakuhachi over one shoulder was seated on a stone nearby. None of them had noticed him a moment before.

"If all the Tsuno packs knew what was about to occur, you would be helplessly outnumbered. However, Kishenku's capacity for betrayal extends even to his own kind and works to your advantage. Kishenku has revealed his return from the dead only to a few Tsuno and keeps the location of the City of Night a closely guarded secret. He does not intend to share his power, it seems. If you are careful, you may be able to defeat the few who follow him."

"You again," Naseru said, frowning down at the monk.

Isei's katana was already drawn. He watched the little man for any sudden movements.

"Who is this?" Sunetra asked, taking a wary step away from the monk and drawing a knife. "Vordu mentioned a komuso earlier."

Isei stepped forward but Naseru stopped his yojimbo with a gesture. "I have met this monk once before," Naseru said, eye narrowing. "So you are real? Not just a dream after all."

"As real as anything in this world," the monk answered. "I have come to receive your answer regarding my earlier offer. Ally with me against Vordu and the Tsuno, Hantei Naseru. I will help you destroy them."

"Why should I believe anything you tell me?" Naseru said, turning back down the path toward the Temple. "That dream was nothing but a web of illusions created to draw me here."

"It was not my dream. It was yours." The komuso laughed and stepped in Naseru's way. "I simply chose to make an appearance there. Your brother may be the shugenja of the family, Hantei Naseru, but you also carry an Oracle's blood. That dream was a warning from your Lion ancestors who died a thousand years ago. A warning intended to prevent what is about to happen today. As you guessed, the seal upon the City of Night was broken the instant you laid eyes upon the sphere. That is why you came here, Hantei Naseru, despite all logic to the contrary. You *know* that you are needed. How does it feel for one who has lived a life so rigidly based on logic and contingencies to realize that your most important decisions are made for no reason at all? How does it feel for a man who has struggled so hard to define himself as a unique individual to realize that he is led by destiny, guided by the strength of his ancestors? How does it feel, Hantei Naseru, to realize that as much as you enjoy your image as the consummate villain, you are doomed to die a hero?"

"Get out of my way," Naseru said in a low voice.

Isei stepped to Naseru's side, ready to attack. The komuso backed away but did not step from the path.

"Give me your answer," the komuso said. "I will not serve a master who is unwilling to accept my aid. Ally with me now or I will take my offer back to Kishenku."

Naseru shouted and drew his sword. Isei had already leaped to the attack, but the komuso moved swiftly to one side. Naseru lunged behind him, and his blade passed harmlessly through the komuso.

"Your father's blade could not defeat me," the komuso said. "What makes you think you will fare better?"

The komuso dropped the staff and tore the basket mask from his face. As he did so, his form melted, shifted, and grew to demonic proportions. In an instant, it stood a head taller than Isei. Its flesh was covered in overlapping blood-red plates, and it held long blades in two of its four long arms, with two more sheathed across its back. The creature's steel lips twisted in a smile as it looked down at the shock and terror in their eyes.

"You are Fushin," said Naseru. "Onisu of Betrayal. You are the beast that murdered my father."

"Daigotsu murdered your father," the onisu corrected, shaking its head slightly. "He merely possessed my body at the time. As I told you, to serve the Shadowlands is to be a tool, used and tossed aside. I aspire to become something more. I had hoped you would understand. But here we are."

"Stand together!" Naseru shouted to Isei and Sunetra. "This creature is formed of betrayal. So long as we are loyal to one another, it cannot defeat us."

"I know the Wolf informed you of my weakness," the demon said with a smile. "A pity you know nothing of my strength."

Fushin gestured with his two empty hands. A wall of shadows surrounded the trio, shutting away the light of the crystal city. As Fushin retreated into nothing, two figures stepped from the darkness. One was the slim, petite figure of Otomo Hoketuhime. The other was a fierce-looking samurai in battle-scarred armor, the mon of the Seppun family emblazoned upon his back banners.

"General Saigorei," Isei said. His katana shook in his hands.

"Isei-san," Saigorei said, his tone disappointed. "The little boy who died during the first wave at Oblivion's Gate. The only reason you claim any courage at all is because you care so little about your life. I can scarcely blame you. It must be terrible to have peaked so young. There is nothing left for you, Seppun Isei. Not even death will be a new experience for you. You are even more a soulless shadow than I am."

"And the little Crane who fancies herself a Scorpion," Hoketuhime said fluttering her fan before her perfect face. "You will always want what you cannot have. Your Crane parents have forgotten you. Your adopted Scorpion kin barely tolerate you. Naseru will never love you. He sees you as a tool to be used, and if you died he would find another to take your place.

"Ignore them," Naseru said. "They are only illusions!"

Isei looked at Naseru uncertainly. Sunetra said nothing, only stared right ahead at the illusion of Hoketuhime.

"They are real enough, my son," said Toturi, stepping out of the shadows where Fushin had once stood. "Fushin creates nothing. These phantoms speak only the doubt your companions carry in their hearts. These samurai do not follow you because they admire you or even respect you. They follow you because they have nothing else."

"You dare take the shape of my father?" Naseru shouted.

"I have just as much right as you do. You play at being my son if it will gain you advantage in the courts, but you wear the Hantei name."

"A name given to me by your treaty, *Father*," Naseru retorted, rising to the illusion's taunting despite himself.

"I could take the Toturi name from you, this is true," he said, "but only you could prove you do not deserve it. Look what you have done to your brothers and sisters—your perverse machinations to bar them from a throne you do not deserve. This Empire lies in chaos because of you. Who do you think you are?"

Naseru knew this was false, a dream created by a demon, intended to torment him, yet he still found it difficult to look into his "father's" eyes. He could not push the creature's words out of his mind.

"How can you follow this man?" Saigorei said to Isei. "How will you ever see the light of glory while you stand in the Anvil's shadow? You have seen the way he toys with others, the way he plays games with the lives of those better than himself. He is no Emperor. Come now; fight me. Fight one last battle of your own choice, Isei. Be your own man. Escape this shadow. Let me kill you so that you can be free from his command."

"Stand your ground," Naseru ordered, fixing his glare on the shade of Toturi. "Isei, you know Saigorei would never shame himself by insulting another man's courage."

"I know," Isei said in a hollow voice.

"Then push it aside. Let your anger fuel your courage and prove the demon wrong."

Isei nodded firmly.

"You are not safe here, Sunetra," Hoketuhime said in a mocking voice. "Naseru uses you as a spy because you are expendable. One day, he will destroy you. Abandon him while you have the chance."

Naseru turned to Sunetra and forced a grin. "I will not even justify that pathetic attempt to sway your loyalty with a comment. You are a Scorpion. You are better than that."

"Thank you," Sunetra said, blood-red lips quirking in a satisfied smile.

"Move as a group," Naseru said. "Step past them."

The others nodded and moved forward slowly, staying within the ribbon-marked path.

In the darkness, Fushin sighed. "Mere shadows, it seems, will not suffice. The time for subtlety is over."

The darkness parted, and a pack of six Tsuno warriors stood before them. The beasts looked confused, uncertain how they arrived there. Then their eyes settled on Naseru and the others. With a triumphant roar, the beasts charged. One Tsuno bore down on Naseru, knocking him back with a heavy shoulder. Naseru gathered his wits quickly but saw that his sword lay several feet away. Standing above him, the Tsuno lifted its sword high.

25 VENGEANCE?

The fight in the pass had been horrible. The few Unicorn guards had been overwhelmed. The proud horsemen lay slaughtered in the pass beside their steeds, torn to pieces by the oversized weapons and claws of the Tsuno. There were no signs of any dead Tsuno. Either there had been no casualties or they had already carried away their dead.

The devastation reminded Irie of Kyuden Tonbo. Even the jovial Shono had become quiet and withdrawn at the site of the carnage. Shono had dismounted once, pausing to say a prayer over the body of his dead cousin's youngest son. Irie wanted to say something to him, to reassure him that his kinsmen would be avenged, but the words would not come. How could she know if those words were true?

When they arrived at the mouth of the cave, they found Vordu's castle had been thoroughly pillaged. They dismounted and carefully made their way inside. Shono's eye and Irie's sword burned a bright green, lighting the darkened halls. A pair of dead Unicorn samurai lay in the hall, their swords still gripped tightly in their hands. Irie whispered a short prayer that their souls would find peace in the next realm.

"Naseru?" Shono called out, advancing carefully with his katana held low. "Vordu? Isei? Any of you still alive?"

Grim silence answered Shono's call; then a loud clatter erupted from farther down the hall. Irie quickly moved to stand beside the Unicorn, holding her weapon ready for whatever might come. A small storage closet opened and a skinny old man stumbled out, a thick woolen blanket over his shoulders.

"Lord Shono!" the old man said, falling prostrate on the ground. "Thank the bright fires of Lord Yakamo! You have returned!"

"I suppose I should not be surprised you survived, old man," Shono said with a grin.

"Who is this?" Irie demanded.

"This is Hantei Naseru's servant, Bakin," Shono said. "If Isei's tales are true, he's the toughest old man since Hida Kisada. Are you injured, Bakin-san? Can you walk?"

Bakin nodded rapidly as he rose. "If you demanded it, Lord Shono, I would do somersaults. I am most relieved to see you."

"Likewise. Where are Naseru and the others?"

"They have gone into the Way of Night. They left before the Tsuno arrived."

How convenient, Irie thought, that Naseru had left before the attack began.

"My steed is waiting outside, Bakin," Shono said. "I want you to take him and ride for the Sun's Arc Way. Find Commander Chen. Tell him we are under attack. Take this to him as proof I sent you." Shono drew a small block of wood from his pocket and threw it to the old man. It was his official chop, the seal of the Shinjo family daimyo.

"I could not take your steed," Bakin said. "It is too fine a horse for me."

"He'll be safer with you." Shono grinned. "If we die, keep him with my compliments. Now go!"

The old man bowed a final time and scrambled for the door, invoking every Fortune he could remember as he wished them good luck.

Shono and Irie exited the castle and stood side by side, staring into the depths of the cave. The bloody footprints of the Tsuno led into the earth.

"What is inside this cave?" Irie asked, looking at the Unicorn.

"Trouble. Turn back. This is not your fight." He paused for a moment. "Come to think of it, it isn't really my fight, but I've never really had enough sense to run away in situations like this."

"Neither have I," Irie said, grinning despite herself. "I stand with you, Shono."

The two samurai advanced quietly through the tunnels, weapons at the ready. The metallic roars of the Tsuno echoed deep within the mountain.

"So," Shono whispered, "are you going to ask me about my eye?"

Irie looked at him incredulously. "Quiet," she snapped. "The Tsuno will hear us."

"We've got a glowing eye and a glowing sword," Shono said with a shrug. "It's not as if we're inconspicuous."

"Still, this is not the time."

"Just trying to break the tension. Everyone asks me about it sooner or later."

"Then I will ask you *later*."

"Right," Shono said. "Then you will tell me where you got that sword."

They stopped at a large pool on the floor. Shono knelt and touched the pool with one finger; it came up dark brown.

"Tsuno blood," he said. "The Tsuno went through Vordu's wards the hard way."

"Wards?" Irie said, looking around warily. "What do we do? How do we get through them?"

"Not sure," Shono said. "My guess is to stick to the parts of the cavern with Tsuno blood on the floor. Those are the places where they've already been set off."

Irie nodded. It was a grisly but effective strategy. The two samurai moved carefully through the warded area until they came to the enormous crystal gate.

It was closed.

"What do we do?" Irie asked.

Shono's shoulders slumped. He sheathed his sword in resignation. "We wait," he said, sitting on a stone. "Either Naseru will find a way to open the gates, or he won't. Either way, there's no other way in short of digging a way in ourselves."

Irie sighed and sat down next to Shono, keeping her blade free of its saya to help light the cavern. The two sat in silence for a time.

"Why do you follow him?" Irie said, breaking the silence.

"Who?" Shono looked at her blankly.

"Hantei Naseru." She nodded at the gates. "Why do you follow him?"

Shono laughed. "It's a long story. Why do you want to kill him?"

Irie frowned. "How do you know I want to kill Naseru?"

"I see the look in your eyes," Shono said. "I know vengeance when I see it."

"Do you plan to stop me?" she asked, hand tightening on the hilt of her sword.

Shono shook his head. "No. For three reasons. The first is that I don't really like Naseru all that much. I respect him, but I don't like him. I have a feeling he earned whatever trouble you're bringing him. Second, I happen to be highly in favor of letting other people make their own mistakes. If you had wanted my advice you would have asked for it."

"And what is the third?" she asked.

Shono smiled. "I don't think you have a chance in Jigoku of killing him. No offense, but he's the Son of Toturi, and the Fortunes have a way of rallying to his side."

"We shall see, Shinjo."

Beside them, the large crystal gates opened silently.

"Finally," Shono rolled off his seat into a crouch.

The two samurai waited for several moments to see if any

enemies would emerge. When none appeared, Shono and Irie slowly moved forward, alert for any sign of an ambush. They ducked into the ruins.

In the tunnel beyond, two samurai stood against five Tsuno. A third lay prone on the earth. A sixth Tsuno stood with its sword held high, ready to slaughter the man. Irie charged that one while Shono hurried to aid the others. Her crystal blade left a sparkling trail of green light as she cut the beast in half.

"My thanks," said the fallen samurai.

Irie realized to her horror that she had just saved the life of Hantei Naseru.

"You are a Yotsu?" Naseru showed no surprise as he rose. He pulled his kimono over his right shoulder, covering the bloodstained bandages there, and snatched his katana from the ground.

Irie could not speak. She only nodded.

"Then fight beside us," Naseru said fiercely. "The Empire may be at stake!" The Anvil ran past her, hurrying to aid the others.

Irie lunged forward with a fierce battle cry, hewing at the next Tsuno with her crystal blade. The weapon left sparkling arcs of green light as she moved. Shono's crystal eye was also shining brightly. The light of Irie's weapon made the Tsuno hiss and draw back in pain, so she pressed her advantage. The world moved in slow motion as she danced between the massive blades of the creatures. The earth shook as a heavy body hit the ground. A Tsuno blade glanced off of her thigh, but Irie ignored the pain and fought on, burying her sword in the next beast's chest. The creature roared and slashed at Irie with its claws, refusing to die despite its mortal wound. Irie brought up one hand to defend her face as she struggled to withdraw her sword. In that instant, Naseru's yojimbo appeared and slashed the Tsuno solidly across the throat. The monster whimpered and collapsed, red-gold eyes staring at Irie in hatred.

The samurai gathered into a tight group as they prepared to deal with the last of the Tsuno. Shono had slain another of the creatures, leaving only two. Naseru's yojimbo held his sword unsteadily in one hand; his right arm hung limp and bloody. Naseru stood just in front of his yojimbo, his own katana ready for battle. The Scorpion Irie had noticed earlier was nowhere to be seen.

One of the Tsuno gesticulated frantically and barked several words in a strange tongue. A ball of seething purple flame appeared before its snout, and with a gesture the Tsuno sent its spell flying at Irie. Not quite realizing what she was doing, Irie lunged forward and slashed at the air. Her crystal sword scattered the ball of flame into fluttering sparks. Another swipe of her sword, and the Tsuno spellcaster lay dead.

Realizing that their foes were not as overpowered as they appeared, the last Tsuno backed away.

"You have not won, human," it said as it stepped toward the crystal gate. "One day, we will return. We will restore those you have slain. You have gained nothing."

"Only if you survive," Naseru said coldly.

It was then that Irie noticed the Scorpion lurking in the shadows near the crystal gate. She was rapidly working a winch. The gate shut swiftly, crushing the Tsuno beneath the heavy stone.

Irie stood apart from the others as they tended their wounds, pondering what she should do next. Here was her vengeance, right at hand, but somehow it felt wrong. When she had imagined her final confrontation with the Anvil, she never imagined it like this. Naseru was not the coward she imagined him to be. She had fought beside him and witnessed his courage. What sort of a courtier draws a blade and defends his own yojimbo?

"Your stance is familiar," Naseru said, sheathing his blade as he walked toward her. "Elements of the Shiba style, but your battle cry was Mirumoto. Are you a Tonbo?"

"I was, once," Irie said quietly. "But the Dragonfly Clan is dead now."

Naseru bowed his head. "I regret your loss. I should have realized the Lion would seize their chance to gain vengeance on your clan. I never imagined they would be so brutal. There is nothing more I can say, except that you of all people must realize how foolish vengeance is." He eyed her cautiously.

"I came here to kill you, Naseru," Irie said flatly.

"So I surmised," he replied. "Perhaps I deserve it. In any case, all I ask of you is one hour's parole. We are injured, outnumbered. We need every sword we have to stop Kishenku. Especially one as unusual as yours." Naseru looked down at the crystal sword Irie held.

"How did I stop the Tsuno's spell?" Irie asked.

"Night crystal absorbs magic," Naseru said. "Will you stand with us?"

"I will," Irie said.

"Then we must hurry. There is little time left."

26 | A FINAL CHOICE

Kishenku is coming," said Moto Vordu, sagging feebly in his bonds.

Shem-Zhe said nothing. The young shugenja knelt quietly on the floor and watched his master.

"What really happened to Liyun and the other apprentices?" Shem-Zhe asked. "The ones who died in the ruins?"

"They were taken by the spirits. You know that. The ghosts of the city became more restless as we continued our studies."

"And you never thought you were responsible?" Shem-Zhe asked, looking at Vordu with pity. "You never thought that perhaps the ghosts were trying to warn you of the danger?"

"I knew they were," Vordu said. "I did not care. Liyun was just one more mistake I intended to correct."

Shem-Zhe drew a scrap of silk from his kimono and quietly wiped the tears from his face.

"I know you are disappointed in me, Shem-Zhe, but you

must know I did what I did for the right reasons. Look at the wonders we have created here. Look at the power we have harnessed through the night crystal. Can you truly tell me that what we have gained has not been worthwhile?"

"Was it worth lives of your daughter and grandson?" Shem-Zhe asked. "The lives of the villagers the Tsuno slaughtered to capture them?"

"More mistakes to be corrected," Vordu said. "Untie me, Shem-Zhe. I can still seize the power of the crystal sphere. We can destroy the Tsuno and restore all the damage they have done. Everything could be as it was before Kishenku returned. All will be made well."

"What about the ward that the Scorpion found protecting the pedestal?"

"You would believe a Scorpion?" Vordu said, aghast. "I have studied the pedestal countless times and found no such thing. The Scorpion is a fool."

"Strange to hear you call someone else a fool, Vordu-sama," Shem-Zhe said sadly.

Vordu was silent for a long time. "So the apprentice now thinks himself greater than the master?" Vordu laughed ruefully. "I thought you were unlike the rest of them, Shem-Zhe. I thought you shared my vision."

Shem-Zhe looked away.

"Fine, then," Vordu said, closing his eyes as he listened to the howls of the approaching Tsuno. "I will not attempt to use the sphere. But if nothing else, at least let me help you keep them out of the Temple."

"How?"

"This entire building is made of the purest form of night crystal I have seen," Vordu answered. "It is a natural conductor for magic. If the two of us combine our power in a ritual prayer, we could suffuse the Temple with holy energy. A prayer against the Taint is a simple enough spell, and the Tsuno carry the Taint. So long as we maintain our prayer they will be unable to set foot in the Temple without being consumed by the energies."

"What about Naseru and the others?"

"If they are in the ruins, they are already dead. If they live, our spell will not harm them."

Shem-Zhe looked at Vordu's cloak, still heaped in a pile where Seppun Isei had discarded it. "All right," he said, "but without your amulets. I will be the focus of the ritual. You will add your magic to mine."

"Agreed," Vordu said, nodding eagerly.

Shem-Zhe rose and drew a short knife from his belt to cut Vordu's bonds. The young shugenja paused, eyes meeting those of his master. Where once there had been only polite deference and submission, there was now steel. He held the tip of the blade in Vordu's face.

"If this is a trick, Vordu-sama, I will end your madness here and now."

Vordu nodded soberly. Shem-Zhe released the older man from his bonds, and the two sat cross-legged on the floor. Chanting in unison, they summoned forth the power of the fire kami. Whispering to the spirits, they encouraged them to suffuse the crystal structure of the Temple, filling it with the holy power of the Celestial Heavens. Almost immediately, a tortured cry echoed through the Temple's corridors. The Tsuno had already gained entry and the ritual was destroying them. Vordu opened his eyes and smiled as they continued the spell. His apprentice grinned back, though he said nothing.

For a brief instant, Shem-Zhe's grin changed to a look of utter horror. Vordu looked back in confusion. The younger shugenja flew backward, carried by some invisible force, to crash violently into a tall shelf of scrolls. Shem-Zhe lay still, buried under parchment and broken wood. Vordu looked over his shoulder in alarm. A tall Tsuno stood in the doorway of the Temple, armor and horns covered with fetishes and bone amulets.

"Greetings, Vordu," the Tsuno said in a surprisingly elegant voice. Leaning on a gnarled staff, it strode into the chamber.

"Kishenku," Vordu hissed, shuffling awkwardly to his feet. "How is this possible? The spirits we summoned—"

"Are quite effective at destroying creatures Tainted by the Shadowlands," Kishenku replied, pausing several feet from the Unicorn. "Did you forget that I come from a time before the Tsuno allied themselves with the Dark Lord? I have no Taint, Vordu."

Vordu looked quickly at the crystal sphere, then back at Kishenku. The Tsuno laughed.

"By all means, please, attempt to use the sphere on me," the Tsuno said, baring its teeth in a mocking smile. "The arrival of Izumo's descendant has restored its power. All that it requires now is a simple touch, a focused will to direct it. Of course, the trap I spent so many centuries weaving has also become active. Touch the sphere now, and your soul will be snuffed out quicker than a candle flame in a hurricane."

"You trapped it, just like Naseru said."

"Of course. It was difficult to call upon my magic as a spirit, but I had plenty of time. I knew someday I would require a pawn to gain entrance to the city, but I had no intention of letting that pawn rob me of the very prize I sought. The sphere is much simpler to use than I made it out to be, Vordu. Even a fool like you could use it now."

Another figure entered the chamber behind Kishenku—a small monk with a wide basket hat.

"Might I introduce Fushin, Onisu of Betrayal?" Kishenku said with exaggerated politeness. "I believe you have met."

The monk laughed quietly when he saw Vordu, then played a short trill on his flute.

"Report," Kishenku said, looking sidelong over one shoulder.

"Naseru and the others have been occupied," he said. "Your remaining troops should be able to handle them, but you never know. I could slaughter them quite capably, if you summoned me fully into this realm."

"I think not, Fushin," Kishenku said. "You are quite dangerous enough as a formless spirit. Given form, you would betray me and take the sphere for yourself."

"True enough," the onisu said, shrugging in acceptance of his own nature. "What will you do with him?" He dipped his flute toward Vordu.

"I have not yet decided," Kishenku said, red-gold eyes burning down at the old shugenja. "I do owe you my life, human. I will make you an offer. Even I cannot touch the sphere safely until the magical trap I put in place has been removed. If you aid me in unraveling my spell from it, I promise you a swift death."

"What of my family?" Vordu asked. "You promised to release them."

"I have already released them," Kishenku said. "I have released them from this savage mortal coil. Aid me, and you shall see your family in the gray fields of Meido."

Vordu's jaw worked wordlessly for several seconds. "You promised me they would not be harmed if I helped you."

"And you promised not to betray me," Kishenku said in a mocking tone. "Consider this a renegotiation of our prior deal. Make your choice. Aid me or try to use the sphere against me. I have lied to you in the past. Perhaps I am lying now. Perhaps the sphere is not warded at all."

Moto Vordu shook his head slowly. He felt lost, betrayed, defeated. Slowly, he extended one hand to touch the crystal sphere. Kishenku made no move to stop him. A bright light filled the room as the old shugenja's gnarled fingers touched the cool surface.

This time, the Tsuno had not lied.

As Moto Vordu died, he prayed that Hantei Naseru would have the strength to stop the madness he had unleashed.

27 LIKE UNTO A GOD

"What happened here?" Shono asked, wincing at the charred Tsuno corpses littering the halls of the Temple.

"They're burned," said Irie.

"Perhaps one of these is Kishenku?" Isei suggested.

"That is too much good fortune to hope for," Naseru said.

The Anvil hurried ahead, sword ready. The group paused to collect themselves in front of the door to the chamber that contained the crystal sphere.

"If the Tsuno is inside," Isei said, "then he already has the sphere."

"No," Naseru said. "I do not think Kishenku has used it yet."

"How do you know that?" Shono asked.

"Because we are still alive."

"So what is our plan?"

"If our earlier battles are any indication, the light of night crystal pains the Tsuno," Naseru said. "If we rush Kishenku, the light of your eye and Irie's sword may distract him."

"Then what?"

"Hopefully something will come to mind."

"Sounds risky," Shono said uneasily.

"We have no time for another plan," Naseru answered. "Follow me or turn back now."

Without further hesitation, the Anvil threw open the door and charged.

In the center of the chamber, Tsuno Kishenku stood beside the sphere. The charred body of Moto Vordu lay beside the pedestal, still smoking. The Tsuno's lip curled in a sneer when he saw them. The Tsuno waved one hand negligently, and a wave of force cascaded through the chamber, throwing Naseru and the others against the wall. Naseru grunted in pain as he sat heavily on the floor. He was uncertain what hurt more—the impact against the wall or that his plan had unraveled so quickly. His hand rested on something soft; he had landed on Moto Vordu's discarded cloak.

"I am pleased to meet you, Hantei Naseru," Kishenku said in a dry voice. "You bear the blood of Soli Izumo and the mighty Akodo, the two greatest betrayers of my kind. You should witness this."

Tsuno Kishenku placed his left hand upon the crystal sphere, and the Temple walls flared with an angry red light. Kishenku's body radiated pulsing energy. The Soultwister threw his head back and hissed in ecstasy as the power suffused his body. Sunetra hurled several knives at Kishenku from where she lay. A wall of fire roared in a circle surround him, melting the missiles in mid-air. Kishenku gripped the sphere with both hands, slowly lowering his gaze to scowl at his human attackers through the flames.

"You are a man who sought to change the Empire, Hantei Naseru," Kishenku said with a throaty chuckle. "You have succeeded. Are you not pleased?"

"I will be more pleased," Naseru said, "when you have returned to the realm of the dead."

Naseru's hand tightened on Vordu's cloak. He could feel the tiny night crystal amulets woven into it. If the amulets could absorb magic like Irie's sword, then perhaps he still had a chance. Seppun Isei crouched on the floor nearby. His eyes flicked to the cloak, then met his master's. The yojimbo nodded.

Naseru rose to his feet and placed his free hand on his sword.

"Still defiant," Kishenku snarled. "You are a worthy end to your line, Naseru. My congratulations." The Tsuno extended one long finger, and a beam of sparkling black flame shrieked toward the Anvil.

"Now!" Seppun Isei shouted, leaping into the beam's path.

The bolt struck the yojimbo with a loud sizzle. Naseru dodged around Isei and charged the wall of fire, throwing the cloak over his head. Kishenku screamed in rage as he realized the Anvil's plan. The fire intensified. Naseru did not falter but ran directly through the flame. He could feel the skin on his legs and back burn as he ran through the fire, but he ignored the pain. Leaping, he drew his sword and slashed at Kishenku. The blade shattered on the invisible barrier that surrounded the Tsuno.

Fire raged all around them. Naseru saw the skin blister and peel from his hands. The heat was so intense that his hands felt like they had been dipped in freezing water. He stumbled forward, his injured legs no longer supporting his body. He reached out for something to break his fall and felt his fingers touch the cool surface of the crystal sphere.

The pain was gone.

As quick as thought, Naseru's body was healed. Naseru and Kishenku now each rested one hand on the sphere. A maelstrom of conflicting energies swirled between them as both attempted to control the power of the City of Night.

Kishenku roared and lashed at Naseru with his free claw, but an invisible barrier deflected the attack. The sphere, it seemed, was unwilling to let any harm come to either of its potential masters.

"A contest of wills, then?" Kishenku growled, forcing a wicked smile. "Whoever maintains control the longest becomes a god. Whoever falters first, becomes a memory." The Tsuno laid his other hand upon the sphere and glared down at the Anvil. "Let it be so. I do not fear you, human."

"Nor I you," Naseru said, slowly rising to his feet and placing his other hand on the sphere as well. "Your race was proud and strong until your arrogance destroyed it. You were unable to control the sphere last time. What makes you think this time will be different?"

"I did not fail last time; I merely did not go far enough. This world the Five Races created is unnatural, aberrant. It is the existence of this mortal realm that drew the attention of Jigoku. If the universe would be returned to balance, this world must be unmade. Destruction was *always* my intent."

"It saddens me that a creature with such ageless wisdom can be so utterly mad," Naseru said, eye narrowing. A drop of sweat trickled from his temple as he concentrated on the sphere. He could feel Kishenku's will like a physical force, trying to push his hands from the crystal. He knew he could not resist much longer.

"You presume to judge me?" Kishenku roared. Naseru's knees buckled as the Tsuno's will hammered him. "Your life is the sputter of a candle compared to mine. You cannot comprehend the mysteries I have long since ceased to dwell upon."

Naseru's right hand fell from the sphere. The Tsuno smiled, casually removed his left hand, and extending his fingers near Naseru's throat. As soon as Naseru faltered, Kishenku would crush him.

"Already you begin to weaken. You cannot maintain your grip, human. How can you possibly compare your will against that of a soul that has existed for millennia?"

"By being unpredictable," Naseru grunted.

Naseru flicked his wrist, and Tadaji's night crystal dagger appeared in his hand. For a brief instant, he felt resistance from the magical field, and then the dagger struck true, shearing through the barrier that protected Kishenku. Naseru stabbed the blade deep into the back of the Tsuno's right hand. The Soultwister roared in pain and drew his hand away from the sphere. Kishenku's red-gold eyes widened as he realized his mistake. Naseru concentrated for a single instant, and Tsuno Kishenku became nothing more than ash floating in the air.

Naseru sighed in relief, then looked down at the sphere. He could still feel the power radiating inside him, unopposed by the Tsuno's will. He could sense Shono, Isei, and Sunetra standing around him. He could hear their heartbeats quicken when they saw what he had done. He could feel the weight of the mountain above him. He could hear the sounds of birds in flight, miles away. He could feel the eyes of the gods upon him, and he could smell their fear.

"Use it," said the komuso's voice in his ear. "If someone should use this power, why not you? This is your destiny, Naseru."

"Fushin," Naseru whispered. "Where are you?"

"Me?" the onisu laughed. "I am only a dream, but you could summon me fully into this world. You could even destroy me, I think. You can do anything you wish. You possess the power Kishenku sought for ages, unspoiled by Izumo's meddling. The Empire is yours. The *universe* is yours."

"I do not want this power."

"Oh? Then let go of the sphere."

Naseru could not bring himself to do so. He pictured all the mistakes he had made, the work he had left undone. He imagined ways to make the Empire better and knew that all was within his power. His battle was only beginning.

The onisu snickered. "Power is not easily set aside," Fushin said. "You like to view yourself a hero, but your base nature will not allow you to surrender what you have gained. You are a god now, Hantei Naseru. Why should you deny it? Use the sphere. You can take your father's throne and more! Wipe away the Shadowlands. Drag Fu Leng down from the Celestial Heavens. Take his place if you desire! Change history so that Hantei XVI never returned to the Empire and your father never died. Your merest thought, your slightest whim, can be reality. You already used the orb's power to heal your flesh when Kishenku's magic burned you, without even realizing it. You simply wished the pain gone, and so it was. All of your problems could be fixed so easily."

"No," Naseru said through gritted teeth as he struggled to keep his mind free from thought, to pry his hands away from the sphere. "This power destroyed the kitsu. If I use it, it will surely destroy Rokugan."

"Then start with something small," Fushin said. "Erect a monument to your sister's bravery. Cure the madness that torments your brother, Sezaru. Kill Akodo Kaneka. You know you want these things, Naseru."

"Naseru, what are you doing?" Sunetra shouted.

Shono cast a nervous look at the exit. Irie pressed the air with one hand, as if touching an invisible wall. He could sense Isei lying on the floor, killed by Kishenku's magic.

"You can restore him," Fushin suggested.

"He came back from the dead once, and it destroyed him," Naseru said. "Isei died like a samurai, and I would not rob him of that. If I made the changes you suggest, how much more would I destroy?"

"Naseru!" Irie shouted, hammering the invisible wall with one fist. "Step away from the sphere!"

"It is your power that keeps them away," Fushin said. "They are jealous. You know that none of them deserve this power."

"*No one* deserves this power," Naseru said in a strained voice.

"But someone must have it. Now that the sphere has been awakened, someone will find it. Why should it not be yours? What will happen if you step away? Shinjo Shono will make a curious god, I think. I voice only your own desires, Naseru. Your own fears. You know I am right."

Naseru looked into the depths of the sphere, and for a moment, he was tempted to do as the onisu said. Then he saw his own reflection in the crystal surface. One eye stared back, one black silken patch.

"If I truly desire this power as much as you say," Naseru said. "Then why did I not restore my eye?" Naseru's voice was stronger now, steadier.

Fushin was silent. He had no answer.

"Even one step down this road is one too many," Naseru said. Focusing his will, the Anvil drew upon the sphere's power one final time, turning it on itself.

A loud pop echoed through the Temple, and the crystal sphere crumbled into dust.

"You are a fool, Hantei Naseru," Fushin whispered. "You will regret this day...."

The onisu's bitter voice faded into nothing.

28 | A NEW GUARDIAN

Horiuchi Shem-Zhe sat up with a groan and pushed aside the wrecked remains of the scroll rack where he had landed. "What happened?" he said, peering about groggily.

"Shem-Zhe!" Shono said, laughing as he helped his fellow Unicorn out of the pile. "I feared you were dead!"

"Vordu-sama was not so fortunate, it seems," Shem-Zhe said, looking at his fallen master. Someone had lain the old shugenja's cloak over the body.

"He is fortunate the Fortunes were so merciful," Shono said. "How is Isei, Naseru-sama?"

Naseru said nothing. The Anvil knelt beside the fallen body of his yojimbo. He held the man's katana and wakizashi across his lap. The Anvil's normally unreadable features were full of sorrow.

"Isei stood by me since my days in the household of the Steel Chrysanthemum," Naseru said, his voice thick. "He was my ally when no one else would dare stand by me. He doubted his own bravery at every step, but I never knew a samurai with more courage." Naseru looked up at Shono. "Seppun Isei was my friend, and that is a rare thing indeed."

"He was a fine warrior, Naseru-sama," Shono said, bowing his head respectfully.

Bayushi Sunetra placed one hand on Naseru's shoulder. Horiuchi Shem-Zhe whispered a short prayer for the souls of the dead. Yotsu Irie merely stood in the background and watched silently. She had arrived too recently to share their memories, but she could share their grief.

"You should leave here, Naseru," Shono said. "I sent Bakin to retrieve reinforcements from the Sun's Arc Way. Commander Chen will be here soon."

"I cannot leave Isei," Naseru said.

"Naseru," Shono said more urgently. "Chen commands one third of the Khan's armies. If he finds you here, he will kill you as a favor to your half brother."

Naseru grinned wryly. "Since when were you concerned for my welfare, Shinjo Shono?"

"Saving the Empire puts you on my good side, Naseru-sama," Shono said. "Besides, I think I stand to earn a healthy profit from your involvement with the House of Foreign Stories. Now leave before it is too late."

"I will attend to your friend," Shem-Zhe added. "With Vordu's death, the Way of Night is now my responsibility. I can hold Seppun Isei's body in state until you have escaped, and then send him to Kyuden Seppun once Moto Chen's attention is elsewhere. His soldiers will not disturb the dead. You have my word."

"You have my most profound thanks, Shem-Zhe-san," Naseru said, rising and tucking the yojimbo's swords under his arm.

"It is the least I can do. I helped Vordu and did not recognize his evil in time. I would not know peace if I did not do all I could to help the heroes who stopped him."

"Will you continue your research here?" Naseru asked.

"Difficult to say. There is much still to be learned from these ruins . . . but the danger is also great. I think that if we continue, we will search more slowly than before. If the Khan threatens to seal the cave, so be it. Better to not go forth than to go forth recklessly."

"Good advice," Naseru said. "You are a wise man, Shem-Zhe. Shoan would be proud. Now I think I shall take *your* advice and leave."

"Stay well, Naseru," Shono said. "If you ever sit in your father's throne, I'll be the first to kneel before it."

Naseru gave a final bow, he turned, and left the Temple. Irie and Sunetra followed. Making their way to Vordu's castle, they mounted steeds, and galloped out of the Way of Night. At the end of the pass, they reined their steeds to a halt and took a final look back. Naseru turned to Irie.

"I assume from the fact that your sword is still in its saya that you no longer wish to kill me," he said.

"Things are far more complex than I first imagined, Naseru," the Yotsu said quietly. "I had imagined you as an evil man, but I was wrong."

"Perhaps you are not so wrong. For a moment, when I had my hand on the sphere, I was tempted to use its power to destroy the Shogun's army. I nearly became the very thing you pictured me to be."

"But you did not."

"Only because I remember the anger I saw in your eyes when you told me who you were. How many more orphans would I have created? How much evil would I have unleashed? I would have been little better than the Tsuno. Power, any sort of power, is a destructive force, Irie. It requires wisdom to be handled safely."

Naseru took the swords from beneath his arm. "These blades were once wielded by the yojimbo of the Hantei Dynasty. They were passed from one guardian to the next. I offer them to you now, Yotsu Irie."

Naseru held the swords out with both hands. Irie looked at the swords, uncertain what to say.

"Surely there is someone more worthy," she said. "Sunetra, perhaps?" She looked at the Scorpion.

"I would make a poor yojimbo," Sunetra said with a small smile. "I prefer the shadows."

"You have only just met me," Irie said. "How can you offer me your trust?"

"I have made a career out of judging character, and yours is strong enough," Naseru said. "With you as my bodyguard, I would never forget the tragedy of the Dragonfly. With you as my advisor, we could prevent such a thing from happening again."

Irie looked at the swords. "Are you serious?"

"Indeed," Naseru said gravely. "Please take my offer, Irie-san. Though I appreciate your courtesy in refusing twice, if you refuse a third time, I will be deeply hurt."

"Hai," Irie said, accepting the blades. "I would be honored, Naseru-sama."

"Isei would be proud to see you carry on his legacy."

"Before I begin my duties, I must return to the Yotsu dojo," Irie said. "I must report to Lady Seou."

"Of course," Naseru said. "I will await you in Ryoko Owari."

Irie rode away to the east. Naseru and Sunetra continued to the south. Once the Way of Night was well behind them, they slowed their pace. After a time, Naseru noticed Sunetra watching him curiously.

"Yes?" he asked, looking back at her. "Is there a problem?"

"You surprise me," she said softly. "What you did today . . . all of that power . . . I cannot even imagine doing what you did."

"That was not power," Naseru said. "That was slavery. True power is the ability to control one's destiny, not to be chained to your slightest whim. I envy the architects of the City of Night. If they were truly able to use the sphere to create this world, their will must have been truly indomitable. The fact that they were able to set the temptation of the sphere aside makes me respect them even more. It was all I could do to destroy it."

Sunetra nodded.

"But that is in the past," Naseru said pertly. "I must visit my brother, Sezaru, and tell him what I have seen. No doubt he will be most keenly interested to know the origins of the

Tsuno, assuming he did not already know. I wonder if he did not know that the onisu was hunting me all along." Naseru thought of the strange letter he had received from his brother so long ago, and he laughed despite himself.

"And what will you do after that?" Sunetra asked.

"Return to the City of Lies. I am sure that while I am gone Bayushi Kaukatsu has put no end of schemes into effect to undermine my power base. I shall have need of a good spy in the days ahead, Sunetra. Are you up to the challenge?" The Anvil smiled at the Scorpion.

"That depends," she said, tilting her head slightly. "Are you willing to let me in on any more of your secrets?"

"You will have to wait and see," Naseru said. He kicked his horse into a gallop, leaving Sunetra's pony behind.

Sunetra laughed and followed.

EPILOGUE

Three days later, the Temple of the Ninth Kami, the Shadowlands

Lord Daigotsu reclined in his throne, fingers laced before his handsome face. His dark eyes were clouded as he pondered his minion's report.

"So you say that Naseru chose to destroy the sphere rather than draw upon its power?" Daigotsu asked.

"Yes." Fushin bowed deeply before the throne. "Somehow, he knew that the kitsu sealed the sphere away because it had become flawed. He must have realized it could no longer be used to create, only to destroy. Perhaps one of the kenku told him?"

"I doubt it," Daigotsu said. "Kenku are too secretive. If they aided him at all, they would have been far subtler. If Naseru was able to destroy the sphere despite your temptations, then he must be more dangerous than we thought."

"So he is strong-willed," Shahai said with a small chuckle. The Dark Lord's consort lay back on her cushions. Her pretty face regarded the onisu with a mocking smile. "A strong will cannot save you from a knife in the belly."

"You might be surprised," Daigotsu said, still pondering.

"Shinsei once said that a smith might have many hammers, but he needs only one anvil. A strong will can inspire others to fight. Naseru might become troublesome if he can rally others against us. Heroes are bad enough. Heroes who create more heroes must be dealt with severely."

"So you will turn your attention to the Anvil rather than the Wolf?" Shahai asked.

"In due time. I am no fool. Toturi Sezaru is the more immediate threat, though even he does not occupy my mind at present."

"Who does?"

"Fushin," Daigotsu turned to look at the onisu.

The onisu looked up quickly. "Yes, my lord?" he said.

"When you encouraged the Anvil to use the power of the sphere, what did you tell him to do?"

"Various things, my lord," Fushin said. "I suggested he destroy the Shogun. I recommended he restore his father to life. I told him to build a monument to his sister. . . ."

"Did you tell him to tear Fu Leng from the Heavens?" Daigotsu asked in a mild voice.

Fushin said nothing. The onisu's metal lips pressed into a thin line.

"Fushin, it is in your nature to betray, for it is from betrayal that you draw your strength," Daigotsu said, rising from his throne. "The Celestial Order despises a vacuum. Had Naseru destroyed Fu Leng, the Anvil would have replaced him as the new Dark Kami. And from such a betrayal—a mere demon betraying the very powers that created him—your own power would have grown a thousandfold. Was this not your plan?"

"I planned no such thing."

"Fushin, you forget: I created you." The Dark Lord drew a long obsidian blade from his belt. "My eyes are always upon you, and as surely as I created you, I can create another to replace you. You have defied Fu Leng. Now it is time for Betrayal to learn the true meaning of loyalty."

The Dark Lord gestured, and Fushin's ghostly form became solid at last. The Nightmare of Betrayal reached for its swords, but Daigotsu was quicker. The massive red demon fell solidly to the stone floor, its life drained by the Dark Lord's obsidian blade.

"Now Shahai-chan," Daigotsu said, looking over one shoulder as he flicked the ichor from his blade. "What shall we do about Toturi Sezaru?"

Legend of the
Five Rings.

The Four Winds Saga

Only one can claim the Throne of Rokugan.

WIND OF JUSTICE
Third Scroll
Rich Wulf

Naseru, the most cold-hearted and scheming of the royal heirs, will
stop at nothing to sit upon the Throne of Rokugan. But when dark
forces in the City of Night threaten his beloved Empire, Naseru
must learn to wield the most unlikely weapon of all — justice.

June 2003

WIND OF TRUTH
Fourth Scroll
Ree Soesbee

Sezaru, one of the most powerful wielders of magic in all Rokugan,
has never desired his father's throne, but destiny calls to the son
of Toturi. Here, in the final volume of the Four Winds Saga,
all will be decided.

December 2003

Now available:

THE STEEL THRONE
Prelude
Edward Bolme

WIND OF HONOR
First Scroll
Ree Soesbee

WIND OF WAR
Second Scroll
Jess Lebow

Tales of Dominaria

LEGIONS
Onslaught Cycle, Book II
J. Robert King

In the blood and sand of the arena,
two foes clash in a titanic battle.

January 2003

EMPEROR'S FIST
Magic Legends Cycle Two, Book II
Scott McGough

War looms above the Edemi Islands, casting the deep
and dread shadow of the Emperor's Fist.

March 2003

SCOURGE
Onslaught Cycle, Book III
J. Robert King

From the fiery battles of the Cabal, a new god has arisen,
one whose presence drives her worshipers to madness.

May 2003

THE MONSTERS OF MAGIC
An anthology edited by J. Robert King

From Dominaria to Phyrexia, monsters fill the multiverse,
and tales of the most popular ones fill these pages.

August 2003

CHAMPION'S TRIAL
Magic Legends Cycle Two, Book III
Scott McGough

To restore his honor, the onetime champion of Madara must
battle his own corrupt empire and the monster on the throne.

November 2003

Capture the thrill of D&D® adventuring!

These six new titles from T.H. Lain put you
in the midst of the heroic party as it encounters
deadly magic, sinister plots, and fearsome creatures.
Join the adventure!

THE BLOODY EYE
January 2003

TREACHERY'S WAKE
March 2003

PLAGUE OF ICE
May 2003

THE SUNDERED ARMS
July 2003

RETURN OF THE DAMNED
October 2003

THE DEATH RAY
December 2003

The Minotaur Wars

From *New York Times* best-selling author Richard A. Knaak comes a powerful new chapter in the DRAGONLANCE® saga.

The continent of Ansalon, reeling from the destruction of the War of Souls, slowly crawls from beneath the rubble to rebuild – but the fires of war, once stirred, are difficult to quench. Another war comes to Ansalon, one that will change the balance of power throughout Krynn.

NIGHT OF BLOOD
Volume I

Change comes violently to the land of the minotaurs. Usurpers overthrow the emperor, murder all rivals, and dishonor minotaur tradition. The new emperor's wife presides over a cult of the dead, while the new government makes a secret pact with a deadly enemy. But betrayal is never easy, and rebellion lurks in the shadows.

The Minotaur Wars begin June 2003.

The original Chronicles

From *New York Times* best-selling authors Margaret Weis & Tracy Hickman

These classics of modern fantasy literature – the three titles that
started it all – are available for the very first time in individual
hardcover volumes. All three titles feature stunning cover art
from award-winning artist Matt Stawicki.

DRAGONS OF AUTUMN TWILIGHT
Volume I

Friends meet amid a growing shadow of fear and rumors of war.
Out of their story, an epic saga is born.

January 2003

DRAGONS OF WINTER NIGHT
Volume II

Dragons return to Krynn as the Queen of Darkness launches her assault.
Against her stands a small band of heroes bearing a new weapon:
the DRAGONLANCE.

July 2003

DRAGONS OF SPRING DAWNING
Volume III

As the War of the Lance reaches its height, old friends clash amid
gallantry and betrayal. Yet their greatest battles lie within each of them.

November 2003